THE ANDERSEN ANCESTRY

ADDIE J. KING

THE GRIMM LEGACY - BOOK 2

Loconeal Publishing

Amherst, OH

THE GRIMM LEGACY

Copyright © 2014 by Addie J. King
Cover Art by Melinda Timpone
Edited by Kathy Watness

Loconeal books may be ordered through booksellers or by contacting:
www.loconeal.com
216-772-8380

Loconeal Publishing can bring authors to your live event.
Contact Loconeal Publishing at 216-772-8380.

Published by Loconeal Publishing, LLC
Printed in the United States of America

First Loconeal Publishing edition: July 2015

Visit our website: www.loconeal.com

ISBN 978-1-940466-39-2 (Trade Paperback)

ALSO BY ADDIE J. KING

The Grimm Legacy
The Andersen Ancestry
The Wonderland Woes
The Bunyan Barter

DEDICATION

To Ray . . .
With you I have everything . . .

CHAPTER ONE

I wasn't expecting a faerie court visitor when I came downstairs for coffee that morning. I was to start my internship with a judge at the courthouse. Summer after the first year of law school was a time for resume-building, so many of us would be working more than one job: one to build the resume, and one to pay the bills—not a time for magical mystery and intrigue. But then, I guess I shouldn't have been surprised.

As I came down the stairs, I noticed the house was in disarray. Cushions and pillows were missing from the couches and chairs in the living room. I poked my head into the dining room and nothing was out of place. Nothing was missing in the hallway, but cushions and pillows were missing from my dad's library.

I grabbed the heavy iron fireplace poker from the library and crept toward the kitchen. I was on guard; the magical happenings in my life just nine months ago were cause to make sure I was armed. Iron can hurt or even kill faerie beings, and I just happened to be living in a house with a portal to the faerie realm in my basement. And, hey, if my intruder was human that iron poker was heavy enough to leave a serious dent in someone. I took a deep breath outside the door and thought, *get a grip, Janie Grimm. If you can argue for your life in front of a faerie court, a simple burglar is nothing. You can do this.*

I crept toward the kitchen door in my Marvin the Martian pajamas, raising the poker over my shoulder to get a good angle. I eased the swinging kitchen door open with my hip and peered inside. As the door opened, I caught the scent of freshly brewed coffee. What kind of burglar starts the coffee pot? I guess if one was going to face an early morning break-in I'd rather have a burglar who left me with coffee.

As the door opened the rest of the way, I saw someone sitting at my kitchen table sipping coffee and reading my newspaper.

"Good morning," he said, as he raised his mug in salute.

I lowered the fireplace poker. It was Geoffrey, the father of my friend and sometimes date, Aiden.

Just months earlier I had started law school, met Aiden, solved the mysterious death of my father, discovered my stepmother to be the murderer, got kidnapped, and defended myself in a trial before Evangeline, my evil faerie stepmother who was known in the faerie courts as Queen Eva. All of that had happened in September; it was now barely June, but I hadn't seen Geoffrey since then. To say that Aiden and his father weren't on the best of terms was an understatement.

"Is Aiden here?" he asked, putting down the newspaper and leaning back in the kitchen chair.

I waited until I'd poured myself some coffee, and mixed in some sweetener and creamer before I answered. Was he fishing for information about his son, or about my own personal morals? "No, he's not here. He doesn't live here." Best not to delve into anything I wasn't specifically asked for. Aiden and I had never talked about what to say to his father if we saw him again. Of course, we also hadn't talked about his father. At all.

I lifted the mug to my lips, but stopped before I took a sip. Alarm bells were ringing in my head; Aiden had warned me months ago never to accept food or drink from a faerie being, and Geoffrey was definitely one of those. Accepting nourishment could obligate me to some kind of servitude with the provider of the food or drink. I set the mug down on the table without drinking. Better to be safe now than sorry later.

"I didn't mean to imply anything, Ms. Grimm," he said, shrugging his shoulders. "And the coffee is yours. I didn't do anything to it, and drinking it doesn't bind you in any way. I just don't get coffee when I'm in the courts, and I've missed it. Aiden's mother used to make it for me in the mornings when we were together before he was born. Of course, she'd also have fresh cinnamon rolls with it." Geoffrey's voice softened when he referred to his son's mother.

In the months since I'd met them, Aiden and his mother, Doris, had become my surrogate family. My own mother had disappeared when I was a kid, my father died fifteen months ago, and my stepmother was, well, evil. I didn't really have any family. I could understand why someone wanted something from her kitchen; her cinnamon rolls were incredible. No matter what had driven them apart, I could empathize with a longing for her baking.

Since beings from faerie couldn't be forsworn, I could believe his statements or I could use them against him if he was lying. He hadn't tried to trick me, and he'd flat out said I was safe. I sipped my coffee, and then sat down at the table across from him. "What's going on?"

"There's been a prison break from Søborg Castle."

"What's that?"

He stood up and refilled his mug. "Just like your world, we have to have somewhere to safely confine dangerous beings. Søborg Castle is now our place, our prison, if you will. In fact, your stepmother is there now. Many years ago there was a civil war that brought your stepmother to power the first time. Queen Eva was actually an improvement over Celeste, the Seawitch. Eva was instrumental in binding Celeste into the Søborg Castle dungeons. As you learned last fall, we are forbidden from holding humans who enter the faerie realm against their will. The Seawitch was amassing incredible power by dragging humans into our realm and getting their agreements after they were already there. By then, they couldn't get away, and she drained their life force for more power."

That couldn't be good. I said as much.

"That's an understatement. The human world and the faerie realm worked together to impose a binding on the Seawitch that allowed us to imprison her at Søborg Castle and force her compliance. She's been looking for a way to escape ever since, and I think she may have found a way to do it when your stepmother's power was stripped."

They stripped my stepmother's power? Wow, they *were* pissed off at all of her shenanigans last fall. I couldn't complain since she'd wanted to kill me and she had killed my father.

"How do you know the Seawitch is out, and why are you telling me?" I asked. "Does that mean Evangeline is free?" That could only be bad. No wonder he was here to warn me.

He held out the newspaper. On the front page the headline read, "Body in Morgue Disintegrates on Table". Yikes. How does a body disintegrate? I didn't want to ask; something told me the answer would be less than pleasant.

"Evangeline's still under lock and key, but the Seawitch? She's here, in the mortal world. The Seawitch gains power from feeding on the life force of mortals. Once she was imprisoned and bound, Celeste could not cross into the mortal realm to feed; she could only take a human's life force if they found their way to her and made a deal they couldn't follow through on. She's been bound for hundreds of years. Sheer hunger is probably driving her at the moment. She's probably not even trying to make deals or take them back to faerie. She's just feeding. Feeding for her takes everything from a body and leaves nothing but water behind. If she weren't so hungry, there would be more bodies left intact, or at least parts of bodies left intact. When that happens, there's normally at least a finger or two left that someone could use to identify the victim."

"Well, that's horrifying on its own, but what happens when she gets enough to eat that she's not starving anymore?"

"That's when things get scary. She's going to start consolidating power, and she's going to go after the descendants of the humans who helped bind her. I'm pretty sure she wants revenge."

Here we go again, I thought. How many people had my ancestors, the Grimm Brothers, pissed off that I'd have to deal with? "So how much danger am I in, Geoffrey?"

He seemed surprised. "You? Tales of what you did to your stepmother will probably keep you fairly safe if you don't get involved. The Grimms were well after Celeste's time. I need your help to try to figure out who she's after, so we can warn them. It's been too long since I've been in the mortal world. I don't know my way around anymore."

I didn't know whether to be relieved or annoyed. I was out of danger, but it seemed he was dragging me back in. Before I could say anything, however, a large frog hopped into the kitchen, yawning and smacking his lips.

"Bert, what's going on?"

Bert had been living with me for the last nine months, on the lookout for magical shenanigans while I'd studied for exams, written papers, and generally tried to go on about my life after my stepmother had lost her crown. He had once been human, but was cursed into frog form by a witch long ago. He had come to help me with my stepmother and he'd stayed. He wasn't my only roommate; my friend Mia had also moved into the house just the day before, after the school year ended. I was counting on her rent to keep up the house. It was too big for me to afford all the utilities and upkeep on my own, even without having a rent payment. The house had been my reward for defeating Evangeline.

"If Mia's going to run around the house in the middle of the night and steal all the soft things in the house, she could at least wear something revealing to make it worth all the fuss. I mean, seriously, she even took my pillow and blanket. There's not a single soft place left for a frog to sleep on."

I set down my coffee and headed for the stairs to figure out what was going on. Geoffrey and his magical mayhem would have to wait a few minutes for me to sort out the domestic drama.

CHAPTER TWO

"Mia," I called up the stairs as I climbed them, Bert hopping along behind me complaining the whole way up. "Mia, get up." Geoffrey stayed downstairs.

There was no answer.

"Mia!" I called, banging on her door with my fist. "What's going on?"

I heard mumbling and shuffling coming towards the door. When it opened, I saw my best friend on the other side with wild, blond, bed-head hair. She had her body wrapped in the comforter like a mummy in down-cushioned wrappings. When I looked past her into the room the mystery of the missing cushions was solved: all of them were piled high on top of her bed with extra blankets and cushions all but spilling off of the mattress. I marveled that she'd been able to climb on top of it all. I'm not sure I could have managed it.

"Mia, what's going on?"

She yawned. "I couldn't sleep on this mattress. It's lumpy. I kept thinking that if I could just put more pillows and soft cushions on top of it I wouldn't notice it anymore, but it didn't help. I've been awake most of the night and I can't fall asleep. What time is it? It's not time to go yet, is it?" We were supposed to be at our internships at the courthouse at eight; it was six-thirty in the morning.

There couldn't be anything wrong with the mattress. It wasn't new, but it had been mine when I'd lived here in high school. I'd taken over my stepmother's old room when we moved in, since it was bigger. I didn't remember the bed ever being lumpy, and I'd always slept just fine on it. Then again, we had learned that Evangeline was trying to slowly curse me for years. She'd affected my memory, she'd killed my father, and then she'd tried to kill me. It wasn't outside the realm of possibility that she'd done something to the mattress as well, no matter how petty or silly it seemed.

"We'll have to tear it apart later today and try to see what's wrong with it, but we both need to get moving here shortly. There's coffee downstairs but, I'm going to warn you, Aiden's dad is in the kitchen." Bert harrumphed his way past me into the room. "You even took my pillow, Mia. Where was I supposed to sleep? I can't climb up on a bed unless there's something next to it that I can use as a step, and I certainly can't climb up there to get my pillow back. What's a frog supposed to do to get some sleep around here?"

She sighed, and pulled his pillow down from the mound of fluffiness on the bed. I hoped we could come up with a decent solution; I knew neither one of us could afford to replace the mattress anytime soon. "I'm sorry, Bert. I didn't mean to take your pillow, but I didn't know what else to do."

I sympathized. She was going to have a long day today. Our internships at the courthouse only lasted for the morning, but we were both working at the Schuster Center for the Performing Arts downtown in the evenings, and our boss had encouraged us to attend the performance that night. We'd be selling ticket subscriptions to the different series of performances as telemarketers, and she wanted us to be able to describe the current run. It was going to be late when we finally called it a night, and she'd be dragging long before we even started thinking about going home.

"What's Aiden's dad doing here? He doesn't live here."

I had to remind myself that Mia hadn't gone through the portal with me when I'd been taken by my stepbrother and stepmother last fall. "I think he came through the portal in the basement. He's faerie. There's a problem."

Her eyes widened as I explained. "I guess I better go get ready then. It's not like I'm gonna be able to get to sleep now," Mia said, as she grabbed her bathrobe and headed for the shower.

I turned to Bert. "Why do I have a bad feeling about this?"

He cocked his head up at me. "Because you're not stupid, Janie. I've got a bad feeling about this as well. But first, I'm going to get some more sleep now that I have my pillow back."

I wished I could. I'd woken up an hour earlier than I'd planned when I'd realized someone was in the house. If I was going to be up this early, I'd much rather have been talking to Geoffrey and calling Aiden to try to figure out what needed to be done rather than going to work. I hated having to juggle real life and faerie emergencies at the same time. And I'd been excited about the internship we'd both landed. Instead, I headed downstairs, and convinced Geoffrey that we'd keep our eyes peeled until we could figure out what was going on.

He didn't act like he wanted to leave until I agreed to fill up a thermos of coffee for him. I'm not sure if it was a desire for coffee, or a hope I would drop some kind of hint about how Aiden thought of him. He kept asking about his son, but I didn't really have a lot to tell him other than that he was fine, and we were seeing each other. Aiden had been very tight-lipped about his dad ever since September. I didn't know the party line, so I didn't say anything extra.

"Look, Geoffrey, I'll keep an eye out, but I don't really have time this morning to show you the sights. I'm supposed to start a new job in about an hour, and I've got to get Mia out of the house and ready to work. This is about the worst timing you could have had."

"I'm sorry, but the nasty evil Seawitch didn't let me schedule it into my calendar." Sarcasm dripped out of his smirk as his said it. "Look, I get that you're busy, but we can't let someone walk around thinking they're safe when they aren't. Take this." He handed me a curved cylinder that looked like it was made from bone.

"What is this?" I asked. It looked like part of an antler of a really big animal, but I couldn't tell for sure what it was. I'd never seen an animal with horns or antlers that big. Could it have been a rhinoceros or an elephant? No, more likely a really big deer or elk. Maybe a moose? Possibly, but I'd never seen horns like that before. Besides, if it was rhinoceros or elephant, I thought I'd seen a report on CNN that said it was illegal to hunt those animals for their ivory. I wouldn't want to get in trouble for possessing it. I said as much to Geoffrey.

"It's more than four hundred years old, so I'm pretty sure they got the horn before that law got passed, Janie, since the laws in your country are a lot newer than that. And be careful with it; I'm not sure it's even possible to replace it."

I held it up to one ear and shook it. "It doesn't seem all that fragile, or all that heavy. What am I supposed to do with it? What does it do?"

He grabbed my hand, stopping my motions in testing it out. "It's a tinderbox, but I wouldn't use it for carrying a tinder for a fire. It's magical."

Of course it was.

He continued, "If you are in need of magical assistance you open the box, and whatever you need will come out. Just don't overuse it. The magic needs time to recharge after it's been used, and if you use it too much it won't be available when you need it." He showed me how to open the cap at the base of the horn, which was ornately carved and fitted perfectly into the end.

I put it down on the counter. "What do you expect me to do to earn it?" Everything in faerie generally comes with a price.

He laughed. "My son has taught you well to be leery of us, but in this case we are merely asking you to do a favor for us in helping to locate the target of the Seawitch. It would be rude of us to ask you for help and not provide you with magical assistance that's available."

Well, when he put it that way, it seemed churlish of me to refuse. And where would I have been if Aiden had taken my reluctance to believe in magic to heart last fall? I took the tinderbox from Geoffrey. If nothing else, I could at least warn the right person and put the tinderbox in their hands so they would be able to protect themselves.

That was the least I could do, wasn't it?

I took the tinderbox and stuffed it in my backpack, telling Geoffrey that he had to leave once he finished his coffee. I needed to get dressed and get to work.

And after I was done with my internship for the day, I'd have to see what Aiden said about all this before I did anything else. I had a bad feeling about this.

CHAPTER THREE

I got ready for my internship, and then Mia and I headed out. It was our first day to work with Judge Neederhorn, and we'd been looking forward to it ever since we'd gotten our acceptance letters.

We were both dressed in suits, ready to blend in with the nameless hordes of lawyers and judges coming in and out of the courthouse, but when we got to the judge's office we were a bit shocked by what we saw.

This guy had a bust of himself outside his inner office door. There was a signed photograph of him on the wall, giving us a thumbs up. The rest of the office was decorated with the kinds of things that made the judge look like a rock star: posters of him taking the place of Freddie Mercury in concert, a painting that superimposed his own face on Napoleon's, a sculpture of him as the Thinking Man. No matter how successful I might someday be, I promised myself I'd never have a nude sculpture of myself in my waiting room. That was more than a little creepy.

His secretary asked us to have a seat as we waited on him; he was late. Based on the lack of reaction and surprise on the faces of his staff, I got the impression this wasn't unusual.

We sat in the lobby for an hour waiting for the judge to show up and tell us what we were supposed to be doing. I asked the secretary more than once if we had the time wrong. "No, you're fine, but I don't have any work to give you until he gets here. I'm sorry you have to wait, but I've written down what time you got here so you get credit for it."

We were getting paid for the internship, but it wasn't a lot. Still, as long as we weren't losing out on an hour's pay, I was okay with waiting.

Nearly an hour after we had been told to be there, an older man with wild gray hair came in wearing shorts and a t-shirt that said, "Justice happens" with a big smiley face wearing an old fashioned

English judge's wig. Trailing behind him were three people dressed very severely in tailored gray suits and talking about different types of fabric. I couldn't figure out why they were talking about material, but the secretary waved us to follow her into the judge's office. As the judge settled himself behind the desk, the three gray suits began measuring his arms, his neck, and his wrists.

"Ah, you must be my summer interns," he boomed, brushing off the three suits. "I have a very special research assignment for you."

I whipped out a legal pad to take notes, and saw Mia doing the same out of the corner of my eye.

"I need you to find me case precedent that allows me to issue an order regarding the potholes on Wayne Avenue. No one has filed anything yet, but there's no reason to wait. We need to do something *now* to get things fixed rather than waiting for some lawyer to dig up a client who might get hurt. We should do something good before something bad happens." He held out his arms for the grey suits to keep measuring.

My jaw dropped. Courts can't randomly order people to do things. There has to be a lawsuit filed. Someone has to ask the court to do something before they can. That was Civil Procedure 101; a court can't order something without a case in front of it. There was no law out there that would allow us to do what he seemed to want to do. It flat out did not exist. There was nowhere to look, nowhere to research, nowhere to even begin. It was not allowed.

Period.

Mia and I gave each other identical horrified glances, before turning back to the judge and asking him if there were any similar suits already pending before the court. No. Were there any lawsuits even closely related to problems with the potholes on that specific road? No. Any pending cases involving accidents near the potholes? No.

I wasn't sure what he expected us to do even as he asked us for a written argument to support his position by the end of our workday on Friday. "And make sure it's footnoted. Footnotes make things look better," he said, as he shooed us out the door. I heard him talking about gabardine wool and silk linings, braided trim and gold thread, with the grey suited men.

We shrugged our shoulders as we asked the secretary to point us in the direction of the law library, and promised to check in before the end of the day. The secretary shrugged as if she was used to his antics, and told us to give it our best shot.

What could we do?

We headed off to the library to spend a few hours trying to find even a sliver of reasonable argument for an unreasonable position. By noon we were both ready to beat holes in the wall with our own heads. Would practicing law be like this all the time? The only thing we could hope for was that the judge would remove his head from his rear end and stop obsessing about his stupid robes long enough to realize he was basically asking us to do the impossible.

Finally, it was noon. We trudged back to the judge's office to check in with his secretary. We could hear the suits rattling off measurements and I saw one of them holding up fabric swatches. Had they really been talking about robes all morning?

I didn't dare ask. Somehow, I had the sinking thought that if I said something it would get back to the judge I disapproved of. While I thought he should be doing more important work than getting new robes, I wasn't exactly experienced enough to have any credibility with a judge looking down the barrel of retirement. He had many more years of experience to draw from. If he said he could do it, who were we to tell him that he couldn't? I could see many boring hours of research ahead of us without an end in sight.

And yet, I had another mystery to solve before I worried about the crazy judge. Who was the Seawitch, and what could Aiden tell me about her?

CHAPTER FOUR

I had a few hours that afternoon to try to make sense of my morning before I had to appear at my night job. I intended to use them by tracking down Aiden and trying to get some answers.

When I'd first met Aiden, he'd been waiting tables at the same restaurant where I'd meet my stepmother for brunch every week. At the time I'd thought him just a cute, albeit clumsy, distraction from a family obligation. I'd thought the biggest danger I'd been in had been from him accidentally dumping water in my lap or dropping my food on my head. In reality, my stepmother had insisted on the meetings as a way to keep tabs on me, try to curse me like she had my father, and monitor any progress I'd made on figuring out the location of the Holder of the Grimm family Legacy. That hadn't worked out so well for her, but Aiden and I were still doing an awkward one-step-forward-two-steps-back approach to each other.

Some of that had to do with how we'd met. I'd been concerned that a relationship forged in magical lands, mortal danger, and fairy tales wasn't something with a strong foundation for a future. Never mind the amount of distraction I'd had in finishing up my first year of law school. Long nights and high stress levels weren't exactly good for a budding romance. And there was also the half-faerie thing.

I wouldn't have had a problem with any cultural background he might have been from . . . if he'd been 100 percent human. Doris, Aiden's mother, didn't talk much about her time with Geoffrey, but one could tell there had been strong feelings there. Why had they split? Had my stepmother required it? Had it been a clash of culture they couldn't get past? What if there had been some obligation he had to leave them for? Aiden had tried to tell me it wouldn't happen that way for us, but I didn't want to set myself up for that kind of heartache. I was just feeling like I was getting my life back together after all the craziness my stepmother had put me through.

Yet I couldn't quite stay away from Aiden. I liked him. Truth be told, I liked him a lot. And here I was running right for him when faerie magic hinky stuff reared its ugly head in my life again.

I didn't know that I had another choice. He was now the active, on-call person for the F.A.B.L.E.S. organization—The Foundation for Ancestry, Biography, Legends, Epics, and Stories. Most of the members had a hand in training him, so they could step back a moment or so and enjoy a retirement I was sure they richly deserved. Many of them had given hours and hours over the years, away from their families and other obligations, and Aiden wanted the position badly.

Too bad it didn't pay very well. He'd had to take on a second job. The restaurant gig hadn't lasted; too many broken dishes made it hard to keep up with the bills and pay for damages. When he found out that Mia and I would be working evenings at the theater, he'd applied for a job as an usher. "That way," he'd said, "we'd see each other on a regular basis, even if we were at work at the same time, and there are no dishes to break."

That made sense, but I knew we wouldn't be able to talk about magical stuff at work. And, as it turned out, we would be working in different parts of the building. We'd only see each other if we carpooled or if we got a break at the same time, which wasn't a guarantee, so I was determined to go see Aiden that afternoon.

I dropped Mia by the house in my stepmother's handed down Escalade. I hated driving it, but I'd sold Dad's old Buick in favor of the newer car in hopes of having less maintenance to budget for while I was in school. Mia was already yawning before we left the courthouse, so I took the quickest way home that I knew, made sure she got inside, and headed back downtown to the warehouse F.A.B.L.E.S. called headquarters.

I parked and headed for the door, rapping sharply with my knuckles on the corrugated old building to let them know someone was waiting outside. I hadn't noticed all the bells and whistles last time. Then again, the last time Doris had been there and we'd all been carrying in food for a potluck. It took a few minutes before Trusty John slid a metal panel back and asked me for a password. I didn't know it.

"Then I can't let you in," he said, looking sadly at me, and shutting the little door in my face. That was odd; last time John had practically tripped over himself in an effort to do anything for me that he could. Did they already know about the Seawitch? What was the reason for all the security? Of course, for all I knew, that was security when there wasn't a group meeting.

I banged on the door again until he opened the viewing panel. "John, it's me, Janie Grimm. I'm here to see Aiden. I have information for him that he's going to want to hear."

John started to shut the door on me again, and I saw Aiden over his shoulder. I started banging on the metal with both fists, yelling that Aiden needed to talk to me and he needed to tell John to let me in. He finally came over and argued with John until I was allowed, grudgingly, into the warehouse.

"What's going on that you guys have the place locked up so tight?" I asked, as I stepped through the door.

Aiden came over to me with his arms piled high with gizmos and gadgets that were going off with all kinds of electronic beeps, chirps, and whistles as I got closer to him. "Are you wearing your necklace?" he asked.

Aiden had given me a necklace nine months ago, when I was still new to all the magic stuff. It was supposed to keep one safe from magical effects, at least long enough to get away. I hadn't worn it since my stepmother had been imprisoned by the faerie court; who needed magical protection when the person out to get you was under lock and key? Besides, Aiden had warned me against wearing it too much, so I'd forgotten completely about it in my rush to go ask him about magic. I should have thought to worn it, and I told him so.

"No, really, it's a good idea that you're not wearing it if you're coming here. There are so many other magical devices we've been testing that it would make everything go crazy."

All his gadgets were already going crazy. I raised my eyebrows as they whirled and whirred and beeped and buzzed. "Um, then why is everything making noise?"

"I don't know." He waved various bits and items and gee-gaws around like the deputy who waved around that wand at courthouse security when someone set off the metal detector. Everything got louder when he got closest to my backpack. "What have you got in there?" he asked.

I sighed. I'd hoped for a few minutes to talk to him normally without bringing up the visit from his father. There was no way around it; I'd have to get right to the point.

CHAPTER FIVE

"I had a visitor this morning, Aiden. It was your dad."

He adjusted the dials on his gizmos to turn down the whirring noises, without looking up. "What did he want?"

"He wants my help. Our help. There's been a jail break."

"Your stepmother?"

"No. The Seawitch."

With that, I knew I had his attention. Even Trusty John dropped what he was doing, his jaw gaping open in shock. "Start at the beginning. What happened?"

I set down my backpack, and John and Aiden moved the magic detecting whatsits to the other side of the room. They calmed down as they got further away. That's when I remembered what was in my backpack. I quickly explained Geoffrey's request for help in figuring out the Seawitch's target.

Aiden's eyebrows were raised so high that they were almost merging with his hairline. "Did you just say the *Seawitch* is out for revenge? That's worse than anything I can think of, honestly. And all my father gave you was a box? What the heck is that for?"

I tried to remember what he'd called it. "I think he said it's a tinderbox."

I hadn't thought those eyebrows could go any higher, but they did.

"He must think highly of you to hand over the Tinderbox. It's pretty powerful." He paused for a moment. "Wait a minute, is that what's in your backpack? No wonder all my detectors are going off. It would be like setting off an atomic bomb on top of a radiation sensor."

John nodded. "Well, I guess we know they work now," he said, as he peered over my shoulder.

I reached into my backpack and pulled out the box. I handed it to him. "How does it work? Your dad said that all I had to do was open it and whatever I needed would come out."

"Well, yeah, but it's still faerie magic. Which means that you might be stuck in a cage for all eternity and open the box, but instead of a skeleton key to get out, you might get a bottomless lunch pail to keep from starving to death. I'm not saying it's not help; it just might not be exactly the help you wanted when you reached into the box."

"So I shouldn't use it? Why would he give me something that wouldn't help?"

Aiden shrugged. "It'll help; it just won't be quite the way you'd like it to help. It's unpredictable, which is pretty much par for the course. That said, I can't remember the last time this thing was used, much less the last time anyone took it outside of the faerie realm."

"He did say something about not using it too often, or the magic of the tinderbox wouldn't recharge itself, or something like that."

He snorted. "It should be good and charged at this point. I don't think I've ever seen it before, although I've seen pictures, and heard enough about it to know just how powerful it is. I wouldn't go anywhere without it until we get all of this figured out, but it would be pretty tricky if you had to use it in public."

Something about what he'd just said triggered my there's-more-he's-not-telling-me sense. "What do you mean by pretty tricky if I had to use it in public?"

Aiden sat down heavily in a folding metal chair, which teetered and wobbled as if it wanted to close up on him like a metal jaw of clumsiness devouring his lanky frame. In all the time I'd known him, Aiden couldn't walk and chew gum at the same time. Oh, heck, he couldn't walk without falling down, tripping over his own feet, or just plain finding some way to cause chaos without trying. He was convinced it was due to his half-faerie genetic inheritance. I thought at least some of it was his own natural self-consciousness, which came from years of klutzy making him worry about every single step, wave, or gesture.

I grabbed the back of the chair to keep him from falling backwards. He righted himself, and nodded at me, red faced at yet another reminder of him being somewhat different from most other guys out there. Truthfully, I think he was more embarrassed about the half-faerie thing than anyone else who knew, including me.

He continued with the conversation, ignoring his own faults and my own inner monologue. "You can't predict how that thing is going to decide to help you. What if a dragon came out of the tinderbox while you were at a baseball game?"

"Well, it is Dayton. They'd probably think it was a publicity stunt." Dayton had a minor league baseball team, which fed into the Cincinnati Reds farm system. The Dayton Dragons had been a highlight of the downtown scene for a few years. I loved going to the games.

He snorted at me. "You know what I mean. A dragon in center field breathing fire on the lawn seats is not necessarily keeping magic under wraps. A hellhound on Courthouse Square would be noticed. And a banshee at the opera? Well, not everyone would know the difference, but enough people would notice. Those kinds of things are frowned on. The magical world gets a lot of freedom in our world because they keep things under wraps. If the Seawitch is going around killing people, sooner or later the bodies are going to pile up. She likes leaving a trail. Major magic in front of the public will raise too many questions."

I settled myself on another chair, managing to unfold it and sit down without hurting myself. "But don't those things happen anyway? I mean, we do have the tabloids that can't seem to report anything but craziness."

"But what happens when it starts getting reported on the eleven o'clock news? In the mainstream papers? Will we start having armed guards at portals?"

The idea of the government taking over my basement was simultaneously amusing and disturbing. I certainly didn't want that to happen. I nodded at him, but then a thought occurred to me. "But wouldn't that make your job easier, Aiden? I mean, if the government could act against magic, wouldn't it be easier to figure out where the threats are coming from, and how to take care of it? You'd have more resources and more help, and more money to use to handle these things."

He shook his head. "You think I'd be allowed to do this kind of work with my background? You think they'd try to negotiate anything? It would be brute force, trying to protect humans from magic. Neither side wants to see it. Especially the faerie courts. They would lose a lot of freedom, a lot of their influence, and, well, a lot of the things that make them who they are if they were confined or catalogued or processed or put in government issued boxes. And, just like us, they'd fight like hell to prevent being put in such a position. We'd have an all-out magical war on our hands. And the non-magical side would have a big disadvantage."

That, I figured, we could do without.

CHAPTER SIX

Aiden was right. No one wanted an all-out war, but I couldn't figure out who the Seawitch was looking for. Maybe she didn't care as long as she got her revenge. But I still had to figure out who she was looking for revenge against. Maybe that would stop things from escalating.

And then there was also the issue of dealing with whatever fallout might be on the horizon with Geoffrey's reappearance. Aiden didn't ask about his father. I felt uncomfortable bringing it up, but I felt just as uncomfortable *not* bringing it up. I took a deep breath. "Aiden, I . . . if you want to talk about your dad, I'm here to listen."

He ignored me, which would have pissed me off if I didn't know him well enough to realize he wasn't trying to be rude, he just didn't want to talk about it yet. Maybe it was because John was listening in. I'd have to ask him later, maybe after work.

"Janie, do you have any idea who the Seawitch might be after? The faster we can figure out who it is, the faster you're out of danger. I don't like the idea of you being the lightening rod on this."

Aw, he cared. "I don't have a clue. What can you tell me about the Seawitch?" I asked. "I don't know the underlying story."

"I don't know it well, but I can tell you the Seawitch would sign contracts with mortals, giving them exactly what they asked for, and then tell them they had to perform some kind of nearly impossible task in order to prevent the forfeit of the very life essence the Seawitch feeds on. Once it feeds, there is no bringing someone back. If they survive, they'll end up a drooling vegetable, with no brain activity and in a permanent irreversible coma."

Why did it have to be contracts? I might have gotten through my first year of law school with a decent understanding of contracts and binding agreements, but that didn't mean I liked them. And his warning about the Seawitch definitely struck a chord. I did not want to sign up for that. Aiden offered to do more research, and to come to the house the next day with his findings. I wondered if Geoffrey would make another appearance, but kept my silence on that issue. I'd push him more on it later when other ears weren't listening in. I wondered why he didn't want John to hear it. Of course, I could be wrong, and he just didn't want to talk about it at all.

John put the tinderbox back in my backpack and Aiden took it from him to walk me out to my car. "Be careful, Janie. You just don't know where danger might come from when you're mixed up in faerie court business. I should know."

"I'll be careful, I promise. I'll see you tonight at the theater. And then we'll get lunch tomorrow and start digging through some of Dad's old books to see if there's anything about the Seawitch."

My dad had been a professor of folklore and history before he'd gotten sick and died. Many of his books were still in the library, as my stepmother had forgotten them in her mad purge of his effects after his death. I'd been meaning to offer them to Aiden; I just hadn't gotten around to saying anything about them. I didn't have much use for them since, after my stepmother was under lock and key, magic had kind of gone away in my life until now. Of course, today was the day I didn't have the time I'd like to sift through them looking for answers. Aiden would do better with the books than I would, and he had more time to get them organized.

He opened my door for me, and I sat down inside the car, behind the wheel. He leaned in to say good bye. I turned my head and kissed him, a short peck on the lips as he leaned in. Aiden's head jerked back, as if he was surprised.

"What's wrong?" I asked, reaching one hand up to his face.

"I didn't expect that," he said, a wry smile on his face. "That's not a complaint. I was just surprised."

I wasn't sure how to take that. "Why surprised? We've been dating. Yes, we've been busy but we like each other, and you looked upset so I wanted to see you smile."

That got me a big, face-splitting grin.

"That's better," I said, smiling back at him. "Now, what time do you have to be at the theater? I have about an hour or so before I have to be there, but I have to go pick up Mia. Do you need a lift?"

He nodded. Aiden's notorious klutziness meant his car was in the shop more than it was working. I was surprised he was able to keep a valid driver's license and insurance with all the accidents he got into, but he didn't think the bus was a good idea. He'd told me he'd tripped going up the steps into the bus once and knocked out his own front tooth. He ended up in the emergency room waiting for stitches when the police had brought in someone who was high on something to the point of trashing the ER. That out of control patient had broken Aiden's arm in the process. I didn't think anyone could have had that bad of luck, but it was Aiden. If there was a way to get hurt, he'd find it, even if he wasn't looking for it.

"I need to be there at four-thirty," he said, "Why don't I just go with you to get Mia? By the time you got her, it would be time to get back downtown again."

He was right, so I nodded. He went around the back of the car and got in the passenger's side. As he sat down, I turned to him. "And we'll get to spend a few more minutes together."

I could tell he was still preoccupied with the mention of his father, but I didn't want to push. I put the car into gear and pulled out of the parking lot. We drove in silence for a minute, until I asked if he had any thoughts about who the Seawitch might be after and whether that person might be in Dayton or not.

"I don't know if they're in Dayton, but it would make sense. This town isn't the only one with portals to the faerie realm. If the Seawitch was looking for someone, it would make sense to go through a portal that would go to the place where the person she was looking for would be found."

That made sense. But how many portals could there be? Visions of hundreds of open, swirling purple pools of air where faerie beings could come through and go after humans made me nauseous just to think about it. How could we normal humans sleep at night? How could we feel safe and secure? Ignorance might be bliss, but I wasn't sure I'd sleep knowing there were so many options for danger to slip into our lives.

Then again, I hoped he was right. The idea of having to search the whole world without knowing a direction seemed worse than the idea of having the Seawitch right in my own backyard. And then there was the idea that maybe I could encourage that person not to give up the fight; my own experiences had taught me there was a way out of the craziness. Maybe I could help them without getting involved and getting into danger. Yeah, I probably wasn't quite that lucky.

I pulled into my own driveway and honked the horn for Mia, who stumbled bleary-eyed out the front door, and wondered if I'd have any better luck at staying out of danger this time around.

Somehow, I was pretty certain it wouldn't work.

Mia got into the car, slamming the door as she let out a jaw-cracking yawn.

"Did you get any sleep?" I asked. She shook her head and laid her head against the arm rest in the back seat, cushioning it with her purse as she closed her eyes again.

Aiden gave me a questioning look, but I shushed him, refusing to answer the question written all over his face. I didn't know how to explain her sudden insomnia and the pillow and blanket theft from this morning.

We rode in silence with Aiden giving me funny looks the whole way.

I parked the car in the garage next to the Schuster Center for the Performing Arts, and shut off the engine. Mia emerged from the backseat, rubbing her eyes and stretching her arms over her head before she followed us inside, silently bobbing along behind us as we headed in to the office. Aiden gave me a peck on the cheek when I headed inside the ticket office, and Mia almost walked into us, zombie-like. She muttered something incoherent, presumably an apology for stumbling into us, and shuffled past to get inside and clock in.

"Is she okay?" he asked, as he turned to watch the door shut behind her.

"She didn't sleep well last night. I dropped her off at home to get a quick nap before I stopped to see you. I guess she couldn't fall asleep." I shrugged. "What can you do? I just didn't want her behind the wheel today, so we carpooled. At least she made it to work."

"Does she have a problem with insomnia?"

"Not that she's ever complained about before, but she just moved in and she said the bed wasn't very comfortable. She probably just has to get used to it. If it's that bad, we'll try switching beds and see if it helps."

He made an incoherent noise, and I couldn't tell what he was trying to say. I'm still working on trying to read him. Aiden can do blank expression better than anyone when he doesn't want anyone to know what he's thinking. Even so, I could almost see the wheels spinning in his head. I knew he was thinking about something . . . the question was what? What could my roommate's inability to get some shut eye be triggering in that brain of his?

I didn't have time to ask. I squeezed his hand and promised to give him a ride home after work in hope that I could pry whatever conclusion he was coming to out of his head.

I ducked in the door just in time to find that the evening was already going to be a long one, and that I'd need to get some coffee into my best friend to get her through the night.

CHAPTER SEVEN

O ur supervisor, a middle-aged lady wearing a cheap navy blazer with a tan skirt that fell below her knees, was standing in front of the room calling the meeting to order and laying out quotas for the night. Tonight was the dress rehearsal for the newest release at the performing arts center, and she wanted us to hit our quotas in the first two hours of our normal work shift, then watch the dress rehearsal in order to be able to better sell ticket subscriptions over the phone over the next few weeks.

I couldn't believe what I was hearing. She wanted us to sell the same quota on our first night about a show we didn't know in half the time with almost no training. Something wasn't right, but I was hoping two hours of insane cold calling would result in sales I wasn't expecting. What could I say? I was most definitely the newbie here, with no idea what that might entail.

I poured a cup of coffee for myself and for Mia the minute our meeting was over, and sat down at my computer terminal to get started. I opened up the screen with the call script and hit the button on the phone to start dialing. I hate this job, but I guess it could be worse. At least I wasn't flipping burgers or standing outside in the heat, or well, there were worse telemarketing jobs. I was glad to be talking about the newest stage production of The Little Mermaid instead of answering the phone for a number that began with 1-900.

The next two hours were a blur of hang-up phone calls, answering machines, and annoyed parents answering the phones just as they'd sat down to dinner. I heard screaming child after fussy baby after tantrum after fighting siblings, like a cycle of insanity chasing itself in a circle of formula, pacifiers, and lack of naps. When I finally hung up and tried to shake my head to clear the ringing in my ears, I noticed Mia had slumped over in the seat next to me, sound asleep. I elbowed her hard in the ribs and she jumped.

"Hey," I whispered. "Wake up and have some more coffee. We'll try to figure out something with the bed tonight, I promise. You've got to get some sleep or you won't make it through the summer."

She nodded, and gave me a weak smile. "Thanks, Janie."

I kept watching her, nudging her when I thought she was starting to doze off. We didn't quite hit our quota, but we got closer than I'd thought we would when it was time for us to go watch the dress rehearsal. The supervisors finally let us gather our things to head for the theater. As we settled in the seats, I promised to at least keep Mia from snoring. I could absolutely handle that if I was going to get paid to watch a stage production tonight. I was looking forward to it as the Schuster Center hadn't been built the last time I'd gone to see anything on stage. I remembered my mother had taken me to watch a holiday ballet show when I was five.

And I was happy to be remembering that. My stepmother, the faerie witch queen that she'd been—no, really—had tried to bind my memories about my mother, keep me in the dark about the truth that killed my father, and tried to keep me from having a long and full life myself. Memories were still coming back to me after all this time. Every time I thought I'd remembered everything, a new memory, like my mother taking me to the ballet, would crop up to remind me, painfully, that Evangeline had tried to take away my memories like she had taken away my father. My mother had died when I was young, so in taking away my impressions of her it was like she'd tried to take my mother as well.

The lights had barely gone down when I saw Mia's eyelids droop. I didn't have the heart to do much more than make sure the supervisor didn't have a direct line of vision to see whether or not she was asleep, and nudge her if she made any sound that even started to hint of snoring. She was exhausted.

The show started and it was wonderful. I only knew the story of the mermaid who gave up her singing voice to gain legs to catch her prince through the Disney movie version. I didn't know all the twists and turns of the story, which wasn't as cute and cuddly as the singing lobster in the movie might have made me think. I wished I'd brought Bert along; he'd have enjoyed the show, I was sure, but there were just too many people from the office sitting together to risk having to explain why I had a frog sitting on my lap. And he'd have been a distraction to me, as well as to everyone else. I'd have to think about bringing him at some point and finding a place for him to watch safely out of everyone else's sight. I figured he'd like it.

When the show ended we all stood up and clapped, whistling and hollering for the cast, trying to make up for the fact we were the only ones in the theater. As I stood, I grabbed Mia's elbow to stand her up as well. I felt bad that she'd missed the whole thing, but I don't think I'd ever seen her quite so tired.

The actors came out on the stage and took their bows. Even with all of us cheering, it sounded awfully quiet, and yet, I almost didn't hear it at first.

The main actress, the one who'd played the mermaid, wasn't bowing. She wasn't dropping into a curtsy, and she wasn't waving at any of us in the stands. Instead, she had her hand to her forehead, shielding her eyes from the floodlights, searching the audience for something. As we quieted down, I heard her asking, "Where is the songstress?"

The *who?* I wondered. As if I didn't have enough mystery people to find, here was another one. Was the universe playing a sick joke on me?

Everyone went silent, the clapping dying abruptly as she began asking over and over, "Where is she? Where is the Songstress?" The more she talked, the more I realized she was using the term as a title or a name rather than as a description.

The actress was holding her face in her hands, her voice climbing into a high whine as she climbed down from the stage and headed toward the only people in the theater who were not on the stage: us. Before she got too close a young man with spiky brown hair stopped her. He quieted her down, and guided her back to the stage where the stagehands and other actors took her back to her dressing room. He came back to the rest of us.

"You folks should probably go on home. The dress rehearsal is over, and the cast and crew have the day off tomorrow. The director will call a meeting to go over the notes tomorrow afternoon, and then opening day is the day after. Andrea is probably just overtired. We've been working long hours getting ready for opening night."

Mia stepped forward in front of me, more awake than I'd seen her all day. "I'm sorry. I didn't catch your name. Did she find what she was looking for?"

"I don't know what she was looking for. I think it was just nerves. She's spent so much time in character lately, and she can be a Method actor from time to time if she starts thinking it will help her performance. I'm Jonah, by the way. Jonah Warren. I'm one of the understudies, for the part of the prince and a few others, but I didn't have a scripted part for the dress rehearsal."

Mia gave him a coy look. "If you are an understudy does that mean you get paid to just be here and practice in case someone is hurt or sick or has an emergency?"

"Pretty much, but being an understudy is a high stress job if you get called on to take over a role for a night, because you don't always know about it until the last minute. Understudies have to learn more than one part, so they generally have to be at most of the performances even if they aren't going to be on stage, so they can rehearse the lines for their different parts as the play unfolds. Otherwise, we're just called on to help out the principals if they need extra practice, or to generally help out around the place."

"Like tonight," she said. She was acting like she'd come alive when he'd come up to us, and I knew I was staring at her in shock. We'd never seen this guy before, and she had been asleep just ten minutes ago, but now she was flirting like a besotted teenager with this stranger. That wasn't like Mia. She was normally more sophisticated with guys than I was, but she also wasn't someone who flirted with a total stranger. This was odd.

I heard yelling from backstage, a female voice, calling out for the Songstress, again. "Are you sure she's okay?" I asked, indicating to the upset actress backstage. "Should someone call a doctor or something?"

He shook his head. "Andrea is a drama queen. She's gotten the lead role and has been lording it over everyone. She probably heard people talking about a singer somewhere and twisted it for her own purposes. She likes attention and she likes having everyone fawning over her. I'd bet the contents of my wallet she's already tipped off a reporter somewhere about mystical connections or something in the theater. Or, at least I would, if there were any contents in my wallet. Understudy doesn't pay much." Jonah began herding us toward the door at the back of the theater as the floodlights on the stage were turned off. It was time to go home.

I let him point us out to the lobby as I dug my keys out of my purse, intending to head straight for the parking garage and then home, but I couldn't leave without Aiden. He hadn't been sitting with us in the theater, and I didn't see him in the lobby with the rest of the staff. I pulled out my cell phone and sent him a text message telling him where we were at, and asking him to meet us in the lobby.

Jonah was talking as I stared at my phone, waiting for a response from Aiden. ". . . always needed to be the center of attention. Andrea hasn't been with the company long, but when she snagged the lead so fast, no one could tell her she was wrong. There's a lot of pressure on her to pull off this role, and her understudy is just chomping at the bit to see Andrea screw it up so she can take over. I wouldn't be surprised if there was some kind of sabotage. It happens all the time in the theater. In fact, Kirsten, her understudy, was the one we all thought would get the role anyway."

Still no response from Aiden to my text message.

"So how did Andrea end up with the part?" Mia asked. "And how come you're not one of the leads?"

Jonah gave her a shy smile. "I wish you were one making the casting decisions. Actors don't always get explanations for why they get cast or why they don't. It's a decision that's made by the director of the play for the direction he sees for the play to go. Just because someone gets the lead in one play doesn't mean they'll always get the lead, although every company has people who tend to be cast more than others. It doesn't even always have to do with ability, so there's no way to know why a decision might be made on casting."

"Well, you should have gotten the part," Mia said, turning on the charm and touching his upper arm lightly with her fingertips, curling up beside him in such a way that there was no mistaking her interest.

For someone operating with almost no sleep it was an impressive show of self-awareness in attempting to impress the opposite sex. They weren't paying any attention to me as Mia flirted with Jonah until my cell phone buzzed in my hand. Aiden was on his way.

I wondered what he'd think of Mia's behavior. It certainly was uncharacteristic of either one of us. I just hoped Aiden wasn't looking for me to act like that. No matter what state our relationship was in I'd feel like a fool if I tried to drape myself on Aiden's arm like that.

Never mind that if I did try to wrap myself around Aiden in that manner it would probably end up with him falling at my feet. And not in the good way.

CHAPTER EIGHT

A iden joined us before I could muster the nerve to ask Mia what was wrong with her, whether she was sleepwalking or she'd had some kind of wacky mushrooms in her lunch. He took in Mia's behavior without commenting on it and said, "We should probably go. The police are on their way and, unless we have something to add to their investigation, we should probably clear out."

"Why are the police here?" Jonah asked.

"Andrea Scolari got tired of the stage hands, the director, and the other actors telling her that they didn't know who the Songstress was or where she was, and she called 911 to make a missing person's report. She actually believes there's a cast member missing, and no one can convince her otherwise. The director told me we should clear out if we haven't been talking to Andrea, because anyone who's talked to her is in for a long night. Apparently, they need to interview everyone she's talked to in order to find out if there really is someone missing or if Andrea is cracking under the pressure. They're going to give the police all of our phone numbers in case they need to ask any more questions."

I didn't want to question it, but I didn't know what else to do. There would be no poking around the theater tonight to get to know my way around, but at least I had some kind of excuse I could use to untangle my roommate from the cute actor.

"Come on, Mia. We better get going. Besides, you were exhausted today. I think we could both do with a good night's sleep." When she acted reluctant to leave I whispered into her ear, "You can see the cute actor tomorrow, you know. We do have to come back to work. And hopefully there won't be any police then and you'll have gotten some more sleep."

She didn't put up much of a fight after that. Jonah insisted on walking us to the car despite Aiden trying to tell him that he had it under control. In fact, Aiden seemed downright upset that Jonah was walking us out, but it wasn't the right time to ask. Finally, we were all in the car with Jonah waving to us as we pulled out and headed home. I offered Aiden the spare bedroom, not feeling comfortable in asking him to spend the night, but definitely not wanting to be alone in the house after that warning from his father this morning. Of course, then there was also the added bonus of him being there to talk to Geoffrey in person should his father make an encore appearance for coffee in the morning. Aiden accepted without much fanfare, but then I worried he was reading more into my invitation than I'd meant. I didn't think we were at the casual overnight stage of a relationship yet. I wasn't looking forward to that discussion.

Mia curled up in the backseat and fell asleep almost immediately, an abrupt change from the animated flirt we'd seen earlier. The snoring coming from the backseat started before we'd even gotten back to the ramps onto highway 35. Aiden gave me a questioning look, but I shook my head at him to keep him quiet on the drive. We pulled into the garage and got out of the car, but Mia never moved. I had to reach into the backseat and shake her awake to get her inside.

Bert met us at the front door. "So, what'd I miss tonight?"

Smart frog. "Well, we got to see the dress rehearsal of the opening production, and some actress ended up calling the police and claiming someone was missing even though we couldn't figure out who she was talking about."

I didn't know frogs could raise their eyebrows. Then again, he didn't really have eyebrows, but he had been human once and it was a very human look of disbelief on his face. "Is she crazy or something?"

I shrugged. "Don't know." It was already eleven at night, and I had to be in the judge's office at eight in the morning. I still needed to have a very awkward discussion with Aiden, and get to bed myself. I wasn't sure if I was up to a detailed recap, but Bert deserved more than the brush off. He'd become a friend.

"Very possible that she's snapped; it's her first lead role. We got out of there before we were stuck answering questions we didn't know anything about until the wee hours of the morning. The play's good, though. I really enjoyed it. And if she hasn't lost her marbles, then maybe we have a lead on where the problem is coming from."

Bert was blocking the hallway, and wouldn't move even as I tried to push past him. "You know, Janie, this could be pretty serious."

"I know. Can you let me by so we're not talking about it on the front porch?"

He didn't budge. "Do you remember the kind of memory fog that your stepmother had you under last year?"

"Of course I do, Bert. Get out of the way so we can all go to bed." Mia was swaying on her feet, ready to drop right there on the porch. I wasn't sure what was wrong with her, but she definitely needed a good night's sleep, or tomorrow would be worse than today.

"Promise me I can go with you tomorrow, and I'll get out of the way."

"Bert, my day isn't exactly like law school where I get a break every hour. I'm working. And it will be boring. Plus, if you leave there's no one here to watch the portal in the basement to make sure we don't have any unexpected visitors. We just had one the other day, and I'd like to not worry about having magical intruders every morning. The next one might not be nice enough to make coffee."

Aiden gave me a funny look, but he kept his mouth shut. He was smart enough to know I was talking about his father.

Bert, however, wasn't discrete enough not to comment on it. "What, you want some kind of doorbell on a magic portal? If something wants in, it's coming in. Seriously, what am I supposed to do, belch at it? I don't have any magic, and I can't lift a weapon. I'm not exactly good at home security."

"All right, Bert," I said, laughing. "You made your point. I still wish there was some way of knowing whether or not someone was in the house before I came downstairs in the morning. And if you're here and we're not, you at least could knock the cordless phone off the handset and call to warn us." We'd practiced this several times after Bert had been stuck in the house last year when I'd been abducted by my stepmother and forced through the portal. He'd memorized the numbers to my cell phone, as well as Aiden's, Mia, and the house number for Doris, Aiden's mom. A list of emergency numbers for the F.A.B.L.E.S. members was listed on the side of the refrigerator just low enough and hidden enough by the wall that Bert would be able to slide in and call any of them if someone or something snuck in, and we'd used initials so no one would be able to use the list to track them all down.

"Yeah," he said, "but then I'm stuck in the house trying to hide from whatever it is that came through while I wait for the cavalry to arrive. I'm better at identifying what's going on and telling you how to handle it than playing security guard."

I couldn't disagree with him there. He definitely had the telling us what to do part right. "Fine, Bert, let us in and you can go with us tomorrow. But no burping, no ribbing, no croaking, and no noise inside the bag until we tell you coast is clear."

"Deal," he said, and hopped out of the way, allowing Mia to stagger past and head for the stairs. I let him go knowing that picking him up would be perceived as an insult after my list of prohibitions for the next day. Bert could be prickly at times if he was reminded of his amphibian state and his own limitations. I didn't want to do that to him.

Mia mumbled a good night and almost fell on the landing, but righted herself and ignored all of us staring at her. No one said a word for a few minutes until Bert broke the silence. "Has someone cast some sort of spell on her to make her a zombie? I mean, she was tired this morning, but I've seen her stay up later and I've never seen her quite this tired before. Janie, what really happened at the theater tonight?"

Had I missed something? Was it a spell that was keeping my roommate from being her normal self or just a lack of sleep in the nervousness of starting our first legal jobs? She had moved in a few weeks ago, but she'd never acted quite that tired first thing in the morning. Even through law school exams, which had involved all-nighters and over-doing the caffeine intake, she hadn't been that exhausted.

I shook my head. There was no way to tell at this point. Everyone has down days, and today had been weirder than normal. I promised myself to keep an eye on her the next day for any signs of magical interference after a good night's sleep. With the portal in the basement it was always possible she was reacting in some odd way to the exposure.

Bert hopped off to the study, which he had claimed as his own sanctuary last month. I assumed he'd retrieved his blanket and pillow and found a way to get them back to his corner. I'd bought a cat bed for him that he called a pillow, with fleece lining and tons of padding, so he'd have a soft place to sleep without having to figure out how to clamber up on a human sized bed.

That left Aiden and I in the hallway, alone, staring at each other, and clearing our throats. As much as I didn't want to send him home, I really didn't know how to start this conversation, either. Could we get back to the worrying about magical interference with my roommate instead of doing uncomfortable relationship discussions?

CHAPTER NINE

"So, um, you still want me to stay?" Aiden asked, staring at his feet.

I had always thought that conversations with boys were supposed to get easier as I got older. I had an odd memory of asking a boy if he sorta kinda wanted to hold my hand behind the playground for just a minute. I was six. I remembered promising him that no one would ever know and no one would see us, and I wouldn't tell anyone. He ran off screaming for his mommy, claiming I had cooties. I'd cried, and Dad had come over to comfort me. Somehow I knew I wouldn't scare off Aiden, but we were on pretty uncertain ground relationship-wise. We'd never spent nights together. We'd gone on dates, held hands, and kissed, but it was all pretty PG-13. He was a good guy, who was still working on his own issues and not pushing me too hard to confront all of mine.

I knew I wanted him to stay, but I didn't know how to explain it. I nodded in lieu of trying to be articulate. Articulate wasn't happening.

He nodded. "No pressure, Janie. I don't want you to feel like we have to do anything, or say anything. I just want to know you're safe. And you're not required to be my father's messenger. If he shows up again I'd like to be here to deal with it. You shouldn't have to. I'll sleep in the guest room if you want."

I could tell that wasn't what he wanted, and realized I didn't either. I wasn't up for a late night, and I didn't think we were ready for anything too crazy, and said so. "It probably sounds nuts, but I'm a little weirded out by the idea of things slipping into the house without any way of stopping them. Your dad came into the kitchen and made coffee this morning. What if it had been someone a little less thoughtful? Say what you will about your father, he came with a message and didn't cause any major issues that we know of. What if it's something not so nice next time?"

"You're wanting someone to stand guard?"

Oh, great. He was thinking of skulking outside my door as I tossed and turned inside. That would so not help me get any sleep, and who knows if Mia would be well rested in the morning. "No, I want you to sleep beside me. Don't get any ideas, because I'm not offering sex. I just don't want to be alone. I'm afraid I wouldn't fall asleep, wondering what was going on in the house with every creak of the stairs. I just want to know there's someone beside me who would have some idea of what to do if something goofy happens. I want to know you're there to help me. And I'll sleep better knowing you're beside me, and not in harm's way. For all we know, the Seawitch could be after you."

"Not hardly, but I'll take it as a compliment that you worry about me. It's a good sign. Yes, I'll sleep beside you tonight if you'll drop me at the warehouse in the morning. I can get Doris to help me get the car out of the shop after you go to work."

Nothing more awkward than mentioning one's mother when about to spend the night with someone of the opposite sex. I had to grin. I knew he didn't mean anything by it. If ever there was someone with less talent than me in impressing a romantic interest it was Aiden. He blushed, and turned to lock the door behind us. I headed into the kitchen to check the back door, and came back shutting out lights and checking the house as I went. He offered me his arm like a Southern gentleman escorting a debutante to a ball. I grinned, and took it.

We went upstairs. Mia's light was already out, and I assumed Bert was already asleep. We went into my room, and Aiden allowed me to go in first and change into my nightclothes before knocking softly and coming inside.

"Obviously, I didn't plan on staying the night, so I didn't bring anything," he said.

Despite Evangeline having claimed she had given away a bunch of my dad's things, she had forgotten a stash of sweatpants he'd hidden in the back of the closet. He used to wear them around the house on lazy Sunday mornings before he'd married her, but she had always insisted he wear matching pajamas after we moved into her house. I found them when I'd taken over her room and closets for my own, but I doubted she'd even known they were there. I offered a pair to Aiden to sleep in. After some back and forth, he agreed.

We settled in for the night, curling up together and trying to get comfortable. I wasn't used to sleeping beside someone else, and it seemed like he wasn't either, but I was glad he was there. Even if I didn't sleep well, I felt safer. I wasn't sure why; Aiden wasn't exactly what most girls would think of as a knight in shining armor, or a burly protector. I closed my eyes feeling more secure than I'd thought I would.

I fell asleep easily, but woke up two hours later trying to place a noise I'd heard. Aiden sat bolt upright when he felt me move, but he didn't know what it was either.

"Did you hear it, too?" he asked.

I nodded. It didn't sound like it was coming from the basement, but it did sound like someone was trying to get into the house itself. We crept downstairs; him barefoot in my Dad's sweatpants, me wearing my Hello Kitty pajamas and my fuzzy bunny slippers. I'm sure we made a less than intimidating pair.

Aiden went in front of me, creeping down the stairs slowly and deliberately to avoid creaking noises. I kept waiting for him to trip and fall down the stairs, but he was being careful. We headed for the kitchen to find it dark. There was no coffee brewing, as there had been when his father had shown up the day before, but we didn't find any intruders, either.

I looked out the sliding glass doors on the patio outside the kitchen, and saw something. It looked like someone was curled up on the lounge chair on the patio and covered in the tarp I'd forgotten to put back on the grill three days ago. I motioned for Aiden to come over and look, and he did, staring over my shoulder. I couldn't see who it was; I couldn't tell if they were dangerous or just tired. Aiden handed me the phone before slipping outside. I knew he meant me to call 911 if anything happened, but somehow I thought he'd trip over our visitor rather than our sleeping guest causing him any kind of danger.

Aiden crept up to the sleeping form, and shook it by the shoulder. A young girl sat up, blinking hard, her unwashed blonde hair sticking up in peaks and horns all over her head. "I was just looking for a safe place to crash!" She stood up, dumping the grill tarp on the ground, and I could see that she wasn't much older than 16. She scrambled away from him, looking terrified, like an abused puppy.

"Are you hurt? Is there someone I can call to help you?" I asked, putting down the phone on the counter and heading outside to check on her.

"Please don't call anyone! Don't tell anyone I was here. It's safer for you; it's safer for me."

She had piqued my curiosity. I didn't want to get her in trouble, but I just didn't feel comfortable letting her go on her own given how young she was. I had to figure out what was going on.

I was able to talk her into coming into the house and getting her something to eat. A glance at the clock told me that it was three-thirty in the morning, but I'd gotten a decent night's sleep the night before. Mia hadn't stirred out of her room yet, and I knew I wouldn't be able to sleep until I knew what was going on with our nocturnal visitor.

Chapter Ten

It had taken quite a bit of convincing to get the girl to come inside. She flinched every time Aiden came near her. He shrugged it off, but I could see it bothered him that she was so uncomfortable in his presence. He finally offered to go check the basement for me, and left me alone with her in order to try to find out what was going on. I offered her an early breakfast, and she gratefully accepted.

I got out a pan and started frying eggs, then two slices of bread in the toaster. She looked like she was starving. I wondered when she'd last eaten. I pulled some bacon out of the fridge and asked her why she was sleeping on our back patio.

"I don't have anywhere to go, and I didn't think anyone would find me. All the lights were off, so I figured everyone was either asleep, or no one was home."

"Why are you so worried about someone finding you?" I asked, but she wouldn't answer. The toast popped up, and I handed her a plate, the butter, and some grape jelly while I tried to come up with another way to ask what was going on.

"What's your name?"

She got quiet for a minute. "It's been a long time since someone asked me that."

What the hell had she been going through that no one asked her for her name? "I need to know what to call you. I can't very well call you Patio Girl."

She chuckled, and I got the feeling she didn't do that very often either. "It's safer for you if I don't say."

"Look, you don't have to tell me anything, but if you're in danger I'd like to help if I can."

"Someone's looking for me. I appreciate the food and the few hours' sleep on your porch, but you really don't want to get involved. Trust me," she said, with a mouthful of grape jelly smeared toast.

I slid a couple of eggs onto a plate and passed them over before starting up the bacon. I hit the button to start the coffeepot as well; I figured I'd be up the rest of the night with Grill Cover Girl. First things, first, however: I needed to get a better name from her even if it was fake. I couldn't just call her Girl Who Eats All My Bacon.

Okay, I could. But I didn't want to.

Aiden came back as I filled the skillet up a third time with more eggs and our visitor chewed through five slices of bacon. I kept cooking, wondering why he had such an odd expression on his face. The girl plowed her way through enough eggs, bacon, and toast to feed me for a week, and then asked if she could use my bathroom before she left. I didn't feel right about her leaving. I felt like I needed to do more to help her. Then again, for all I knew she was looking for a warm place to shoot up some kind of street drug into her arm.

"The bathroom's the second door on the right," I said, giving her permission. I opened the swinging kitchen door to point it out, and watched her walk down the hallway. She took a wide berth around Aiden to get to the door, and then disappeared without a second word.

I couldn't quite bring myself to stop watching the bathroom door from my perch in the kitchen. I didn't want her to feel like I didn't trust her, but I really didn't. I just didn't have any good way of knowing whether she would try to rob me blind, if this was some kind of setup, or if there was something else going on. My money was on something else. Something in my brain tugged at a memory, and I left the kitchen, heading for the study with Aiden in tow, asking what he'd missed.

"I don't know what this means, but I found the story of the Seawitch in your Dad's books. It was an old story told by Hans Christian Andersen. It was first written as an opera, but then Andersen wrote it down in his *Fairy Tales Told for Children* in 1837." He was in professor mode; proud of his own research, but dates and names and publication dates didn't really do much for me in figuring out who or what was in danger, what was going on, or who I had to save.

"Get to the point, Aiden. Who is the Seawitch after in the fairy tale? Shouldn't that be a place to start?" I wasn't sure if it would work, but it sure made sense to start with the documented enemy or maybe even victim in the story itself.

"Good thinking. Let me go do some more reading while you talk to our visitor. I'm thinking we might get to the heart of this faster than we did in your case, because we actually have a bad guy, for lack of a better way to put it, who has their own story instead of randomly showing up over and over in multiple stories."

"What do you mean? I didn't realize that Evangeline was in multiple fairy tales."

"She isn't," he said, as the door to the bathroom opened and our visitor came out. "I'll go look some more but, in your case, keep in mind that multiple Grimm stories had evil stepmothers. It would be difficult to figure out which one would have applied even if we had some reason to believe it was your stepmother at first."

He was right, but now wasn't the time to discuss it. Aiden slipped back to the library, flipping on the light. I heard Bert complaining about being woken up as the girl came back toward me, hugging her upper arms as if she was cold. June weather in Ohio just isn't cold enough to explain that kind of cold, and I was too cheap to run the central air in my stepmother's gigantic house. Evangeline had run it constantly; I much preferred to open an upstairs window and get some fans going if I could.

"Can I get you a sweatshirt or something?" I asked.

Her eyes snapped up to meet mine, and they were clear and bright. No evidence there of drug use in my house, thank goodness. I'd have to double check the bathroom later, but I was relieved. The worry about police officers breaking down my door and arresting me for allowing drug activity or facilitating drug use or anything like that would be one more stressor I couldn't handle at the moment.

She nodded, and I led her into the laundry room. I had a red hooded sweatshirt hanging up that I'd just washed and hadn't taken upstairs yet. "Here," I said, taking it off of the hanger and handing it to her. "It's clean, and will keep you warm."

She slipped into the sweatshirt, her skinny frame dwarfed by the size. Her arms were dirty, and there were smudges under her eyes. Her dishwater blonde hair was greasy, and I could tell she hadn't had a shower in a while, but I didn't want to push her.

"Look, I don't know who you are, or where you're running from, but I would like to help you if I can. You obviously felt comfortable enough to fall asleep on my back patio, which indicates my place is far enough away from whatever your problems are that you felt secure. If you don't want to give me your real name you don't have to. But give me a name to call you, and I promise you can crash on the patio anytime you need to. Promise me you won't break in, or damage the house or anything in it, and I'll give you a hot meal when I get home, if you're here."

She gave me a cautious look. I could tell she was weighing her options.

"Call me Allie. It's not my real name. Don't use it to try to find me because you can't, and you don't want to, believe me. I'll take you up on your offer, but I won't be here every night. If I do, it won't be long before someone gets curious and follows me."

I wasn't quite sure what that meant, but I tried to get her to take my cell phone number in case she needed anything. Allie refused no matter what I said or promised. "It's better for you if I can't be forced to give your number to anyone, and I wouldn't dare write it down anywhere. Just knowing I have a safe place to go when things get to be too much is huge. But is that guy here all the time? Is he your husband?"

Aw, crap. How to explain I'd asked Aiden to stay to make me feel safer when she felt safer sleeping on my back patio covered in my grill tarp than wherever it was she stayed on a regular basis. "No, Allie, he's not my husband. We're dating, but he stayed because I had a bad day yesterday and he wanted me to feel better about myself."

"Oh," she said. "Do guys actually do that?"

I smiled. "He did."

"You mean he actually let you sleep and didn't make you do stuff?"

Oh, God. What was she trying to tell me? I didn't feel qualified for this conversation. I glanced at the clock and saw it was nearly five-thirty in the morning. Before I could say anything about it, I heard raised voices coming from the library. Aiden and Bert were arguing, presumably about some part of their research. Allie looked terrified. She stepped back, stumbling over the kitchen chair as she hurried out of my kitchen and through the patio door.

"But Allie, wait, it okay. It's just Aiden doing some research and getting excited about it." I tried to chase her out the door, but she tripped and fell just before she got to the grass, scrambling to get back up, then she was off faster than I could run in my bunny slippers on dewy grass.

She was gone. And I had a sinking feeling in the pit of my stomach about what she might have been hiding from. I just hoped I was wrong.

Aiden came up behind me as I called out for Allie to come back, that it was okay.

"What happened?" he asked, putting one arm around my shoulders.

"I don't know. One minute we're standing here talking, and the next minute she's all but tripping over herself to get out of here as fast as she possibly can. I don't understand. I thought she was starting to open up. She gave me a name to call her; we'd talked about her coming back for food if she needed it, and then all of a sudden she was running out the door. Other than hearing you and Bert argue, I can't figure what scared her off."

Bert hopped towards us through the kitchen. "What's going on?" I tried to explain.

"Are you nuts? Did you just invite a homeless girl to sleep on our patio and eat all our food when we've got a magical bad guy out there gunning for something? I mean, isn't sleeping here more dangerous if something decides to come after you for trying to help someone?" Bert asked.

He was right. I hoped I hadn't just put Allie in danger, but something told me that she was in plenty of trouble of her own, without our own issues. And somehow, I liked the idea of someone else keeping an eye on the house from the outside. While she probably wouldn't call the police, I could push her even harder to have a number to call someone if she saw something wonky.

"I just couldn't stand the idea of her out there without giving her a good hot meal and something clean and warm to wear. I think she's in a lot of trouble."

"Who's in trouble?" I heard a voice behind me. It was Geoffrey, making his way through my kitchen toward where we were standing outside the sliding glass doors on the patio. "And who decided to cook breakfast this early in the morning? Is there any left?"

Oh, great. Emotional crap to shovel when I'd hoped to talk to Aiden about what he'd found before trying to get another hour or so of sleep. "Good morning, Geoffrey. The coffeepot's started if you want a cup," I said, turning to go back inside.

Aiden sighed, and I saw his shoulders slump as he followed me. I don't think he really wanted this conversation either.

"Well, that's all well and good, but why is there a pile of wooden matches on the patio?" Bert asked.

"What?" I turned, not sure what he was talking about.

"There's a pile of matches here on the patio. Where did they come from?" He hopped over for a closer inspection and I followed.

He was right. In exactly the same spot where Allie had fallen, as if they'd fallen out of her pockets, was a small pile of wooden matches. They were the same kind I remembered from Girl Scout camping trips when I was a kid, those strike-anywhere matches that were supposed to work no matter whether they'd gotten wet or not.

Curiouser and curiouser, I thought.

CHAPTER ELEVEN

W e all trooped back inside and I shut the door behind us, locking the sliding door and closing the shades over the glass. I was hoping this would be a short visit, but it didn't take a mind reader to figure out that Geoffrey and Aiden had a lot of emotional stuff pent up behind their skulls. The tension was thick enough to see as a fog in the air. I wasn't sure if there was enough night left to deal with family therapy in the kitchen. I tried to start with something a bit more neutral.

"So, any idea about those matches?"

Geoffrey gestured toward the coffee pot and I nodded, giving him permission to take a cup for himself. "I don't know. I don't generally use matches for anything."

Aiden snorted. "He means he isn't in the mortal realm much and uses magic when he's in faerie, so they can't be his."

Geoffrey's face hardened. "No, I used to smoke when I was with your mother. That was a long time ago. She'd keep a pack of cigarettes around for me, and a lighter. I never used matches, because I didn't trust them. It seemed they'd always get damp, or ruined, or would be otherwise useless when I needed them. Son, there's a lot you don't know about me. I'd like to change that, even though my past bad habits aren't really what I was thinking about starting with."

"When did you quit?" his son asked.

"Right about the time your mother and I split for the last time. I didn't have anywhere else to go except back into faerie, so I went. There isn't really a corner store where you can pick up a pack of Camels in Queen Eva's court. And when one is obligated in service of the queen it's really hard to call your time your own. Even if the queen was otherwise occupied you just never knew where she might show up and require your services. It was better to just wait until one was called rather than risk being too far away to respond. And failing to respond timely without a good reason was grounds for all kinds of creative punishments. But I digress," he said. "Who was it that came to visit you at this hour?"

"You mean other than you?" I asked. "I'm sorry, Geoffrey, but you've come into my house twice without my permission and it's making me feel a little insecure in my own home. Your son does not live here." *Never mind the lack of shirt, baggy borrowed sweatpants, or the bare feet,* I thought. "So that does not give you carte blanche to just sashay your way into this house. It's not your house. It does not belong to the faerie courts. You made sure of that, and when you come in here like this it makes me feel like I'm not safe."

"You aren't safe," he said, stirring coffee with a spoon he took out of the drawer under the microwave.

"See, there's the point. You know where things are in my house even though I have never given you permission to come in through the front door. You come through the portal in the basement and, for all I know, there's no way to lock up the basement door against magic. If you wanted in, you're already past any threshold this house might actually have."

Bert had told me months ago that houses have something called thresholds, which protect users from magic because of the sense of *home,* of belonging, of roots people bring to their personal spaces. That connection to a space gives the inhabitants some protection against magical elements that could otherwise cause them serious harm. The problem was Evangeline's house never really was much of a home. She was a faerie queen, and I'd never considered this house home even though I'd lived here for nearly half my life.

The idea that the father of the man I was dating pretty much had free access to come in and go through all of my personal effects kinda squicked me out a bit, and he could get in even easier than the cat burglar lurking outside in wait. I wondered if he could actually leave the house or not, but since my stepmother had never really created a home for anyone here it was very likely she'd been careful to never do anything that might create, maintain, or strengthen any kind of magical barrier to keep the bad guys out. Not really a big deal considering she was one of the bad guys.

"Geoffrey, you've got to understand why I'm a bit weirded out about you coming in the house in the middle of the night. Is there any way to limit access to the portal? Otherwise, I'm starting to think that moving into this house was a bad idea." Never mind that I couldn't afford the upkeep on the house and I wouldn't feel comfortable selling it to someone else with a portal to faerie in the basement. Talk about buyer beware. I was sure a home inspection would never find something like that.

He nodded, looking pensive and thoughtful. "I can understand why you're concerned. I can approach the High Council about how to address this, but I don't think the issue has ever come up before. I don't know what they would think about it; portal access has never been negotiated with humans before." He crossed his arms over his chest and leaned against the countertop in his impeccable three piece suit, not a single thread out of place. "Besides, I'm here to talk to my son. That's my reward for delivering the message and securing your agreement to help yesterday."

Aiden's father and his perfect dress reminded me again that I was standing there in my pajamas and fuzzy slippers, with wild bed-head hair, and standing next to his son, who was also dressed as if we'd spent the night together; the implication being we'd done more than sleep. Of course, at this point we weren't getting much sleep, but I'd almost rather be doing what it looked like we'd spent the night doing.

"All right, guys, there's enough going on that we really need to just divide and conquer here. There's time for emotional shoveling later, but there's someone out there, in danger, now. That has to come first," I said, hoping they'd follow along. See, I had this plan to get them to work together and show each other they were capable of trust so they could talk about other things.

It could work. Really.

Bert harrumphed in my direction. "Subtle she isn't, but she is right. We can stand here and let you guys sing kumbaya and have a good cry, hug each other, and go on as men, or we can get busy. Geoffrey, she told you yesterday Aiden didn't live here, yet you insisted on coming back so soon, hoping to catch them together. I think you planned your entrance in exactly the way you did yesterday to make Janie feel less than secure in her house and invite Aiden to stay to make her feel safer."

Geoffrey looked embarrassed. "With all my years so close to the queen, and in learning diplomatic manipulations, I apologize to all of you."

Aiden's jaw hung open. I didn't have that problem. "Are you apologizing for being figured out or for trying to manipulate me into inviting your son to spend the night despite the fact he's never done so before? Or, better yet, are you apologizing for coming into my house in the middle of the night without my permission, drinking my coffee, or plain scaring me to death?" I was pissed. How dare he move us all around like pawns in a chess game. I was nobody's plaything.

"Can I just plead guilty, apologize, and promise something?" Geoffrey asked.

Aiden's face was red. "I have a lot of things to say to you, sir. Not all of them are nice, and many of them are things I'd rather say in a private conversation. Some are things I've said to you in the past, including a request to stay away from me. However, you have failed to take anyone's wishes into account except your own. You've seen me. Now, I assume you have more you wish to discuss with me?"

"I do," Geoffrey started but Aiden interrupted before he could get very far.

"No, you don't get to do that. Your reward for getting Janie's help was to see me. You got to do that. You're done for the time being. You will, however, tell whoever it is that you're reporting to that you've gotten your reward and that you're done."

"But . . ." Geoffrey trailed off, uncharacteristic for his normal, dapper, composed self. Then again, I remembered his complete lack of composure last year when Aiden was being tortured by my stepmother. Of course, Aiden had been a bit distracted at the time. I didn't think Aiden had seen his father's reaction, and I don't think he realized just how much Geoffrey cared in those moments when he was begging Evangeline to let his son go.

I still hadn't been able to tell him what I'd seen on his father's face that night.

Aiden was in full rant, however, oblivious to my mental

meanderings. "You took off and left Mom when I was just a baby. You came back and demanded I go with you to faerie, and then ignored me most of the time I was there. You disowned me when I made the choice to live in the mortal realm near the one parent who had actually treated me with kindness and love, and now, when I'm finally interested in a girl, you keep popping up to remind her about all the ways I'm different, that I'm not completely human, that I'm a freak."

His rant sounded completely human to me; it sounded like a boy who'd had to grow up without his father. I guess that transcended just about anything, but Aiden kept right on going. I'd never seen him get that worked up before.

"You have no right to be in my life. You are nothing to me, to use your own words against you. You have some leeway because you helped Janie. But now you've put her back in danger and you are making her feel unsafe. So here's the deal. Janie's helping. You knew if you got her involved that I'd be on the edges of this. I bet you even volunteered. But that doesn't get Mom involved. So we'll help you on our terms. We won't back out, and I'll even use the F.A.B.L.E.S. resources to move this along as much as we can. But you'll find a way to help Janie control access through the portal in the basement, and you'll stay completely away from Mom."

Geoffrey sputtered and protested, but Aiden wasn't budging. I guess I didn't even get a say. Of course, I wasn't in the middle of his demand that Geoffrey stay away from his mother, and I liked the idea of controlling access through the portal. I'd sleep better at night if I knew something could be done to make a faerie being ring some kind of doorbell or announce themselves or whatever.

Bert nodded. Apparently Aiden was doing a pretty good job of negotiating. I wasn't sure what was worse; that I agreed with Aiden's tactics even though he was missing the full story, or that I was agreeing with a frog. Neither one made me sound like I had all my marbles.

CHAPTER TWELVE

Aiden made Geoffrey leave before anything else could be said, and then suggested we try to get a few more hours of sleep. As much as I hated admitting it, he was right. This split work schedule was going to make me crazy if I kept interrupting a good night's sleep for nocturnal visitors.

But how does one go to sleep after all that? I wasn't even sure I could get my brain to stop spinning long enough to drift off. Would it be worth trying to get the two hours of sleep left in the night, or would it make it worse later in the day? I was wondering if I'd have to take Mia's route of the day before and come home to nap between jobs. At the moment, it was sounding like a good thing. I just hoped Mia was having a better night than I was. We'd need at least one person to be alert tomorrow. Er, today. Either way.

Aiden took my hand and led me upstairs, away from the portal.

"Aren't you even going to say good bye to your father?" I asked, pulling back from him.

"No."

"Aren't you going to make sure he leaves?"

"No. If I forced him, he could pop right back here and there wouldn't be much I could do about it. Bert's watching him. He'll tell me if Geoffrey stays or goes. And if my father wishes to have any sort of future discussion with me, which I know for a fact he does, he'll leave and press his luck another day. I'm done with him now." His voice rang with a note of finality.

"Aiden, regardless of whatever happened in the past I think he really does care for you."

He started to protest, but I silenced him with a hand over his mouth as I told him of the raw pain I'd seen in his father's eyes last fall. I told him I'd seen behind the smooth, urbane, guarded surface in the court. I told him that no matter what was between them, they should talk about it. And I told him I'd give anything I had, anything

I owned, and anything I ever hoped to own, to be able to speak with my father just one last time, to be able to tell him, now, about everything I'd gone through, about everything my stepmother had done, and about how I'd gotten justice in his name.

And how I'd never have a chance to tell him any of those things, because my father was dead.

Aiden took it all in, and sighed. "Yeah, I know, Janie. I know it's hard for you to see a father and son who don't get along and don't talk and don't see each other. But there's a difference. Your father was a very good man, and when he died the world lost out on his kindness and his goodness. My father is a cold, heartless, manipulative bastard who is only out for himself, and whatever advantage he can press to get what he wants. At some point, it's healthier to detach from that kind of ulterior motive, because that's actually the smarter thing to do. Trust me. I've been dealing with his crap for longer than you can imagine."

"That doesn't change my point, Aiden." But I allowed him to pull me up the stairs and guide me to my bedroom. My bed was calling me loud and clear. I was really hoping that meant I wouldn't have to worry about being tired enough to fall asleep. Mia had the walking zombie look down pat yesterday, and I really didn't want to try to emulate it.

We went back upstairs and curled up in my bed, Aiden's arm curled protectively around my waist as I finally drifted off into a dreamless, exhausted sleep.

I woke up just in time to race Mia through the shower and head out the door. For some reason, even though I'd gotten about half the sleep I normally get, I was wide awake, bright eyed and bushy tailed. I finished in the shower, got dressed, and went downstairs to make coffee. Mia was barely stirring when I went into my father's study to do a little research while I waited for her to get ready to leave.

Aiden wandered into the library while we waited on Mia, selecting a book from the shelves and thumbing through it while I called to Mia to hurry up. "Come on, we're going to be late!" I yelled up the stairs.

"I'm coming," she yawned, shambling down the stairs to me.

I had to pull her aside and tell her to fix her shirt. She'd fastened the wrong buttons, giving herself a drunken, off-kilter look that reminded me too strongly of people leaning sideways in tomato juice commercials. She hurried to fix her blouse before Aiden noticed, but I could have told her not to bother. His nose was buried in the book, and it looked like it was going to take dynamite to get his attention again. I hurried them both outside to the Escalade, so we could get going.

Bert hopped out of the library and reminded me of my promise to tag along. I scooped him up and set him in my shoulder bag. "Promise me you'll be quiet, Bert."

He nodded. "I already said I would. What's a frog gotta do for someone to take them seriously around here?"

Mia looked like she'd passed another bad night, but she hadn't come downstairs, so I hoped she'd gotten some sleep. If she had, however, it didn't look restful; the dark circles and bags under her eyes were a dead giveaway she was going to be asleep on her feet by the end of the day again. I started the car and backed out of the driveway as I offered her my own bed for a nap later in the day.

"Thanks, Janie. I appreciate it. I can't believe I'm having such a hard time falling asleep and staying asleep once I do close my eyes. I've tried everything. Hot chamomile tea, warm milk, soft music, no music, turning up the heat, turning down the heat, opening the window, more pillows, less pillows . . . nothing works. It can't hurt to try a different bed. I'm about to resort to sleeping pills, and I really don't like the idea of doing that."

"Maybe this afternoon we can tear apart the bed to see if there's something wrong with it. It can't hurt, and if there's something wrong with it, then we know it's the bed." I couldn't quite bring myself to add, *and then we know you're not crazy* to the end of that sentence. Mia didn't deserve that. She'd stood by my side last fall when so many others would have had me carted off to a rubber room for talking with frogs and listening to animal musicians, rapid and magical growing hair, and faerie portals. She deserved better than that from me.

Bert stuck his head up from where I'd stashed my bag between the front seats of the Escalade as I drove toward Brown Street to head downtown to drop Aiden at the F.A.B.L.E.S. headquarters before we went to the courthouse. "I looked at your bed yesterday, Mia, and I didn't find anything wrong with it. In fact, you left a pile of stuff hanging off the side of the bed and I was able to crawl up on it and nap most of the day."

I wasn't sure what Mia thought of a frog in her bed, because she had an odd expression on her face. If it had been any frog other than Bert I think she would have been kinda grossed out. She didn't say anything. I didn't either. I wasn't sure what could be said to that.

"I got it!" Aiden called out, interrupting my mental argument with myself over whether Bert had crossed the line by getting into Mia's bed or not.

"What?" I asked, stopping at a red light.

"The matches, your late night visitor, her appearance, it all makes sense. I think she's the Seawitch's target. She's the Little Match Stick Girl." He said it like it was supposed to be capitalized.

"I've never even heard the story before," I said. "How do we know that it's her?"

The light changed to green, and I didn't even notice until the cars behind me started blaring their horns at me. "A poor girl has to sell matchsticks to stay alive, but lighting the matchsticks allows her to see the face of her grandmother. When she runs out of matchsticks, she dies and goes to heaven, where she's reunited with her grandmother."

"But what about the Seawitch?" I asked. "How does she figure into the story? And that's a terrible story. Who would tell a child a story like that?"

He continued. "It's a Hans Christian Andersen story, Janie. Just like stories about the Seawitch. Also, Andersen was from Denmark, which is also where the portal to Søborg Castle is located. That's the prison where the Seawitch was held until she broke out. That's gotta be the connection. So it's no coincidence Allie came looking for help last night. She showed up on your doorstep. That's the power of magic."

That's the power of a scared teenager finding an out of the way place to get an uninterrupted night's sleep, I thought, but I didn't have much else to go on. He could be right. Stranger things had happened. And when they'd happened to me, I hadn't had any specific story reference to link me to my stepmother, just my own ancestry. It was worth looking into.

Aiden read me the story as I navigated early morning downtown rush hour traffic to drop him off. He asked to borrow the book to do some more reading, and I agreed. It was one of Dad's books, but it wasn't doing me any good at the moment, and it wasn't like I had the time to do anything about it. He might as well do some more digging.

And at least now we had something to point to, something to protect. I promised to pick him up at noon to take him back to the body shop to pick up his car. Hopefully, he'd have found out more by then.

CHAPTER THIRTEEN

We were right on time to meet with Judge Neederhorn, and report to him our lack of progress with his corny research assignment.

We came into his office with our notes, expecting to see him in a suit and preparing for a day of court hearings. Instead, we walked past a line of grumpy lawyers to get into his inner office. They were all grumbling about how hard it was to get anything done in his courtroom. If today was anything like yesterday I could completely understand why they felt that way.

The judge's hair was even wilder than it was the day before. Albert Einstein would look positively immaculate next to him. He hadn't even tried to tie it back in a ponytail. *Just how did this guy get elected,*? Were voters really that gullible?

He ushered us inside and we looked for somewhere to sit down to present our finding, or lack thereof, but every surface was covered in fabric swatches. Gray, green, navy, purple, and maroon material lay draped over every available surface, as if we were working for a fashion designer instead of a judge. There were pinstripes and herringbone, heavy material and lightweight material, a virtual cornucopia of choices for judge's robes, covering everything, even his bookshelves. Mia and I traded a look of horror before we launched into an explanation of why we couldn't find any law to support his desire to fix things without having an actual existing problem before the court.

He listened attentively, as we shot down every suggestion he'd made the day before, and then told us that he was satisfied with the thoroughness of our research. "You two will work out just fine."

If I'd been a teakettle, steam would have been rolling out of my ears and my nose would be whistling. I clamped a lid down on the sudden surge of anger. How dare he treat us like that? It was true we were beginners, but he didn't need to treat us like we were idiots, having to prove ourselves even after we'd already gotten the job.

Shouldn't he have tried to weed out the idiots in the application process?

As if he'd been reading my mind, he jumped in. "I only got your two applications for the positions, so I didn't have a lot of choice. I'm glad to see you're at least reasonably well versed in the power that a court has or doesn't have. So let's get down to business." He began laying out a research problem regarding the questioning of a criminal defendant by a police officer from another jurisdiction and whether or not the *Miranda* warnings were required before the interrogation.

This sounded more like the type of research project we had been expecting. But why had he only gotten two applications for a clerkship? Those normally carry quite a bit of prestige . . . and Mia and I wouldn't have even considered applying without a paycheck. Most clerkships for first year law students aren't paid. We were smart, but we certainly hadn't been at the very tip top of our class; neither one of us had made law review—which was reserved for the very top of the top in a law school class—and we'd specified from the beginning that we needed paid jobs before we could agree. Maybe he'd decided to take us on sight unseen despite our letters of recommendation and decent grades? Was there some other reason we were attractive candidates? Was he connected to the faerie courts?

No good would come of that train of thought. We knew he'd been a magistrate for twenty years, but had only recently been elected as a judge. That was checkable. And the long line of lawyers outside meant he really was hearing legitimate cases. Or at least he was supposed to be hearing them. Nothing to do but to keep our mouths shut and ears open. We needed more than a half-day's exposure to him to figure out for sure if he was the real deal or not.

We headed off to another day of research in the law library, located on the top floor of the courthouse, and down the hall from the appellate court chambers. It was quiet, and the librarian smiled at us as we walked in. We dropped our bags, with me being careful not to squish Bert inside, and sat down to scroll through case law on Lexis Nexis, a computer based legal research database.

Bert kept on sticking his head out the top of my bag, and I kept reaching down to shove him out of sight. I could tell he had something to say, but the librarian was watching us pretty carefully. I finally left Mia at the terminal and slipped out to the restrooms with my bag to see what he wanted.

I checked under all the stall doors, and found them empty. I took Bert into the handicapped stall and shut the door before I opened my bag to ask, in a whisper, what was up.

"I noticed magic earlier," he said.

"When?" I hissed, trying to keep my voice down and listen for anyone who might come in to use the facilities. The last thing I needed was for someone to come in and think I was talking to a guy in the ladies' room. Of course, that did sound better than the reality of talking to a male frog who could talk back in the ladies' room. I wondered how fast it would take someone to demand I be placed in a rubber room and given medication to *fix* me.

"I couldn't see the room, but it was when you were talking to that judge before we left to get on the elevator to come up here."

The judge! I should have known it! "We were in the judge's chambers, and he was telling you how he had to test you. I noticed magic when we were there."

I heard the door open, and I held my finger over my lips, shushing Bert while someone came in, used the facilities, flushed, and then used the sink. I could see him getting angry, but he kept his mouth shut until we heard the door close. I opened the stall door quickly to make sure we were alone again before shutting and locking it behind me to talk to him.

"You brought me into the restroom to talk to me? Was there no other option?" he asked. "Don't take me out of this bag. There's no telling what kind of germs have been tracked all over this floor."

Was Bert a germophobe? Was he really that freaked out about touching a bathroom floor? I'd never noticed him being so picky before. And he was centuries old. Our world today had to be cleaner than anything he'd been used to when he'd been human. I shook my head.

"I'm up in the law library with Mia. There's no one else around, but the librarian keeps giving us the hairy eyeball. I don't have access to the conference rooms like I get at the law school library, and I don't know the courthouse well enough to know what my other options are. Give me a break. Now, this magic you noticed, was it coming from a person, or was it coming from the room, or something in the room, or what?"

He thought for a moment. "It was all over the room."

He had to be talking about the cloth draped all over the place. Aiden's father had been the court tailor to my stepmother. I wondered if he'd know what it might be. I made a mental note to ask about it the next time I saw him. Something told me that no matter how upset with him Aiden might be, we'd see a lot of Geoffrey over the next few days.

"I also noticed there was someone in the room that seemed to be touched by magic, but I couldn't tell who it was."

"You're kidding, aren't you? The judge is magic?"

"That's not what I said. Someone in the room has been touched by magic, but I couldn't get a handle on who it might be. For all I know, there was someone else in the room who found an invisibility spell, or who might have that ability."

"Is that even possible?"

"Janie, are you serious? You're asking me what's possible after all the stuff you went through with your stepmother? What isn't possible, with magic?"

He had a point, in that magic made a lot of things seem less insane, but invisibility? Were we being stalked by something? Or was the answer right in front of my face that the judge was somehow up to no good? Of course, just because he detected magic didn't mean it was evil or out to get us. I'd learned that much as well in the last few months.

Bert kept acting like he had more to say, but I shushed him as I heard the door open again. Loud, slow footsteps sounded outside the stall and, for some reason, chills ran up the back of my spine. I had a bad feeling about this.

CHAPTER FOURTEEN

It was a public restroom; anyone could come inside. So why was my heart thumping like a bass drum in the back of my throat? Why was I holding my breath?

I was doing it because Bert had noticed magic in the courthouse, and suddenly, I could smell it, too. The scent of magic is specific to each person; people smell things that are appealing to them—warm, homey, comforting scents that can lull an unsuspecting mortal into trusting the magical being who actually means them harm. I'd had a hard time adjusting to what it smelled like to me; it smelled like my father. Dad always smelled of old, dusty books and cheap peppermints no matter what cologne he'd worn or what he'd been doing that day. And I smelled exactly that in that courthouse restroom. We were in trouble.

Bert was shaking in my shoulder bag as I scooped it up and silently stood on the toilet seat in the stall, using the handicap bars for balance, not daring to breathe as the slow, heavy, footsteps grew closer and closer.

Under the stall doors I saw a dowdy pair of women's platform loafers, the kind most actual lawyers tended toward rather than the towering spikes TV lawyers paraded around in. The shoes stopped right in front of the handicapped door and I heard her test the door, but whoever it was walked away, used another stall, washed their hands, and then I heard the outer door open and close, as if someone was leaving.

And then I heard a sound that made me think of glass shattering. I didn't see what it was and I couldn't tell what had broken, but something was definitely cracked.

When I heard the outer door close I let out a sigh of relief, admonished Bert to be quiet, and stepped down from the seat of the toilet to head out. If something magical was in the building then I needed to do what I could to keep Mia from falling under its sway again. Last time I hadn't been able to protect her from a magically induced coma. This time, I swore to do what I could, given that she wasn't at her best due to sleep deprivation.

I cracked open the door, peering out carefully before slipping out of the stall. Slipping, however, turned out to be exactly the right word, as my foot slid out from under me. My arms windmilled, trying to keep my balance, but I failed and fell in an undignified heap on an icy floor. The floor was slick with frozen water, but I also saw there were glass shards all over the floor in front of the sinks.

I heard Bert groan as he landed as well, and the legal pads and wallet in my bag pummeled him as the bag landed beside me. "What the hell was that?" he asked.

"I don't know," I said. "Shut up, and let me look."

He stuck his head out of my bag. "It's ice."

"Thanks, Sherlock Frog. I got that much." I stood up carefully, rubbing one sore hip as I stretched, and brushing off my slacks. "It's June, though. Why would there be ice in the bathroom? And what the heck happened to the freaking mirror?" The broken glass didn't reach as far as the handicapped stall. I held onto the door as I stood, not wanting to slip again and fall in the broken glass.

"Magic," he said.

I counted to ten, slowly. I knew he wasn't trying to be deliberately vague, but I'd already come to that conclusion and him being a smart ass wasn't going to help. I picked up my bag and tried to gingerly walk toward the door, holding on to the edge of the sink to keep from slipping again. I hoped he was okay, but at that point I just wanted to get out of this bathroom and check on Mia. For all I knew she was a sitting, er, sleeping, target for whatever had caused the ice to mysteriously appear in the ladies' room.

No one else was in the restroom with us, and the ice stopped at the door. Most of the mirror was missing from the wall above the sinks. I stepped gingerly over the broken pieces, and ran out the bathroom door and hurried back to Mia in the library, hoping she'd been oblivious to my dilemma and working on our research project. I stopped briefly to tell the librarian it looked like there had been some sort of water damage and something had cracked the mirror. I couldn't see her shoes, but I could tell I would be looking at everyone's feet in the courthouse for the next three months. Even so, I figured we'd be in the library for the rest of the summer, so we'd have to at least try to appear to stay on the librarian's good side. She didn't act like anything was amiss; she just thanked me and picked up the phone to call maintenance.

I wondered how long it would be before the magical stuff started to interfere in my ability to get stuff done. I was just glad magic had stayed quiet during exams, and that school was out. If I was juggling school on top of everything else at the moment I didn't know if I'd be able to keep everything up in the air, or if I'd drop a few things.

Mia was right where I'd left her, staring despondently at a computer terminal, a highlighter cap hanging from her lips and her glasses perched precariously on top of her head. She looked up as I got closer. "What happened? You look pale."

"I fell down on the ice on the floor of the bathroom," I said, trying to give her a look that indicated that something was up while still warning her not to ask about it. "I'm just glad I stayed out of the broken glass on the floor. The mirror broke."

"Huh?" she said.

"You heard me right. Something's going on right here at the courthouse and I have no idea what it is. For all I know it could be completely unrelated, but someone came in the restroom when I was there talking to Bert, and I noticed the smell of magic." She nodded. "And I take it you don't want to discuss it here. Did you talk to Bert?"

I nodded.

"Does it have to do with the judge?"

I shrugged. "Not sure yet. Maybe. Need to ask Aiden some questions." I felt like I was being pretty cryptic, but for all I knew the librarian herself was the magical being that had caused the ice in the restroom. If it was, however, why had she left? Was she targeting me, or was it just an involuntary reaction to something else magical, such as Bert? Was she following me and looking for whoever the Seawitch was after? No way to answer any of those questions while we sat there at the library.

Mia held up a stack of papers she'd printed out. "Good news is that the research part of this is done, and we've got our answers. Let's head back to the judge's chambers and see if he has anything else for us today."

It was only ten-thirty in the morning, and we were supposed to work until noon. Maybe he'd let us watch court if he didn't have anything else. Of course, he might want a written memo on our research rather than just an oral report and opinion. Either way, it was time to leave the library.

I wondered if there was a way for him to give us weekly assignments that we could complete at the law school library instead, where we were more familiar with our surroundings. I just didn't like being in an unfamiliar place when I didn't know what was going on. Though it wasn't like familiar surroundings had kept me safe from kidnapping by the stepbrother I'd never known I had. He'd snatched me right from my own apartment last year, dragging me into the faerie realm where I'd had to face down my stepmother.

We headed back to the judge's chambers, where he complimented us on our speedy research, though Mia had done most of it while I'd been talking to Bert, but it wasn't anything obscure. He asked us to draft an opinion on the issue for him, so he could use it in issuing a decision, and he wanted it the next day, so he let us leave early to figure it out.

I didn't complain. Even if we were up late that night finishing it, I was more than ready to hunt down Aiden and ask him what we should do next, as well as trying to find out what might be in that book he'd taken from Dad's library this morning. I hoped he had all the answers.

We headed out to the parking garage and hopped in the car, heading straight for the warehouse to see what we could find, and so we could talk freely. I wasn't even sure the house was all that safe anymore with Aiden's father popping in and out. Who knew what might be lying in wait to eavesdrop on us in our own home?

Mia looked tired, but she was at least trying to get through the day. The bags under her eyes were more pronounced than the day before, and the dark circles were even darker. The whites of her eyes were bloodshot, but she was upright and awake after multiple cups of coffee while we'd been waiting on the judge to talk to us after we'd come back from the library with our research. Her knee twitched as she fidgeted in the seat. I was glad I was the one driving; she was so keyed up from caffeine I wasn't sure she'd be able to stay under the speed limit, and neither one of us could afford to get a ticket.

CHAPTER FIFTEEN

Aiden wasn't surprised to see us when I banged on the door of the warehouse. He let us in, then ushered us over to the folding conference tables we'd once had a potluck dinner on. Doris was sitting at the table, and stood to give me a giant hug as I came up to her.

"How are you holding up, my dear? I hear you've spoken with Geoffrey." She didn't really show any reaction, so I wondered what her feelings about Aiden's father were now. I wanted to ask her more about it, but it just wasn't the time.

"Yes, ma'am, I have spoken to Geoffrey, and he asked me to help out. I assume Aiden's told you what he wanted?"

She nodded.

"Aiden, Doris, there's more." Bert jumped out of my bag as soon as I set it on the floor. "There's magic at the courthouse, and I don't know where it's coming from." The two of us described what he'd noticed in the judge's chambers, as well as what Bert and I had experienced in the ladies' room.

Aiden and Doris listened attentively, but Mia was already dead asleep, sitting in a chair and leaning her head on her arms on the table. I'd thought she'd be more interested, but maybe all the lack of sleep was just catching up to her. I hated the idea of having to fill her in at home later, but she desperately needed whatever sleep she could get if she was going to function on less than a full pot of coffee at work tonight.

"The Snow Queen? Here?" Doris asked, sitting down heavily in her own chair and acting as if something Really Bad was going on. I'd never heard of the Snow Queen, and said so.

"The Snow Queen figured in multiple stories by Hans Christian Andersen. Honestly, I'd have never thought about Andersen stories until last night, but it seems you have many of them going on. I think it's safe to say that the Seawitch might be after some relation of Hans Christian Andersen. Which is odd, because I can't find any reference to Andersen having married or having children," Aiden said, going into nutty-nerdy-professor mode. He took out the book he'd taken from my father's library, as well as one with stickers on the spine like the ones in the Dayton Montgomery County library. It made sense that he'd use the library for research; the main branch was right down the road, within easy walking distance of the F.A.B.L.E.S. headquarters.

"Is the Snow Queen evil?" I asked, hoping I wasn't facing more than one enemy at a time. How hard could this become? At least school wasn't in session with marathon study sessions and study group meetings and prepping for classes; until I realized I'd have a late night tonight putting together the memo the judge wanted. If Mia had done most of the research while I'd been in the ladies' room talking with Bert and freaking out about some magical baddie taking a leak, then I definitely needed to step up and do the writing tonight while she got some sleep. It was only fair, but I wasn't happy about it.

"Well, sorta," he said. "The stories about the Snow Queen kind of all build on each other, and some of them don't even talk about the Snow Queen at all. She's known as the Queen of the Snowflakes, which are sometimes called snow bees, rides around in a white sleigh carriage, and lives in a land of permafrost. The only time I've even heard of her crossing into the human realm was in Andersen's own story, when she numbed a young boy and caused him to forget about his family, but the boy eventually returned to his love."

"Okay, but how does that relate to what's going on here?" I asked, lost.

"I don't know; it's just another Andersen story that seems to be popping up here."

A soft snore came from where Mia slept with her face down on the table. "Andersen . . . oh, my God, how could I be so blind?" I exclaimed.

Doris and Aiden looked up. Aiden nodded at me. "I think you're right. I just came to the same conclusion about an hour before you guys got here."

"There's one way to be sure," I said. "And we need to be sure before we scare the daylights out of her. We need to go back to the house."

They agreed, following me out to the parking lot. Bert wanted to control the music, so I let him. Who knew he'd be playing Wagner's Ride of the Valkyries? I didn't even know I had the song on my mp3 player, but it definitely fit the feeling that we were riding to the rescue of our damsel in distress. I hadn't said anything to Mia on the way out, just roused her enough to get her moving and hurried out. She was almost asleep again as we hit the highway, and Bert kept cranking the music louder and louder as we drove.

Luckily it was a short drive. Bert didn't have much chance to find more, uh, *inspirational* music. I was a little leery of what he might come up with. While I was ecstatic to have figured it out, I was still hoping I was wrong, and Bert's taste in music could be distracting even if it did put a smile on my face.

I wasn't wrong.

We all tromped into the house without much delay, and I dragged Mia upstairs to her room, Aiden and Doris following me as we went, Bert humming the Wagner song under his breath until I told him to shut up.

"Wait a minute, why is everyone coming into my room?" she asked, finally starting to act alert again as we all pushed our way inside. "It's a mess. I haven't put back all the pillows and blankets I used last night."

Aiden and I ignored her complaints as we shoved blankets, mattresses, and sheets to the floor. Doris started picking things up and folding them to get them out of the way. Good thing, too, because the minute the mattress was uncovered we flipped it off, staring at the box spring.

"Huh," I said.

There, staring back at us from the box spring from Mia's bed, were three homely little dried peas.

CHAPTER SIXTEEN

That was why she hadn't been able to sleep. That was why she'd stolen every pillow and blanket and soft surface in the house. She'd been a walking zombie because she'd been unable to sleep because of the lumps she felt through all the many layers on her bed. While I'd been worrying over finding the person Geoffrey wanted us to warn and protect, she'd been right here under own noses the whole time.

My best friend, Mia Andersen, was the Seawitch's target.

I scooped the peas up from where they rested on the dust ruffle that covered the box spring, and Aiden helped me put the bed back to rights. Mia stood there dumbfounded and gaping at us as we made her bed for her. Doris continued to fold up the blankets and stack up the random pillows and cushions, allowing for the bed to be put back and for Mia to sit down.

She sat staring at her own hands. "How is this even possible?" she asked. I had to remind myself she'd slept through our earlier revelation. She still didn't know she was a target. "I remember making this bed when I first unpacked my stuff. I don't recall seeing anything there. And how would I have felt it through the mattress and all the layers?"

It was a good thing she'd snored through our discussion. I could let her in on the whole issue gently later, and let her get some sleep first. "Mia, in this house, anything's possible. It's an old house. Who knows how it got there. And remember, my stepmother had this place for several years. It could just be some wacky practical joke she cooked up in case I ever moved back in. This was my room after all. She had no way to know I'd take a different room. You'll have to help me keep watch in case there's something else in the house I haven't noticed yet. She had years to set booby traps all through the place."

She yawned. "You're probably right. I feel like I've missed something, though. Should we be doing something else?"

"Mia, I think the best thing you can do is to get some sleep. I need you rested and helping tomorrow. And we've both got to get a handle on whatever's going on. That means no walking zombie roommate."

Mia gave me a weak smile, but it wasn't taking much to urge her under the covers despite her concerns. She crawled in as she still voiced apprehension. "How can I sleep when we still don't know what's going on? Shouldn't I be helping you?"

I put my arm around her and hugged her close. "The good news is that we know people who can help."

Aiden nodded, and Doris joined him. "Of course we'll help, sweetie. Now that we know what's going on we can figure out a plan to help. With Janie we knew she was the target, so that part was done for us. The best thing you can do, Mia, is try to get a few hours of decent sleep," said Doris, sounding, for all the world, like the mom and grandmother she was.

"How could I possibly sleep at a time like this?" my friend asked.

"Because you need to," I said, pulling up the covers and tucking her in.

She didn't fight me too hard, but made me promise not to go far. We shut the door behind us, and I turned off the light hoping she'd be able to get some shuteye. We headed slowly down the stairs, and I left Aiden at the base of the stairs as I ran for the coffeepot.

Most people probably would have wanted a stiff drink, but I wasn't much of a drinker and my own late night was catching up to me. I also hunted down the bottle of ibuprofen, because otherwise my bruised hip from the ladies' room debacle would see me stiff, sore, and cranky in the morning. I brewed a strong pot and poured cups for myself, Aiden, and Doris, who had followed me into the kitchen after a few moments of speaking with her son.

"Seems like a lot of information has been thrown at you in the last two days," she said, sipping from the mug I handed her. "You're handling it well."

"What choice do I have? I have to keep it together for Mia's sake. Even so, I wonder if she would be safer staying somewhere else. I mean, if Geoffrey has found it so easy to cross that portal into the house when we were sleeping how easy would it be for something targeting her to slip in here and kill us all? We've asked Geoffrey to try to do something about guarding the portal or negotiating some limitation on its use, but other than that I'm not sure what else to do."

"Sounds to me like you're approaching this calmly and rationally. It's what Mia needs right now. If you panic, she will too."

I grinned at her, and sipped my own coffee, as I led her back into the hallway and handed a cup to Aiden. "Is that what you guys said about me while I was starting the coffeepot?"

"It's true. We did. And we were right. You needed the time and space to protect yourself, deal with the emotional fallout, and with school. Luckily, Mia isn't worrying about classes, but your work schedule sure makes it hard to fit protecting herself and figuring it all out into a manageable time slot. You were right to insist that she try to get some sleep; she needs it, badly."

Had they handled me this much last year? I hated to admit it but they probably had. And they were right.

"There are so many questions right now, but what we really need are specific answers. We need to figure out what all this means," I said, sitting down on the bottom step.

"What do you know about Mia's family history?" Aiden asked. "We might as well talk about the problems in front of us at the moment. Maybe by the time she wakes up, we'll have a plan for how to tell her, and what to do next."

Except for one thing. In all our conversation downstairs, there was one voice I hadn't heard; one voice that I'd relied on when I'd been the target of magical mischief and mayhem, one voice that generally wasn't as quiet as he'd been lately.

Bert was nowhere to be found. In fact, other than his insistence at going with us today and his original complaints about Mia stealing his blanket and pillow, he'd been suspiciously quiet for the last couple of days.

"Her dad's not around; her mom's always working. Where is that frog?" I asked. "He's normally got good suggestions. And, failing that, he would be pissed at not being included in something this important."

We went on a Bert hunt, and it took some looking to find him; he'd taken up guard duty outside of Mia's closed bedroom door.

Somehow, he'd snagged a pillow and blanket and dragged them into the hallway, ready to spend an evening on guard duty watching for threats against Mia. He had a small olive fork in front of him, which was just about the heaviest thing he could lift and wield as a weapon with his skinny frog arms. He also had the whistle he'd insisted I buy him last week after arguing that he'd need something to catch my attention in our great big house if he saw danger. He just didn't have the lung capacity to scream, never mind get my attention or warn me if he needed to, so I'd gotten the whistle. It seemed a small price to pay for his peace of mind.

Doris and I left Aiden upstairs debating with the frog about whether or not Mia needed that kind of close guard in her own house. Finally, he settled for Aiden bringing his stuff down to the sitting room, but he insisted on remaining where he had a good view of the staircase, and remained staring at it through the rest of our conversation.

It wasn't the normal, snarky reaction I was used to from my amphibian friend. I was used to smart aleck comments, funny retorts, and sarcastic come-backs. I was used to his jibes, his concerns, his jokes, and his friendship. I was not used to watching him peering up the stairs, and waiting for the apocalypse to descend within our own walls with that grim look of determination on his face. Something was up with Bert. I couldn't fault him, but I also needed to figure out what was going on, and with him watching Mia so closely I could turn away and ask questions.

I had the odd thought he somehow expected the Seawitch to attack us the minute we'd figured out her target. Whether it was an abundance of caution, or sheer paranoia, I did feel like Mia was a little safer just because we knew who to watch for.

We just didn't know what we needed to protect her from. That would take a bit more work.

CHAPTER SEVENTEEN

Aiden cleared his throat as we all sat down in the sitting room. I'd sold some of Evangeline's fussy, expensive, for-looks-only furniture and replaced them with comfortable, serviceable, used couches and armchairs. We'd kicked around the idea of hosting F.A.B.L.E.S. meetings in my living room, but so far we hadn't been able to do it. Of course, school had only been out a week or so, and Mia and I were just getting settled into the house. For now, Aiden was putting on his best professor voice, and we were about to kick off the first research session we might have here. I almost felt bad the others were missing it, even though I didn't want to wait for them all to be called and gathered here to get started.

"Hans Christian Andersen was never married. Janie, unlike the Grimm brothers, who have known family trees we could place and follow directly to you, there's really no such thing with Andersen. There's some indication he might have had relationships, but it's hard to tell whether they were just infatuations from afar, if he was just unable to connect with anyone, if he was homosexual, or if he was bisexual. There's a lot of scholarly speculation as to why he felt this way. There's just not a lot of record out there as to his romantic entanglements, and in his private journals, even in his early life, he indicates a refusal to have sexual relations of any kind. Because of that, we really don't have any idea how Mia is connected to him other than sharing a last name and the tell-tale peas under her mattress."

"Well, is it just crazy circumstance, or is there some obscure family connection I don't know about?"

Aiden stood up, then began pacing. I was glad I'd removed all the dainty furniture, all the throw rugs and all the breakables; he was the clumsiest person around. In the non-magical world his half-faerie heritage reared its head as a propensity towards uncoordinated mayhem. He could walk and chew gum without breaking his neck in the faerie world, but he'd chosen long ago to remove himself from faerie court politics where he hadn't fit in well, either, with his human background. I was more interested in figuring out what was rolling through his big brain at the moment than trying to remember what medical and first aid supplies I had in the house.

Doris piped up with questions. "Just because there was a familial connection in Janie's case, doesn't always mean there is one in all cases. The similarity in names could be sheer coincidence. Or she could be related in a more obscure way through some cousin or something. Janie, you were a direct descendant of one of the Grimm Brothers. There could be some story out there we don't know yet."

Aiden was nodding with his mother as she spoke. "Mom, here's the thing. By the time Andersen died, both his parents were also deceased. He didn't have a lot of family, he was never married, and he never had kids. His reputation for never getting involved in intimate relationships means it's very likely there are no illegitimate kids either. He has little to no other family ties and I just don't know where the idea of revenge against the Andersen family came from. It's going to take more research. Even so, I don't think there's any doubt that Mia's the target regardless of the connection and how we got there."

I agreed with him. For now, at least, it didn't matter what the tie was; what we needed was a short term plan to keep Mia safe while we figured out whatever our long term plan might be. Bert nodded. Apparently he was following along even though he wasn't making eye contact with any of us.

Doris raised her hand, rather timidly. "I've got an idea."

It wasn't like her to be timid, and I said so.

"Well, I'm normally the one in charge of all kinds of food related things. I'm the one trying to organize the potlucks and the dinners or getting everyone to the same place at the same time as well as keeping people on task, but I'm not the one who comes up with the plan in the first place. Yet, I've got a plan," she said, wringing her hands.

Aiden grinned. "I've been telling you to speak up more often, Mom."

She smiled back at her son. "I know. I just get a bit, well, flustered, when everyone else is around. Anyway, what you guys need is to have someone watching for magical interference at all times. Why don't I see if we can get someone watching the house on a regular basis? I'm sure Stanley and Harold would be happy to help out. That way, you don't have to worry about coming back to a house that might or might not be inhabited by something magical. And if we all split up the shifts we'd be able to watch enough without making it too obvious."

"I'm okay with obvious if it keeps the faerie magic boogeymen away," I said. "I think posting a watch won't prevent anything, but I'm okay with posting people to watch if it means we get some kind of advance warning before getting walloped with whatever might be out to get us." I had to swallow a laugh. Stanley would eat this up. I wondered if he'd been bored ever since my stepmother had been imprisoned.

Stanley was one of the members of F.A.B.L.E.S., and he was a valuable contributor whenever anyone needed anything, but he was a bit on the paranoid side. In fact, he made Oliver Stone look positively optimistic. He was convinced that magic was to blame for most of the conspiracy theories of the twentieth and twenty-first centuries, everything from the JFK assassination to the aliens at Roswell. He saw a magical explanation that blamed Dick Cheney, the CIA, and the National Security Council for any and all magical occurrences. I wouldn't be surprised if he carried his own food and water everywhere he went, even in the real world, so he'd never have a reason to be tempted by anyone or anything who might have any connection of any kind to faerie.

Visions of Stanley hunkered down with a pair of binoculars, dressed all in black, and bumbling around like a geriatric version of the Keystone Kops re-enacting *Mission: Impossible.* It made me snort, attempting to hold in the laughter as I tried to pay attention to Doris and Aiden laying out a plan for surveillance. It caught me by surprise when they said they weren't going to be bringing in the rest of the F.A.B.L.E.S. crew.

"Why wouldn't we want everyone else in on this? Why stop at just a few people? I'd think there'd be strength in numbers. And is that enough to keep Mia safe?" I asked.

Doris spoke up, and I was even more surprised at her answer.

"We had no warning about this. Even in your case, we had some idea of something coming and something targeting you. We knew it was the witch, we knew what it was about, and we knew it was specifically geared towards you in retribution. We might not have known who the witch was, but we at least had some heads up."

"What are you saying?"

"I am saying that as many resources as we've tried to establish, as many people as we have out there, as much as we have put in place, we heard absolutely nothing about this until Geoffrey came to you with this warning. I'm saying we either have a big hole in our organization's intelligence, Geoffrey pulling some kind of faerie court intrigue, or it could be genuine. We just don't know what to trust."

Aiden started pacing again, but when he paced he would trip occasionally over his own feet. "Mom's right. We don't know."

"But we've seen there's magic around. I told you what happened at the courthouse. We all saw the peas under Mia's mattress."

"Yes, and the matches on the patio the other night," Aiden interrupted my rant. "That doesn't mean it isn't all a set-up. Of course, it could all be legitimate. It's why we need to have enough of a watch for your protection, but we also can't get the whole group involved because if it is a set-up we could be jeopardizing the entire group. And not all of them will understand we're trying to protect them. They'll be hurt and upset that we're keeping them out of the loop."

I thought about what he was saying. He had a point if he was worried about protecting everyone, but I thought he was being too cautious. There was something else going on; something else he was worried about. We hadn't been able to make a relationship work yet, but we'd spent enough together for me to know he'd left out important details.

I saw him exchanging looks with Doris, and I knew I hadn't read them wrong. I meant to figure out what it was before I did anything else.

CHAPTER EIGHTEEN

A iden excused himself, ostensibly to go check the house and make sure we'd secured all the windows and doors. Doris stared at her shoes.

"What's up?" I asked.

She muttered something incoherent.

"No, seriously, I can tell there's something bothering you, Doris. What's going on? Is it that Geoffrey is coming around again? Is it something with Aiden? Or are you worried about something else?" After all the times she'd comforted me, calmed me down after exams with pie and an open ear, it was easy to tell she was upset about something. She was normally the calm one, the one everyone looked to for advice and level headed counsel. The anxiety rolled off her in waves.

She took a deep breath, and looked around as if checking to see if Aiden was returning. "I have to admit to a bit of concern about Aiden's father coming around."

I didn't want to pry, but I had to ask. It was my house, after all, that he kept coming into uninvited. "Is he dangerous?"

She shook her head. "He shouldn't be. On his own, he's not. In fact, he's not that bad of a guy."

I assumed he had to have good qualities for her to have been involved with him, and Geoffrey's reaction when Doris had been mentioned left me believing he'd had feelings for her, too. There's a reason people get together in the first place even if it doesn't last. Of course, there are also reasons why relationships end. I really wanted to ask for all the details, but it was totally none of my business. I just nodded. What else could I say?

"Geoffrey has lived in faerie court pomp and circumstance too long. Like anyone who lives in a political and diplomatic fishbowl, it's really easy to lose sight of what real people need and want. It's true in the faerie world, it's true in the royal courts of Europe, and it's true in

Washington D.C. The more the minions run around trying to please the people in power, the more they're concerned about keeping power, and the less the people in power hear about anything contrary to their initial beliefs."

"What does that have to do with him, and whether or not he's dangerous?"

"Well, Geoffrey has always lived life by a different set of rules. He's always been a favorite. He's talented, he's handsome, and he's a smooth talker. He's good at convincing people to see things his way, but he spent a lot of years serving Queen Eva."

Also known as Evangeline Kravits Grimm, my evil stepmother, who married my father as a power play to restore what had been bound by my ancestor, one of the original Grimm brothers. I knew firsthand just how dangerous and powerful she could be; she'd tried to curse me herself.

"How long did he serve as her personal tailor?" I asked, trying to keep the questions neutral no matter how much I was dying to ask her about how they met or why they broke it off. And yes, a big part of me wanted to know if it was something that Aiden and I could avoid . . . or if we were doomed to repeat the mistakes of his parents.

"He'd served her court for four hundred years before we met. That day I was working part time at a bakery, and I was barely eighteen. I lived in a small apartment, which my father had rented for me after I graduated from high school. He married my stepmother, and they didn't like having me around when their kids were still so small. It was an awkward situation; so the best solution, in his mind, was to get me out of the house. I decided to take some classes at the local community college, and I got the job in the bakery for experience and for extra spending money. Geoffrey had had a disagreement with Eva and he'd stormed out, crossing over to the mortal realm for the first time in his life."

I'd bet that been quite overwhelming for him. Then again, it was Dayton. It wasn't like he'd crossed over to the middle of Times Square with the giant billboards and flashing lights and such. I wondered how he'd handle computers or cable television now, as opposed to what was going on twenty-five years ago. I snapped back from my mental side trip as she was talking about the ridiculousness of his outfit, and how he'd been so polite, so courteous, yet so out of place, and she'd been unable to resist him.

"I was nice to him, and I'd give him some of the leftover bread from the bakery at the end of the night for the first week or so. Then I realized he was wearing the same outfit every day. I'd thought he was homeless or crazy, but harmless, and I realized he needed help. I took him to St. Vincent De Paul's, and helped him find a place to stay. The bakery hired him to clean up at night and he worked hard, but he wasn't happy."

What a story. It really did sound like something out of a movie except for the lack of the happily ever after part. Even though I knew it didn't work out, I wanted it to, for her. She sounded so earnest, so in love, as she told me what I assumed was the short, short version of the story.

"Well, I stayed late to close one night, and when I went to take the trash to the back alley, there was a very tall gentleman with horns, a set of wings, and bright blue skin, talking to Geoffrey in the hallway and telling him that his presence was requested at court. I didn't know what to think, but Geoffrey declined the request, very politely, and said he was done with court life. They argued, and finally the blue man left. Geoffrey came inside, and asked me to go out for a late cup of coffee. We talked, and he assured me he would never leave, that he'd severed all ties to the court, and that he would be in the mortal realm for the rest of his days. We had six months of happiness before it all fell apart."

Apparently he'd broken that promise. "So, what happened?" I asked.

"Well," she said, leaning forward on the couch. "He meant to stay. He wanted to stay, but Queen Evan threatened to kill me to make sure he went back. He got a promise from her that I was safe as long as he came back and served as her court tailor. I found out I was pregnant with Aiden just a few days after he left. I didn't see him again until Aiden was a teenager, and had started to figure out his own magical heritage."

I heard a shriek as she said it. I'd have loved to ask her more, about how he could have left her, about what the exact threat had been, and why they'd given in, and whether or not anyone knew about Aiden's existence when they'd made that decision, but I was up and running toward the noise.

I followed it into the kitchen where I saw Aiden facing the patio doors with his hands up in the air and trying, without much success, to calm down a hysterical girl. It was Allie, crying on the patio.

She was covered in dirt and leaves, and the sweatshirt I'd given her was ripped and torn with blood on the collar. Her nose had been bloodied, and she had a black eye.

"Whoa, what's going on here?" I asked, hurrying toward Allie whose hair was matted and muddy.

"He came at me, and I was just trying to get a decent night's sleep on your patio. He was trying to hurt me; him, and the other ones."

The other ones? I shoved that to one aside for the moment. I didn't believe for one second Aiden had done anything to hurt her, but there was no doubt she was terrified and in desperate need of some first aid, a hot shower, something to eat, and all kinds of other help.

I saw Bert's froggy little face at the edge of the kitchen island, as I put my arm around her shoulder and guided her past Aiden. Bert shook his head, and made himself scarce. Aiden finally backed out of the room stuttering apologies and promising to look in on Mia. I assumed Bert was doing the same thing as Allie finally dissolved into tears as the door slid shut behind her.

Doris took charge of the kitchen, yanking food out of the refrigerator and beginning to prepare something to eat. I wondered if Aiden had filled her in on our patio guest. I don't even think Allie cared very much that Doris was there; she calmed down the very minute Aiden left the room. The fact she was so much more comfortable with women than men broke my heart. I had a pretty good idea at that point what was going on. And it just about made me sick to my stomach to think it was possible in my own backyard.

I was beginning to believe that Allie was a victim of sex trafficking, the selling of exploited young people for sex. I was sure there was something going on, and I couldn't turn away. I wasn't naïve. I knew it happened. There'd been a speaker at the law school talking about how it happened not just overseas, but right here in the U.S. with runaways, and lost boys and girls. I wasn't sure what to do, but I had to help

Then again, we already had a target on our backs with Mia. I wondered how I could get Allie help without endangering Mia. And was I putting Allie at risk by letting her into our house where more violence could happen? All I knew, as I guided her to the bathroom to help her wash off her face, was that I couldn't turn away from either one of them.

CHAPTER NINETEEN

I was really ready for this day to be over. It had certainly been a long one. I rinsed out the washcloth I was using to clean up Allie's battered and bruised face, and realized that sleep might well be something I didn't get much of for a while.

"What happened, Allie?"

She shook her head and mumbled something about not getting me hurt.

I set down the cloth. "Allie, I want to help you. I'm not worried about getting hurt at the moment. Right now, I need to know if you need medical attention. Your face is pretty banged up, but it doesn't look like anything's broken. My concern is how you were walking, and how gingerly you sat down when you got in here."

I saw the panic on her face as she tried to cover it, but it sounded like she just didn't have the energy.

"The man who startled you is my friend. His name is Aiden. He's not a bad guy; he's, well, he's pretty close to being my boyfriend." I realized then that it was probably true, even though he'd never pushed me to admit it. "He would never hurt you."

A small voice, one barely audible, she said, "He looks a lot like the guy who did hurt me. I thought it was him and I just couldn't go through it again."

No way could Aiden hurt someone that bad. And if it was Geoffrey I'd kill him myself with my own bare hands no matter how much help he'd gotten us, or how good his warning about Mia might have been. "The other lady that's here tonight is Aiden's mom, Doris. She's making you something to eat right now. Do you want to take a shower? Maybe a hot bath."

She nodded, and I realized she needed help getting out of her clothes. I helped her as much as she'd let me while the water ran in the bathtub. More bruises and more cuts, more sore spots, and more stiffness appeared as she lowered herself into the bathtub. I saw her wince again as she got into the water. "I'll leave you for a bit, Allie. I want to go check on my roommate, and see what Doris might need. I'm going to lock the door behind me, and you have my word Aiden will not bother you."

She nodded, huddling down in the water. I pulled out a towel and my own bathrobe—a raggedy but serviceable one made of green and brown plaid. It wasn't what one might think of as a robe I'd pick, and they'd be right; it had been my father's. I didn't use it much. "I'll bring you a change of clothes. We'll try to toss these in the washing machine for you."

"Thank you," she whispered.

I knew letting her bathe and washing her clothes would not help her if she decided to call the cops, but I was one hundred and ten percent sure she wouldn't call. Her panicked reaction to Aiden in the room and her desperate grip on me indicated I was just about the only person she trusted.

I edged my way out of the bathroom, creating a big production of clicking the lock into place and making certain she saw me demonstrate how to unlock it. There wasn't much danger of her sneaking out; there was no window in the bathroom, and I had her clothes. She had a quiet place to clean up and recover for a bit.

Doris was putting together leftovers into a quick, but homemade soup. She chopped vegetables and meat like a whirling dervish, the knife flashing and thudding against the chopping board as she went. I didn't stop to chat. Instead, I went upstairs to check on Mia, hoping she'd slept through the entire thing.

I crept up the stairs praying she was still asleep, but her door was open just a crack. I heard voices inside and listened carefully. Bert was talking. Mia was talking. And there was another voice talking as well, a woman's voice I didn't recognize. Mia must have turned on the television in her room.

So much for letting Mia sleep long enough to be rested for work tonight. I sighed, asking myself if it was worth taking the evening off to give her a break and try to keep up with all the craziness going on in our lives at the moment. Then again, if she was awake, watching television and talking to Bert, she must be feeling well enough to go to work.

I didn't bother her since Bert was in with her. I headed on to my own room, picking out an old pair of jeans and another sweatshirt to take down to Allie. Before I could get to my room, however, I realized it sounded more like an actual conversation between three people rather than two people talking and/or listening to the television. I knocked softly on the door.

"Mia?" I asked, as I pushed open the door.

She was sitting up in bed, and Bert was perched on the chair by her desk. The two of them turned to look at me as I opened the door, and I was surprised to see that the television was off. There was a large bird sitting on the open windowsill, and both Mia and Bert had been facing the bird until I walked in.

"Um, Mia, what's going on here? Who are you guys talking to?" I crossed my arms over my chest and leaned against the doorframe.

"I'm talking to the nightingale. Her name is Jenny. She's here to warn us."

All the warning bells and whistles were going off in my head. We'd already been warned by Geoffrey. What else did we need to be warned about? Something smelled fishy to me and I couldn't figure out what.

"Warn us about what?"

Mia explained. "Well, the person who the Seawitch is targeting is right here in this house. That we've found them, and others know we've found them. I don't know how anyone knows that since we don't know who it is, why they're being targeted, or how to protect them."

"Why do we just trust magical beings that show up in this house?" I exclaimed.

"Hey! Some of us have proven trustworthy!" Bert yelled. "Isn't it worth getting the information to find out what's going on?"

It was true. He had. And he was right. But why were we getting warned about something we already knew about? Or did we? Was there something in the warning I was missing?

Someone knew Mia was the target, someone besides those of us who had just figured it out. I wondered what was going on, how much we'd figured out correctly, and what we'd be able to figure out before we got surprised.

While I was running all the options and twists and turns through my head, Bert didn't let me come to any conclusions. "We've got to gather what intel we can from whatever source we can, so we can sift through all of it and figure out what's going on. Besides which, I've never known Jenny to be untrustworthy. She's pretty straight forward. And Janie, I've never known you to be this paranoid. Even with everything you've been through you shouldn't question what's going on until you can ask in a time and a place where no one else could be listening in."

In other words, Bert hadn't spilled the beans to Mia and was keeping her from panicking. I decided to go along.

"Okay, so we shouldn't ignore information. You're right, Bert. I'm just sick of all the cloak and dagger stuff, and being kept in the dark. Can't we just be told all of it when someone asks for our help?" Yeah, I knew I was whining, but I couldn't help it. How many times do we have to flail around like rag dolls until we got danger figured out? "Okay, fine. What's the bird got to say?"

If ever a bird could look offended and purse its lips, this bird pulled it off. "Well, I'd heard you were smart, Janie Grimm, and I'd heard you were kind. I'm not seeing much to support that at the moment, but I'm really here to help, not to give you bad information."

"Who sent you?" I asked.

"I don't know if you remember, but there was a man who spoke up for you at your trial. He was the one who was asking questions when you were trying to prove your case. He is well known as someone with connections in the courts, connected to a woman whose name is Winterkiss, and she wanted to send you a warning. I'm under orders to give you any and all information I can, and if I don't have the information you need I'm to return to Winterkiss so she can get the answer."

Heckuva lot of help, I thought, *if I could trust Winterkiss.* But why would she be trying to help me if Geoffrey already was? It didn't make sense. Would they be trying separately to help me? Or did one of them have a different agenda? It seemed Winterkiss was trying to make sure her help was accepted; or was it that her help was more accessible? Who knew when Geoffrey might pop up, or not. Or was Winterkiss trying to take over? No way to answer any of these questions.

"All right. I believe they said your name was Jenny? What can you tell us about the target of the Seawitch and about what they might want? What do you know about the Seawitch's plan? And, just out of curiosity, what's the connection? We've figured out that this relates to Hans Christian Andersen, but he didn't have any kids. Never married. What's the truth?"

I saw the bird's eyes widen. I had the feeling this might take a while.

CHAPTER TWENTY

"Well, just because Andersen didn't have kids doesn't mean there aren't people running around with a connection to him. There's a whole history there that most people don't know, and cannot be explained in just a couple of sentences. Suffice it to say, he had a sister. She married and had children. That's the short version, and any more than that will take more time to explain than I have. What I can tell you is the portal in your basement no longer comes out on the pathway where your stepmother brought you through. We've moved it to the back room behind the throne where you conferred with her before your trial."

"Why would you do that?" I asked.

"Well, you are the only human who has a grant of safe passage through that portal. Anyone else who comes through with you will have to negotiate, or you will, for their safety," the bird said.

Mia and Bert were looking at her in disbelief. Apparently, this wasn't what she'd been telling them. "Okay, so why me? And why the limit? I'd think you'd have granted safe passage to the person who is the target of the Seawitch, especially if you're all so keen to protect that person. Why should I believe it's safe from other members of the court if you've moved the portal to a place where it's even easier for court members to access?"

Mia was nodding. "Yeah. What she said. If we all get targeted by the Seawitch, then Janie's the only one who gets safe passage? Why should any of the rest of us help her?"

Mia still wasn't getting the reality of the situation. Was it better for her not to know what was going on? I didn't know. I just knew I was up to my eyeballs in all kinds of messes I needed to figure out how to handle.

"Jenny, if you would, please go back to Winterkiss and ask her if she could extend safe passage for the target of the Seawitch as well. If she cannot, please ask her if there is a way to negotiate safe passage for that person. Once you have an answer, if you could return to this house without telling anyone else your information and give me the answer, I would appreciate it." I figured if Winterkiss was bluffing, or if she was trying to test me, I would show her that I could negotiate with high court faerie without just accepting their statements at face value. Also, if I hadn't asked Jenny to return, she could have asked the questions and then not returned, and her promise to help would still have been fulfilled. Faerie court members tended to operate within the parameters of the exact promise they made. There was no room for implied promises or implied conditions.

She bowed her head, and Bert nodded at her. "Thanks, Jenny."

She flew out the window. I turned to my friends. "Mia, did you get any sleep?"

My friend nodded, and I saw that no matter how tired she'd been even getting a short nap had done her good. She still looked tired, but she no longer appeared as if she would fall over at a moment's notice.

"What time is it?" she asked.

"Time we need to start getting geared up for work tonight." Yeah, I'd thought of both of us calling in sick, but we both needed the money and if we didn't work we didn't get paid. Even though we didn't have rent to pay, we still had electricity bills and water bills and had to put gas in the car and food on the table. Plus, if Allie kept popping around our grocery bills would keep going up.

Oh crap. I'd forgotten about her, downstairs, with no clothes. I told Mia to go ahead and get up, that we had a guest, and we needed to start getting ready to go. I ran back into my room and scooped up the clothes I'd set aside for Allie, then hurried down the stairs.

I stuck my head into the kitchen. "Sorry, Doris, got sidetracked by new information." She nodded at me, and Aiden lifted his coffee mug in salute.

"I figured I'd hide out in here, so I didn't spook her. There's something really odd about her. Have you figured out what's happened to her, why she's living on the street?" he asked.

Even though I had figured it out, I didn't want them to think badly of her, and she hadn't yet confirmed it, so I shook my head. "I just know she needs help. I'm going to take her some clothes, but it's getting close to time for us to go to work. We're going to have to get her fed and out the door here soon, as much as I hate to say it. I don't know her well enough to feel comfortable with her in the house on her own, and with everything else going on I'm not sure it's safe for her to be here without us anyway."

Doris nodded. "I'll pack up some sandwiches she can take with her." She hurried around and started to put together a large packed lunch, one that would keep me for three days solid. *Here we go again*, I thought, remembering how the Bremen Town Musicians had cleaned me out the year before. Magical hinky stuff was wiping out my pantry and fridge. Go figure.

I made my way down the hall to rescue Allie. When I rapped on the door, I heard her splashing around, then getting out of the tub. I grinned to myself. If she was still in the water she had to be as wrinkled as a prune, but I bet she felt better after having gotten clean and being able to relax in a locked room without anyone bothering her or threatening her or otherwise stressing her out.

"Allie, it's Janie. Can I come in? I've got clothes for you. I'll throw yours in the laundry with mine tonight after work, and you can come pick them up tomorrow."

She unlocked the door, and glanced around. My guess was she was looking for Aiden, but maybe she was just conditioned to be that cautious about her surroundings. She let me in. "I didn't realize I was so tired. Thank you for letting me take a break and relax."

I was relieved to see there was no evidence of drug use; her eyes seemed clear and focused. I handed her the pile of clothes I'd grabbed upstairs and turned my back while she unwound the towel she was wearing when she'd opened the door, and dressed. I turned back when she cleared her throat gently.

"Doris, the lady you met earlier? She's packing up some food for you to take with you. I didn't expect to see you this afternoon, and Mia and I have to go back to work in a bit. I'd like to talk to you some more, though. I want to help, but I'm not pushing. I want you to know this house is a safe haven for you. We are happy to give you a bite to eat, a place to shower, and a listening ear. We'd also love to help, but I can't give you free run of the house while I'm at work until we get to know you better."

Allie gave me a small smile. "I understand. I'd feel the same way. And I appreciate all you've done for me. I feel like I haven't done anything to help you in return. Is there something I could do?"

A small kernel of an idea bloomed in my brain. It couldn't hurt. "Well, this house is huge. I inherited it, and it's in a great neighborhood, but it could be a target. It's easy for someone to look at this house and think it's full of all kinds of things that might be worth a lot of money. There really isn't. We're grad students. We don't have a lot of money. And truth be told, replacing these old, antique windows aren't in the budget. If you're in the neighborhood, keep an eye on the house. Even if it's just to run down the street and bang on a neighbor's door to ask them to call the police. Just getting the cops there before someone can tear the place up would keep us from spending tons of money we don't have."

She nodded, eagerly. I saw in her face an earnest yearning to help me, to pay me back somehow for the food and gentle help I'd been trying to give her. Having my own personal neighborhood watch group on the prowl ready to call in any sign of someone coming near the house made me happy, although I knew I couldn't quite explain why I was so worried about being a target. Then again, it was Dayton, where good neighborhoods and bad neighborhoods merged together, with pockets of both interspersed throughout the city. We weren't all that far from downtown. Who knows who might be out to hurt us?

Allie asked me if I could help her braid her long hair, which had lost its mousy look with a good washing. Instead, it was rich and brown with natural lowlights, and it was thick and heavy in my hands. As I braided quickly, the cramps in my hands reminded me it had been many years since I'd braided teammates' hair in the back of the bus on the way to a soccer game. It was a good memory, and one I'd forgotten about with all the memory tampering my stepmother had done last year. It made me even more determined to see if there was anything else I could do to get this young girl into a better place.

"I should probably go, so you can get to work," she said, even though she seemed reluctant to leave.

I led her out of the bathroom, poking my head into the kitchen, where Doris handed me a large brown paper grocery sack filled with food. "Honey, there are sandwiches in there, and a handful of apples, sleeves of crackers, hard boiled eggs, and some fried bacon. You can eat the bacon cold, but I wouldn't wait too long on the eggs. This should hold you for a bit, so you won't have to worry about food."

"And, if you want, you can always sit on the back patio when we're not here and relax. I'll even leave a book out in a plastic bag so if it rains the paper won't be damaged, but you'd have something to read if you wish." I had no way of knowing if she was a reader or not, but I knew I would have appreciated something like that. She just kind of nodded. "What do you like?"

"I used to like reading just about anything. I haven't read a book in a long time. I'd like that."

"Well, I'll tell you what, why don't I leave one or two in a big freezer bag under the picnic table? And that way, if you're not into one of them, you have something else to read. Don't feel like you have to sit here all the time, but if you're looking for a quiet place to get away, it's here."

I didn't tell her I'd already stashed twenty bucks in the back pocket of the jeans I'd lent her. They hung on her a bit, as she was a few pounds lighter than I was, but they'd do for a day or so until I could get hers washed.

"I should go. You said yourself that you need to get to work. I've been gone too long as it is. They'll be looking for me, and I'll have to have some reason why I was gone or things will be bad. I'll come back, but I'm trying not to make a pattern of it. I'll check on the house when I'm in the area. Thank you for the bath, clothes, and food. I'll return them as soon as I can," she said, edging out the back door.

I noticed she didn't go around the house to the street, but slipped through the back yard and alleys instead. Maybe that was her being careful not to lead anyone to our door. Whoever and whatever she was so afraid of, I wondered what they would do if they showed up when our latest magical threat showed up. I chuckled to myself as I closed the door after her. That might be the one good thing to come out of all this if it resulted in Allie finding her freedom from whatever had such a tight hold on her.

I was starting to get used to the same feeling in the pit of my stomach when Allie left; happy I'd been able to do something, no matter how small, to help her, and sad I hadn't been able to do more. I shook my head to clear it. I could only help Allie as much as she would let me. I had enough other problems for the moment, including making it to work on time. I hurried to the steps, calling for Mia to hurry up.

CHAPTER TWENTY-ONE

On the way to work I filled Mia in about what had just happened with Allie. Aiden went with Doris when we left the house, but Bert had insisted on going along with us, and I noticed he was sticking very close to Mia. He'd very seriously argued that we should be lining our pockets with salt and iron, and he'd fought back until I went back upstairs to get the magical immunity necklace Aiden had given me the year before. I had to eventually concede Bert was right; if there was some magical baddie out there, it wouldn't be a stupid idea to have some protection every time I left the house. Then again, I was starting to wonder if I should wear it in the house as well.

I'd also given Bert the job of explaining the salt and iron thing to Mia while I'd run upstairs for the necklace. Salt and iron ward off faerie beings, and disrupt their magic. It made sense, but if the Big Bad was really as big and bad as the warnings I'd been getting about the Seawitch, then a little bit of table salt and a couple of loose penny nails in my back pocket weren't going to do much to stop her.

There was no music on this car ride, as there had been earlier. The triumph of just a few hours ago in figuring out the target of the Seawitch had given way to a grim determination to fight whatever was ahead of us. I didn't know exactly what that would entail, but I certainly knew more than Mia who was still in the dark as to her importance in all of this. I wondered how long her ignorance would last until she realized Bert wasn't acting like himself, and was practically glued to her instead of tagging along with me.

What was wrong with that frog anyway? He was normally my snarky advisor, my humorous sidekick, my back-up, and my friend. Suddenly he was Mr. Serious, and paying attention to just one thing. I looked down at where he sat on the floorboard, and realized he was curled up next to Mia's leg, a grim look on his face, his brow wrinkled in determination.

Holy shit, I thought, as light dawned. He'd always made cracks about Mia in the past, but never in her hearing. He'd made comments before about finding her attractive. And now he was all but velcroed to her leg while we drove to work. It was obvious. I couldn't believe I hadn't gotten it before now.

Bert was in love with Mia.

And if I was right, he'd been in love with her from just about the moment he met her when she was screaming at the idea of a talking frog that was licking the back of her hand. Yeah, he did. Probably not his finest moment, but he had been trying to convince her that he was real and it certainly did the job.

I blinked hard as I pulled into the parking garage at the Schuster Center for the Performing Arts to start another shift selling ticket subscriptions. Bert insisted on climbing into Mia's shoulder bag for the evening. Normally, he'd have been in mine. Of course, maybe that was out of habit from when I'd been the one in danger. I felt a small twinge of jealousy, but I had the immunity necklace. She didn't. Maybe I should let her wear it, but I couldn't think of a good reason to take off jewelry and hand it to her to wear as we got out of the car and walked to the office. Other co-workers were arriving at the same time, and it would definitely have been odd; never mind that Mia would never have understood why it was so important in the first place. I'd have to either explain she was the target or somehow explain why I needed the necklace less than her. I knew Bert would back me up, but I wasn't sure if she would understand.

And, having known Mia since high school, I was pretty sure she didn't feel the same about Bert as he felt about him. This was not going to end well.

Just as we started our evening of cold calling previous ticket buyers to upsell them to full seasons, someone came into the box office phone banks. It was Jonah, the understudy we'd talked to the night before who had ushered us out of the theater last night before the police arrived to deal with the star's accusatory meltdown.

"Hey, Mia," he said, making a beeline for her desk.

She saw him and blushed. "Hey, Jonah. I hope you're having a better night tonight."

Double shit, I thought. That was more of a reaction than Bert had ever gotten from her. I could almost see the steam rising from her bag where it sat on the floor near her feet. No question Bert was listening to the whole exchange, and all the awkward attraction between them.

Something bothered me about Jonah. I couldn't put my finger on what it was, but Mia was definitely reacting to something. "Hi, Jonah," I said, in between calls. "You trying to get us in trouble?"

He grinned, leaning one hip against Mia's desk. That meant his shadow fell right over Bert's hiding place. I could feel my own heart cracking in sympathy for him, but I just didn't know quite what to do. There were too many people around to say anything about Bert. We were stuck at our desks for another three hours or so until we could clock out, and it was at least another hour before we had a scheduled break. There was literally nothing I could do except try to make the point that we were working and he should leave us alone.

It worked, sort of. "Well, I wouldn't want you to get into trouble, but I'd love to see you after you get off work. We've got an evening off, and I'd like to spend it with you," Jonah said, as Mia's headset went off warning her to start placing her next call.

"Check back with me at eight, and we'll see how the evening's gone," she said. "Maybe we could all just go out for a cup of coffee and get to know each other."

He gave me a strange look, as if trying to signal me to make some sort of excuse so they could be alone, but I wasn't having any of it. "See you at eight, Jonah," I called out, after putting my current call on hold.

I had to give him credit; he didn't skip a beat, although I could tell he was disappointed. "Well, we could all sit down for a cup of coffee tomorrow night, as we've got a brief to write for our day job tomorrow. Sorry to disappoint, but we'll be working late tonight even after we get off duty."

I saw the disappointment in her face, and in Jonah's, but it was true. We did still have to write up our research for the judge in the morning, and we needed to keep working on figuring out what was going on with the rest of our issues. Uh, the magical ones.

Why, oh, why, does everything have to happen all at once? Life had been fairly calm ever since my stepmother had been locked up. If things could just start happening a little at a time, that would work out just fine for me. If Allie had shown up just a month or two sooner maybe I could have helped her without feeling like I had to push her out the door in order to solve the latest magical mystery, protect my roommate, deal with Bert's romantic entanglements or lack thereof, deal with my budding—or not—romance with Aiden, all my own inner issues, and deal with Mia getting asked out on a date we didn't have time for her to go on. Yeah. Like that would ever happen.

As Jonah strolled off, blowing Mia a cheesy kiss and acting like some weird famous person, I realized there was no way I was lucky enough for things to stop happening long enough for me to get a handle on everything going on.

I was going to have start prioritizing. And making some decisions . . . such as letting Mia in on the truth.

CHAPTER TWENTY-TWO

We got to our first break and Mia wanted to go find Jonah. I couldn't talk her out of it, so we went looking.

"Janie, I'm a big girl. I can go myself. It's not a big deal."

"Yes, it is. What if our otherworldly baddie decided to hurt you in order to convince me to bow out? You're in danger, too. I know you didn't choose this," I said, nearly choking on the irony of trying to keep her safe without talking about everything too much out in the open.

"What are you going to do to help? It's not like you're the next G.I. Jane or some kind of female Bruce Willis. What would you do if something jumped out at me?" she demanded.

"Well, Geoffrey told me I have a bit of a reputation after what happened with Evangeline. Maybe they'd think twice even if I couldn't do anything," I explained. Well, he had said that, but I was tagging along because I hadn't told her how much danger she was in, and I just didn't trust Jonah. I didn't really care what my presence did to her chances for a date with him when I didn't think she should be going out with him in the first place.

She rolled her eyes at me, but I heard a whispered "thank you" coming from her purse. She kept walking, as if she hadn't heard it, but I knew she had by the set of her shoulders and the stiffness in her back. What was I supposed to do? She was my best friend, but I couldn't let her run all over the place until I'd had a chance to figure out what was going on myself, and then let her in on the fact she was the person I was trying to protect.

I followed her, giving her some distance, as she headed toward the backstage area. There was no show that night, but there were people all over the place checking props and sets and working on the mechanics of the behind the scenes stuff. I doubted many of the actors were around, and was hoping Jonah had taken off as well, but again my luck was against me.

"Hello, beautiful," Jonah said as he walked up to her, a big smile on his face.

Gag me, I thought, but she ate it up. I started toward them slowly, trying not to be too obvious that I was keeping an eye on her. Covert training was so not my specialty. I had to chuckle as I wondered if this was more Stanley's style. I'd have to ask him for pointers. He'd eat that up.

"And hello to your friend, too," Jonah said. "You ladies get off work early?"

Mia shot me a dirty look, but then turned back to him. "No, we're on our break and thought we'd take a look around. It's interesting back here; you'd never suspect all this goes on behind the scenes." She indicated to the numerous people fixing minute parts of the set and lining up props backstage. "I never thought about what might have to happen to be prepared for a show. I figured there wouldn't be anyone here today, that you guys would all try to enjoy an evening off." She placed her hand on his arm, leaning into him and looking up into his big blue eyes.

I checked my watch. We only got a fifteen minute break, and we'd used up five minutes just getting here and in arguing about me going with her. I hoped the next eight minutes would go quickly, because then I could tell her we had to go. As a good friend, I couldn't really prevent her from talking to a guy who, at least on the surface, was good looking, employed, nice, and interested in her. She'd think I'd flipped my lid.

And then there was also the encouragement I'd gotten from her last year with Aiden; in fact, I was still getting it from her. Never mind Aiden's heritage, or our uncertain relationship, or my own commitment issues. She'd been encouraging me to get over all my own hang-ups, not just about Aiden himself, but about actually caring for someone enough to be in a committed relationship.

There was just something about Jonah that I didn't like. I couldn't explain it, but the hairs on the back of my head weren't just standing up; they were doing the tango.

Something he said brought me crashing back to the conversation in front of me.

"Well, I guess tonight's off. You guys have to work later than I thought," he said.

That didn't make a whole heck of a lot of sense. We got off work at eight p.m., working four hour shifts. Most of the shows at the theater didn't even start until seven or seven-thirty. Jonah, as an understudy, was required to be at every performance, so he'd be there to jump into a role should something happen to an actor. If the play ran at least two hours, the curtain calls wouldn't even start until after Mia and I were already home, dinner eaten, and solidly working on the brief we needed to turn in first thing in the morning. There was no reason for him to stop trying just because we were working until eight p.m., and if he'd already had something else going on that night then he shouldn't have asked.

Then again, if he had the night off as all the other actors did, why in the world was he hanging around here unless he was specifically targeting Mia? And I didn't know him well enough to trust him.

Or was I being too paranoid?

"I was kinda hoping you guys would get off work early since we're off, but it's not looking like you will. I guess we'll have to do it another time, won't we?" Jonah asked, and then bent low over her hand, clicking his heels together as he brushed a kiss on the back of her hand. "I shouldn't have assumed that you'd be off early tonight just because I was."

Weirdo, I thought. Who does that? Then again, I could see Aiden being that courtly if he was making a joke, but most of the time we were too awkward together to even goof around. It was a move I would definitely associate with Geoffrey, with his courtly mannerisms and overly exaggerated politeness. It was the kind of thing my stepmother would have required in her court.

Or was I reading too much into this?

Probably, but at this point I saw just about everything as a potential threat to my friend and I was determined to do everything I could. At the moment I'd rather be paranoid than ignore the fact someone really was out to get us.

She giggled like a schoolgirl. "It's a date. Come see me at my break tomorrow night if you have time, and maybe we'll coordinate our schedules."

Jonah turned away and she waved before turning to me and giving me a glare. "Janie, why don't you like him?"

I couldn't come up with a good explanation. "He just rubs me the wrong way, Mia, and with everything else we have going on right now I'm just concerned that now is the wrong time to be bringing strangers into the mix. Who's to say where the danger is coming from anymore? We just don't know who to trust, and until we have a better grasp on what's going on I don't like the idea of bringing new people around. You just don't know who he is, what he might be, or if he could handle the craziness that's been dropped in our laps."

We headed back toward the office, and I could see the anger coming off of her in waves. I knew why she was mad; I didn't even have to ask.

But I'd rather be a hypocrite than have a dead friend. And I still hadn't told her she was the actual target of the Seawitch. Boy howdy was that going to be a not-fun conversation. I sighed and followed her back to the office. Our break was over.

CHAPTER TWENTY-THREE

Mia had a good mad going on by the time we got back to the office, and I chose not to poke at her. There was time enough for her to get even angrier after we'd gotten everything done for the day. In truth, I was just putting off the inevitable. I was going to have to tell her eventually, no matter how much I didn't want to scare her.

We spent the rest of the shift ignoring each other, distracted by the phones and the ticket sales. It wasn't long before we were done for the evening, and it was time to go home. Mia picked up her purse and left, as I struggled to grab my things and follow her. Everyone else was trying to do the same thing on a night where there wasn't a ton of traffic due to a show or anything else going on downtown.

I finally caught up to her at the car, and I couldn't help but glance into the backseat as I approached the Escalade just to be sure there wasn't some kind of magical voodoo witch doctor faerie thingy lying in wait to disintegrate our bodies and eat our life essence. I hadn't forgotten what Geoffrey told me the Seawitch did to her victims.

I needed to start out with an apology, at least until she could hear my side of the story. "Mia, I'm sorry. You were very supportive when Aiden and I first started talking, and when all the crazy faerie magic stuff first started happening to me. There's more that you don't know about."

"I'm listening," she said, as she leaned up against the side of the car.

"Can we please get in the car and talk on the way home? It's just not safe."

"Safe for who? Or to you mean it's safer for you because I won't yell when you're behind the wheel?" she demanded.

"No, Mia. There are some things we figured out today while you were napping that I need to catch you up on. There just hasn't been a good time to do it. I didn't think it was a good idea to talk about it on our break, because I didn't know where we could talk without someone overhearing it and, as you well know, it's hard sometimes to tell when someone could be magical. I mean, look what happened to me with David last year!" We'd invited someone to join our study group last fall only to find out he was my faerie stepbrother, Evangeline's secret son, who kidnapped me and took me through the portal in my basement.

"And you think somehow the understudy of the play that just happens to be in town at a time we just happen to be working in the ticket office is somehow there to hit on your roommate at a time the faerie courts asked for a favor?"

From that perspective, it sounded kinda dumb. But she didn't have all the right information. "Can we get in the car and talk about this?" I asked.

"No. I want to know what's going on."

"It's not safe to talk about this out in the open. For your sake and mine, can we please get in the car and start driving? I promise you can yell at me as much as you want when we get home. And I'll do all the writing on our brief tonight since you did so much of the research. Please."

I think she took me seriously, although she didn't comprehend why it was so serious. "Fine. But don't think you're getting out of explaining. And I'm not waiting until we get home, either."

"No problem. I'll start talking as soon as we get out of this parking garage." I still wasn't comfortable driving the Escalade, and needed to concentrate enough not to ding it up on the way out of the garage.

"Whatever." She got in the front seat and crossed her arms. Through the window I saw Bert stick his head up from her purse, which was still in her lap. I went around to the driver's side while I dug out the keys.

This was going to be a less than fun car ride home.

CHAPTER TWENTY-FOUR

The minute I pulled out of the garage, she was talking.

"So what is going on that I don't know about?" Mia asked, as I headed for the highway.

Here we go. "Mia, what's your last name?"

"Don't be stupid. You know what it is."

"Yes, it's Andersen, right?"

She sighed. "What does that have to do with anything?"

I turned on my signal to merge onto the exit to the highway. "Well, Aiden's done some research. Have you ever heard the story of the Princess and the Pea?"

"I'm sure I have. Some princess was too prissy to sleep on piles and piles of mattresses because they were lumpy. What does that have to do with anything?"

"Mia, they were lumpy because there were peas under the mattress only a true princess could feel. That's why you haven't been sleeping; your mattress was lumpy because there were dried peas under it."

"It's an old lumpy mattress. How long since it's been used? Who knows what might have been on it that we didn't see."

Oh my, was she in denial. I merged onto the highway, careful to watch my rearview mirror, not just for oncoming traffic, but for cars that might have followed us. I didn't see anything, but, then again, if it was someone who knew what they were doing I might not know how to spot them. I tried to keep watching while I brought up the next piece of news. "Mia, Aiden thinks I ran into the Snow Queen at the courthouse. All the ice I told you about in the restroom?"

"So what?"

"And then you know about Allie, right? And how we found matches on the patio after she left the first night."

"Again, I say, so what?"

This was harder than I thought. She knew about magic, had

known since last fall. It wasn't denial about magic itself, but somehow she had no idea what was really going on.

"Mia, all those stories were compiled and written up by Hans Christian Andersen. The Princess and the Pea, The Little Matchstick Girl, The Snow Queen; they're all stories that Andersen published."

Bert was silent. I wondered why, but at the same time I wasn't sure what he could add to the conversation. He burrowed down in Mia's purse and waited.

She was quiet, so quiet I could almost hear the gears in her brain grinding to a halt. She was quiet most of the rest of the way home. It wasn't until we pulled into the driveway that she said anything else. "So you think because my last name is Andersen I'm the target of the Seawitch? No way. I mean, I've never heard of any connection between us."

I pulled into the garage and parked the car, hitting the button for the automatic garage door to close behind us as we gathered our things to go inside. "Mia, when's the last time you talked to your father?"

"Not since Christmas," she said. "You know he's not my favorite person."

I did know. We didn't talk about it much. Her dad hadn't been around through most of high school and college. Her parents divorced when she was in junior high, and that was when she'd moved into my school district and we had become friends. She didn't talk about her father much, mostly because she blamed him completely for the divorce and thought he treated her mother badly. I didn't disagree, but I'd been gently trying to push her to spend some time with him. I wish I could spend time with mine.

"I think you do need to contact him, and see if there's anything you should know about your genealogy. Is there some family history or legacy we need to know?" I asked, as I unlocked the back patio door, noticing Doris had put together a baggie of paperback books and left them on the chaise lounge, but there was no sign that Allie had been back yet. The house was dark and quiet, and there was no sign of anyone in or around the house either. I let out a deep breath I hadn't even realized I'd been holding as I pushed open the door and walked inside.

Mia's face was flat and expressionless. "You want me to contact the man who ran around on my mother, the man who didn't show up for anything before the divorce, and made sure to be even more absent when it was finally said and done. You want me to call and talk to the man who made sure his child support was always sent in just before the electric was about to be shut off, or just until Mom had filled out the paperwork to take out a loan to fix the furnace or the water heater or whatever had just about died. You want me to contact the man who told me that I was a mistake and ask him for help?"

"Yeah, I do, Mia. Unless you know how to have a séance and raise your grandparents from the dead to ask, then you're kinda stuck with calling him. I don't see how you can get out of it. For all we know he could be the one we're supposed to protect, but with all the magical stuff happening to you, I don't think that's the case." I put down my purse on the kitchen table, and Mia did the same.

Bert hopped out, finally joining in on the conversation. "Mia, this isn't about your dad. It's about keeping you safe. Janie wasn't trying to keep things from you or hide things. She was trying to help you, like you did with her last year. Think about it; she didn't really want to spend any time she didn't have to with her stepmother."

I turned on the lights in the kitchen as Bert talked, and opened the fridge to find Doris had left us a couple of plates of sandwiches leftover from packing for Allie. I pulled them out and set them on the island countertop while we talked.

"How is it that he's not the target? I mean, if it is true I'm the target this time around, why wouldn't the Seawitch be after him first?" she asked.

"Truthfully, she might be," answered Bert, before I could jump in and say the same thing. "But that doesn't mean she won't head straight here if she gets to him."

She sat down heavily, dropping her head to the top of the table. Her voice was muffled, as she said, "I don't want him to get hurt. I don't hate him *that* much."

"Then call him," I said. "Find out if anything weird has been going on. Find out if he's okay. And ask if there's anything interesting in the family history. You can tell him someone has asked if you're related to the dude from the fairy tales. See what he says. You don't have to tell him all of it."

She sighed. "And here I was hoping the only time I'd have to see him was when he showed up for the awkward and obligatory Christmas meeting. I've only seen him once a year since the divorce, and that's only because I couldn't bring myself to say no at Christmas."

I knew she would kick herself forever if she didn't call and at least make sure he was okay, or find some way to warn him. "Mia, if nothing else, you can always tell him there's been some scary stuff going on at the courthouse, which is true, and you just wanted to make sure he was okay. He'll be touched that you cared."

Bert nodded. "Call. Do it now, before you can talk yourself out of it. Find a way to reach out to him. If all this blows over and he's still a piece of slime you can ignore him until Christmas. What harm would it do?"

Mia stood up. "You guys are right. I know you are. I'm just hoping he doesn't take this as an excuse to butt into my life. He's not welcome. And, Janie, just because I'm not yelling doesn't mean I'm over how you acted in front of Jonah, but we'll talk about that later. I guess I have to make a phone call, but I don't trust him. You mind if I put it on speakerphone for all of us to listen in?"

I shrugged. I'd never met the man, so I had nothing to go on except Mia's complaints about him over the years. "Sure. But I'm going to eat a sandwich while you do that, and I'll be setting up my laptop to work on that brief while you talk."

I hoped he was as clueless as she thought he was.

Or maybe I didn't.

CHAPTER TWENTY-FIVE

While Mia pulled out her cell phone and dialed, hitting the button to put the call on speakerphone, I turned on the laptop and dug out our research. I wasn't sure if I hoped he had new information for her or was in the dark. Either way, she wasn't going to have a fun time making this call.

"Hello?" A deep voice answered.

"Dad?" she asked.

"Who's this? Is this some kind of a joke? I'm not falling for it."

Oh, man. He didn't recognize her voice? This was going to be rough. I saw her wince.

"Dad, it's Mia. I don't know how to say this so I'm just going to say it. Is there anything about our family history I need to know?"

Silence on the other side of the phone line was so thick and oppressive I thought it might be very possible to cut it with a butter knife. "What's going on, Mia? Are you okay?"

I suddenly had a very bad feeling about all this, as well as a sneaking suspicion Mia was going to learn something about her father she would never have guessed in a million years. I had a pretty good idea how she was about to feel. I hoped I was wrong, but I'd been there just nine months ago. I started typing, setting up the formatting for our brief and framing the first paragraph to define the research.

"I'm fine, Dad. I'm not calling to make small talk."

He sighed. "I didn't think you were. You never do call me unless you don't feel like you had a choice."

"Dad, I'm serious. I need to know if there is anything I need to know about our family history. It's important. I'm okay, but I need to know and I didn't want to wait until next Christmas."

"Honey, you don't have to wait until Christmas to talk to me. I'm always ready to listen." There were loud sounds in the background. It sounded like gunfire, but that could just be an action movie with a good sound system or a loud videogame.

"Dad, where are you?"

"At work."

"Where are you working now?" she asked.

"At a movie theater. I'm the manager, and I'm on my cell phone in the front of the screen."

"You're talking on the phone in a theater full of people?"

"No. We run the movies from beginning to end when we first get them to make sure there's nothing wrong with our copy. This is the new Bruce Willis movie that opens tomorrow night."

She accepted it, but it seemed odd to me. It was only nine o'clock in the evening, and I was pretty sure there would normally be a regular showing going on at the time; most seven o'clock movies wouldn't be over yet, even on a Tuesday night. I started summarizing our legal findings from her research that morning.

"Whatever," she said. "Dad, really, I just wanted to know if there's anything I should know about our family history."

"Like medical stuff?"

"Among other things," she said, getting impatient.

I noticed her face was getting redder and redder as the conversation kept going. Either her father really was clueless or he was really playing it close to the vest on this. Was he fishing for more information or was he just trying to milk the few and far between contacts he got with the daughter who all but hated him and avoided anything even approaching the idea of appearing to be related to him. I kept typing, hoping she'd continue to forget I was here long enough to settle down to ask him what she wanted to ask him.

"Honey, you're on a speakerphone, aren't you?" he asked.

Why did that matter?

"Of course I am, Dad."

There was silence on the phone. "Who else is listening to me?"

I leaned back in my chair, away from the screen.

"My roommates are listening."

I saw Bert's head pop up. He'd been awfully quiet, but it was the first time Mia had ever actually referred to him as her roommate. I wondered how he took that one. Roommate could be a category he didn't want to be in, but she'd never categorized him as anything before, so he could see it as a step up.

"I'm sorry, Mia. I don't know your roommates, and I don't trust cell phones. We're going to have to meet."

"What is this, like something out of Mission Impossible? I just want to know if there's anything out there that I need to know."

"And I'm telling you that I would be more comfortable discussing some of this stuff face to face."

She was getting madder and madder. I started to wonder if she was going to stroke out. Her hands were shaking. "Dad, I don't want to see you. You know that. I only agreed to one awkward Christmas dinner a year so you would leave me alone the rest of the year."

"You're the one who called me. I assume there's a reason you're calling me. It's information you want. The price of that information is actually being in the same room with me long enough for me to lay eyes on you and tell you in person the answers to the questions you're asking. I'm not asking for much. I'm asking for a dinner with my daughter. And I want to meet your roommates."

"That wasn't part of the deal."

"You're asking these questions in front of them. I assume you'll be telling them the minute I walk away, so I'd like to be introduced to the people you're going to share this information with. Sue me if I actually do want to meet my daughter's closest friends. Isn't that what fathers are supposed to do?"

"Yeah, maybe if the daughter is still in pigtails and the father stopped running around on the mother long enough to be around to meet those friends. Once the daughter is over twenty-one and the father hasn't been around he kinda loses those fatherly rights."

Oh, Mia, I thought. She'd been sitting on that one for a while.

He cleared his throat. "You don't have all the facts, Mia. I know what you think of me, and I know you think your anger against me is justified. Let me tell you that I'm not denying you have the right to be upset with me, but you don't know the whole story. I'm willing to tell you some of it, heck, even most of it, but I won't do it without an opportunity to see you, to assure myself of the people you are with and to make sure I know my only daughter is in good hands with the people she chooses to surround herself with."

"Fine. Lunch. Tomorrow. My house." She gave him the address. "I don't get off work until noon, so if you're early you might want to find something else to do until I get here."

"No problem. Thank you for meeting with me."

She hung up the phone without saying good-bye, and let out a long drawn out shriek of frustration. "I hate that man."

"I know," I said. I'd written a good eighty percent of our *Miranda* brief regarding the police interrogation the judge was hearing motions about, thanks to her meticulous research from the morning, and all I had yet to do was to finish the conclusion. It wasn't a difficult memo to write; it wasn't long, and it wasn't complex, but at the moment I really didn't care about the issue. I only cared about Mia, and keeping her from blowing her top. That, and keeping our jobs.

"Why does he always think he can negotiate his way back into my life?"

"He asked for lunch. He didn't ask for visitation rights, or weekly lunches, or a monthly newsletter. You used to get so angry when he didn't show up. Don't shoot the messenger here, but you're getting what you wanted years ago. He's showing interest." I pushed the computer back from where I sat and stood up to get a bottle of water out of the refrigerator. I also got out a beer, and poured it into a small tumbler before setting it down in front of Bert.

"He's your dad, Mia," Bert said. "Maybe he just doesn't know how to show you he cares without being in front of you to show you."

"He doesn't get to call himself Dad. He didn't earn that title. I only call him that because my mother insisted on it. I do it now even if I don't want to, because calling him Tobias Andersen doesn't feel right after years of my mother nagging me to call him Dad."

Bert choked on his beer. "Your dad is Tobias Andersen?"

"Yeah, what of it?"

"*The* Tobias Andersen?"

"The one and only lying scumbag who runs out on his wife and daughter," Mia snapped. "Yes, that's him. Why? Are you saying he's run out on someone you know? Because that fits his MO."

"No, Mia," Bert said. "He's been working with F.A.B.L.E.S., and other groups like it, for years. Probably since before you were born.

Probably since before he even met your mother. He's an enforcer."

"He's a movie theater manager."

"No, he's not. He's the boogeyman for faerie court members who aren't as strong as Queen Eva. He's the one who protects humans against magical malfeasance. And he's the one we seriously considered calling in last year to protect Janie from her stepmother, but her stepbrother and stepmother moved faster than we did." Bert stuck his face down in his glass long enough to gulp his beer loudly and belch. "Sorry, excuse me, but beer makes me burp more than it did when I was a human."

Not only were we learning there was more in our own lives we never knew, but suddenly Bert had manners. I was beginning to believe angels really could dance on the head of a pin; that hell really could freeze over, and that Santa was real.

CHAPTER TWENTY-SIX

"Mia, I'm sorry, I know you didn't want to call your dad." What else could I say? I hadn't wanted to have lunch with my stepmother all those times either, but it had turned out that those meetings had led me to the truth; she was evil and out to get me. Was Mia's dad evil? No way to know, but I figured we could be prepared for the situation if we had to be.

"You know what, Janie? I don't care what you know or don't know. I just want to get through this lunch. I don't like the idea of meeting him here, but I also have a funny feeling I'll end up yelling at him and I think that's best not done at a restaurant or coffee shop. He deserves it, and I've laid off of him for years, but if Bert's right he's more than just the deadbeat I've known all my life. I just don't know that I'll ever want to see him again." She slipped her cell phone back into her pocket and snagged a sandwich from my plate.

What could I say to that? I certainly had no room to talk about family members who turned out to be completely different from what they seemed at first. There was no way I was qualified to give her advice. "You know what? I bet there are things we can do here to protect the house."

"Yes, there is," Bert said. "I'm sure you've got plenty of salt and nails and stuff around don't you, Janie?"

I had some. I knew I didn't have enough for what I was thinking. "I'll call Aiden and see if he can get more while we finish our brief, and then we can try to at least ring the house with salt and nails before we go to sleep. I can't believe I didn't think about it before."

She nodded, and took the computer away from me. "That's something you know more about. Why don't I look over what you've got so far and try to get a bit further while you make the call and figure out what we need to do?"

I stood up. "Of course." I called Aiden, hoping that keeping Mia busy until it was time to go to sleep would be what she needed in order to keep moving forward and not worry too much about the upcoming emotional crap she would have to shovel with her father. Aiden promised to stop at the store and come over, borrowing his mother's car, since his was still in the shop for repairs.

Mia and I worked quietly, passing the laptop back and forth across the table as we put the finishing touches on the memo we needed to turn into the judge in the morning, but we didn't talk about anything other than work. I heard a soft shuffling noise in the hallway and, when I went to investigate, I found Bert hopping back and forth outside the kitchen door. If he'd been human I'd have said he was pacing.

"What's wrong, Bert?" I asked, closing the door behind me so Mia could continue to read without interruption.

He stopped and sighed. "I've accepted over the years that there isn't a good solution to my situation. I've accepted my life as a frog, even though I didn't choose this. But I have never in my life wanted to be human more than I do right this minute. I can't protect her like this. I can't help her like this. I can't even spread salt around the foundation of the house to protect her because I don't have hands and opposable thumbs; at most I can hold an olive fork and poke someone. I doubt I've got the arm strength to even break skin to protect her. I feel so helpless. And she's interested in that Jonah guy. What's he got that I don't?"

I couldn't say it, but Jonah had, well, human-shaped legs, human skin, and didn't eat flies.

"Bert, I think she's too distracted right now to even think much about what she wants. A pretty looking guy is giving her attention. That doesn't mean you automatically lose. You just have to keep showing her your good points." Did I want them to end up together? Why was I encouraging this? I didn't know, but I did know I couldn't see the long, drawn look on his froggy little face. I wanted my wisecracking amphibian friend back, and if hope would do it, I was willing to see if I could cheer him up. I knew that was selfish.

"I've always wondered, if I got the chance to be human again whether I would take it or not. I've been a frog longer than I was a human. I'm used to this life, even though it is a bit lonely. And now here I am wondering what it would be like to go back to that life in order to build one with a woman. And not just any woman," he said, as he resumed hopping back and forth. "I'd want it to be Mia. It's funny, though, because when I was a human I wanted nothing to do with the idea of settling down. I was the well known bachelor, the play boy, and the womanizer. I always had women interested, and I just wasn't interested in any of them. And now I finally find the one I want, and there's no future because I'm a damn frog!"

I saw tears in his eyes, which he hastily reached up and wiped away. "Bert, help me keep her safe now. That's what you can do for her. The questions of being human or not, of being in a relationship with her or not, doesn't matter if she's not safe, if she's not here for those things to happen. And don't sell yourself short. You were the one who called in the cavalry for me last fall. I'd never have gotten out of that cage without your help getting Aiden there. You might not have been my knight in shining armor, but you made sure the knight got to the right place at the right time."

He seemed to brighten up at that thought, just like I'd hoped that he would. The doorbell rang, preventing any further discussion. "That's probably Aiden," he said. "I'll go keep Mia company and see if I can't help on your brief while you get the door."

I opened the kitchen door for him before I went to answer the front door. He was right. It was Aiden. He was carrying grocery sacks full of salt and had an overnight bag slung over his shoulder. I crossed my arms in front of me and raised one eyebrow at the implication.

He went red from his collar to his hairline, the flustered, embarrassed, splotchy shade that redheads get when they get surprised or embarrassed. "I'm not presuming anything, honest, Janie. It's late. I was thinking that if you wanted me to stay it would be better if I had my own clothes and a change of underwear for the morning, that's all."

"Um-hm," I muttered, incoherently. I leaned up against the doorframe. He was cute when he got this flummoxed.

"Really, Janie. If you're uncomfortable with me spending the night, it's okay. I'll go back home. I just thought I'd be prepared."

"Regular Boy Scout, aren't you?"

"Eagle Scout, but that's not the point. The point is to make things easier for you guys. If you want me on the sofa, that's fine. I'm just not feeling comfortable with you girls here by yourselves, and I didn't think you were comfortable last night about it, either."

"What about your mom's car? Won't she need it in the morning?"

He shrugged. "She said to take it tonight. I don't think she has to be anywhere in the morning, and I'll drop it off when I leave. That is, if you'll let me stay."

It sounded like he wanted to stay. I wanted him to; I just wasn't thrilled about the presumption he'd made. Then again, he had dropped whatever he was doing and came running over here with bags of salt when I'd called. Why was I so worried? He was a nice guy. I guess I didn't want to lead him on, especially since there wasn't a lot of certainty in our relationship at this point. I just didn't feel right about him acting like our relationship was a foregone conclusion.

But was that my own fear of commitment talking or was that how I really felt? Either way, now wasn't the right time to deal with all of that.

It was Mia's turn for shoveling the emotional crap tonight, not me. And before we went any further with all of this I needed to do what I could to protect the house.

"Come on in. Let's get more salt around the house before we do anything else," I said, giving him a small smile. "We'll figure out the rest later, and I'll fill you in on what happened this evening. Believe me, you're not going to believe it all. I'm not sure I do, myself."

He dropped his bag in the living room and handed me some of the salt.

As we went outside and poured a line of salt around the foundation of the house, I filled him in on Mia, her father, Jonah, Bert, Bert's crush on Mia, and everything else. He was quiet until the end. I felt a snapping sensation in the pit of my stomach as the circle of salt was completed. Aiden said it was because I was recognizing magic.

I hoped so, because I felt like I was a little behind in keeping up with everything that was going on. Things were just happening so darned fast.

CHAPTER TWENTY-SEVEN

Aiden was normally a font of information, but tonight he was drawing blanks. "You guys have heard from someone else in the courts? And it's Winterkiss? Man, I don't even know how to start figuring that one out."

We were in my room getting ready for sleep. Mia had gone to bed while we were outside spreading the salt around, and Bert was wallowing into yet another mug of beer. I had given up on getting Bert to cut himself off. I just hoped I wouldn't come down to frog pee on the kitchen floor and a passed out drunk in the sink. He'd already done that once, before I'd moved into the house, and I'd made him stick to a strict two-beer limit after that, but I didn't have the heart tonight.

"Who is Winterkiss? I remember the guy who works for her speaking up during my trial last year." He'd supported my argument at a time when it seemed no one would speak up against my evil stepmother, but I didn't know his boss. "Is she someone I can trust?"

Aiden snorted as he pulled his toothbrush out of his bag. "No one from the courts is trustworthy. You know that. Every single one of them has their own agenda, their own power play, and their own plan. The question isn't who is trustworthy, but whose interests lie closest to your own, because those are your allies. And that's an ever shifting battle."

"Okay, so maybe I'm asking the wrong question. Let's try this again. What's her agenda? What does she want?" I sat on the bed in my Avengers pajamas, my fuzzy bunny slippers mocking me with their ratty pink cheerfulness. "And why would she help me?

Aiden slipped into the bathroom attached to my bedroom, and answered with a mouth full of toothpaste. "She's always been in the running as a potential rival to the Queen. She's probably one of the front runners to take over the throne now."

"What do you mean, 'front runners'? Are you telling me there's no one on the throne? No one's in charge? That's a terrifying thought."

He spit in the sink, and I heard the water running. "They still haven't resolved the issue of succession. Your stepbrother, Hansel, says the throne is his by lineage, but he isn't strong enough magically or politically to hold it. Winterkiss's got the power to hold it but she's not in the line of succession, so there are those in the court who don't think she's the right person to lead. There are others who are scheming and conniving to take out one of them and advance their own causes, but those are probably the two most significant contenders."

"So, if Winterkiss is thinking of her place in all this she probably believes I'm a natural ally. After all, I don't really like or trust Hansel, and I'm the one who helped knock Evangeline off the throne. So, maybe I should meet with her and come to some kind of agreement?"

He came back into the bedroom. "I'm not sure that's the world's best idea, either. I mean, the rest of the court is split about who they should follow. I'm not sure you should take sides at all, because what happens if Hansel ends up on the throne? You'd have thrown in your lot against him. What if he orders your stepmother released?"

"That's not a ringing endorsement for me to stay away from Winterkiss. You've got to know I'd do just about anything to keep Hansel from doing that."

"Yeah, but Hansel doesn't really like his mother enough to let her out, because he's not stupid. She'd try to take over through him, and he'd only be a puppet leader. If he wants to stay in power he's got to balance the need for her strength and his lineage with his desire to be his own person. That's not an easy thing to do, and I'm hearing he's actually trying to do it. It's gotta be hard to stand on his own when she never let him do it before." He sat down on the bed, on the same side where he'd slept the night before.

I thought a bit about what he said. "You know, I do have to give Hansel credit, although I keep thinking of him as David—the name I knew him under. Telling her to jump in a lake isn't an easy thing to do, and you're right. He's walking a tightrope that may well not work out for him, and the temptation to use his mother as a threat will always be there even if he knows it would be the end of his own independence." I pulled back the covers, and climbed under the sheets.

"I don't remember Winterkiss ever being particularly untrustworthy, but there's another factor here. From what you said, it seems like she's not necessarily working with my father, although they both seem to be trying to get you involved in tracking down the Seawitch. If they think you're the best candidate for the role, then are they competing with each other to help you the most? Do they even know they're both working with you?" He climbed under the covers himself, and I shut off the light. His arm curled around my side and I felt him drop a light, chaste kiss on my cheek as he hugged me tight. "But that still leaves one question unanswered."

"Who is your father working for? What's his agenda? What's his goal? Who is he backing?"

"That's it in a nutshell," he said. "I don't remember my father and Winterkiss being particularly good friends, although my dad's not opposed to cozying up to someone who has the right incentive. He's a master at political intrigue and he's about the smartest political operative I know. I wouldn't bet against him, except I don't know what I'd be betting on. That bothers me."

It bothered me, too. I just didn't know what to say. "I guess I just take what they can give me, and see what they can do to help. If we cross check what they tell us and compare their help and their information, maybe it will help us come up with a plan. God knows I could sure use one at the moment."

We talked late into the night, going round and round at the ideas and the possibilities, and it was late when we finally fell asleep wrapped in each other's arms. We woke up the next morning and I wondered if we were falling into a comfortable routine. I liked talking to him about my thoughts and my fears and my own internal mental meanderings before I fell asleep at night, and now I'd done it two nights in a row. I could get used to him being around more often. I wish he hadn't missed Mia flipping out and Bert's revelation. He might have had some insight on how to handle it.

As we got ready for the day, I asked, "So what's the deal with Mia's dad? Bert seemed to imply he's some kind of faerie slayer badass Van Helsing."

"He kinda is," Aiden said, as he pulled a T-shirt over his head. "He's the guy who normally would protect humans. There are several organizations around that research and help out when there are magical shenanigans going on. The F.A.B.L.E.S. group is just one of them. It's my understanding Tobias Andersen is an independent contractor, kind of a cross between a private investigator, an executioner, and a one man S.W.A.T. team. He's serious stuff, Janie. If he's on your side you're good to go, but he's all kinds of busy."

"Is that why he was never around when Mia was a kid?" I sat down on the bed to put on my shoes.

"Janie, we never knew Tobias Andersen had a kid. If our guys had known he did and that she was in our own neighborhood, Mia and her mother would never have wanted for anything. F.A.B.L.E.S. would have stepped up for him. He's done so much to protect people they would have done whatever they could to give back. If I tell my mother about this she'll be upset for weeks that she could have done something to help and didn't know to do it. You'll be covered in baked goods, because it's what she does when she feels bad about something. She bakes until you can feel the diabetes starting just from stepping into her kitchen. The last time she felt guilty about anything similar was when she felt like she hadn't done enough to protect you. Do you remember how much food there was?"

It was true. Doris had outdone herself in supplying me with dinner, with baked goods, with pies and cakes and cookies and pastries and cinnamon rolls to the point I had to start working out regularly or my jeans weren't going to fit again, ever. I smiled at him. "I'm not sure whether you should tell her or not. Her food is incredible, but I don't have the money for a whole new wardrobe a few sizes larger."

"I don't either," he said, smiling back at me. And then he kissed me.

It wasn't one of those chaste good-night kisses he'd given me the last couple of nights before curling up beside me and holding me tight. It wasn't one of those quick pecks someone might absentmindedly give a loved one when hurrying out the door. This was serious, and it was intoxicating.

He leaned in, and lowered me back on the bed. All I could think of was him—all my doubts and fears and worries were gone in that moment. His mouth and mine seemed like they fit together in ways I'd never thought of before; we matched each other perfectly, with each move of lips and tongue. He reached up to cup my cheek, and stopped.

"We don't have time for this, Janie. We've got to get going."

He was right, but I didn't want to. Was there ever going to be a good time for us to just sit down and try to work through all of our hang ups and issues, and figure out if this whole relationship thing was going to work or not?

I swallowed hard and took a deep breath. Best not to look too churned up before going downstairs to face a hung-over frog and a pissed-off friend.

CHAPTER TWENTY-EIGHT

I wasn't far wrong, although, thankfully, Mia was keeping a rein on her anger and Bert hadn't pissed all over the floor this time. He'd thrown up in the sink instead.

I turned on the water and rinsed off a very groggy, smelly, hung-over frog as the coffeepot brewed. My life is so glamorous.

Aiden tried to convince Bert to get moving, but he was mostly mumbling gibberish as he blubbered his way around the sink. He must have gotten well and truly soused last night, which meant he'd had more beer than I'd thought he had. Someone else must have poured it for him because I'd thought he'd only had two or three before I'd gone to bed, and I knew he didn't have the upper body strength to open the refrigerator to get out more. Someone else had provided the alcohol to get my friend so drunk he was rolling in his own filth.

"Aiden, did you come down and give him more alcohol?" I asked, exasperated.

"No."

"Mia, did you?"

"No, I went to bed before you did."

"Yeah, but I heard you still moving around, that's why I asked," I said, as I pulled out a wet, cranky frog from the sink and placed him on a clean dishcloth. He promptly fell over sideways.

"It doesn't take much for me to get drunk, Janie," he muttered, and then belched. "No one got me more. You left the six pack on the counter. I drank all of it."

No wonder. He was normally tipsy after two, drunk after three, and this time he'd six. It was a wonder he was still alive. "Bert, are you okay?" I asked. "Do we need to get you medical attention?"

He opened one red rimmed eye and glared at me. "Who are you going to call, Janie? A doctor? A vet? I'm not some dumbass pet. And a doctor wouldn't know what to do with me. Even if I was gravely injured, or poisoned, or dying, there is no one you could take me to in this realm who could do anything for me."

That was a depressing thought. I hated the idea I couldn't do anything for him but, then again, I knew the alcohol binge wasn't his biggest issue here. The biggest issue was his own demons; his feelings for Mia, his feelings of inadequacy for not being human, and whatever else had happened to him in his own long life I didn't know about yet. I wish I knew how to help him. I hated feeling helpless.

"Bert, are you okay to get through the day today or do you want to stay home? It's no problem either way, but I don't want you throwing up in my purse."

"I'm fine, Janie. I'm not going to get sick again. There isn't anything left in my stomach to come out."

Reason number one million six hundred and seventy one why I wasn't a big drinker. It just wasn't my idea of a good time to be that sick in the morning no matter how great the party the night before or how many emotions I wanted to drown. I wasn't against having a drink or two, but more than that got way too expensive for my budget if I was going to be miserable in the morning. Even so, I'd always known Bert to be as good as his word. If he said he wasn't going to ralph all over my wallet I'd believe him.

"Fine. Whatever. Dry yourself off and get in my purse. We've got to get moving," I said, as I poured myself a cup of coffee. "We'll be late."

He did as I asked, as Mia came back into the kitchen. She didn't say anything to me as she poured herself a cup of coffee in a travel mug and packed up the laptop. I could tell she'd finally gotten a good night's sleep, but she was still pissed.

I started to say something, but she cut me off. "Look, Janie, I get why you were being cautious about Jonah, but there's absolutely nothing that even remotely links him to anything that could possibly be going on with my stupid father and whatever the hell is going on with your magical messed up friends. And I just can't get over the fact that you didn't tell me what was going on until after you'd treated me like a two-year-old in front of a man I'd like to get to know better. You're supposed to be my best friend, not my babysitter, so act like it." She stomped out the back door toward the garage.

She was right, but the last two or three days had been insane.

And as I walked out the back door to follow her I noticed Allie sound asleep on the chaise lounge on the back patio. I went back inside and grabbed the pile of clothes I'd run through the laundry the day before and laid it beside her. She had a black eye, which was new. I went back inside and grabbed the rest of the sandwiches we hadn't eaten the night before and a can of root beer, and set them on top of her clothes on the picnic table beside her. I let her sleep, and followed Mia toward the garage. Aiden left in his mother's car right after us, promising to meet us back at the house at noon, just before Mia's father could come over for what would likely be a very awkward afternoon of family drama. I just hoped putting her through all of this was worth it.

We headed to the courthouse in silence, and got to the office only to find the judge had decided to take the day off. We didn't have another research project to work on, so his secretary sent us home. Mia was livid, but I tried to convince her that maybe it was a good thing; we'd have time to get home, change out of the suits we wore to the courthouse, and put together something for lunch before her dad came over.

"Maybe he'll see that you're fine living here and have everything you could possibly need, and he'll leave you alone," I said, as I drove back home. The morning felt like a waste. Only a week into our split up work schedule and I already felt like I was going out of my mind.

She snorted at me. "He's been trying to worm his way back into my life for three years. I've put him off over and over again hoping he'd get the hint."

"Mia, what if Bert and Aiden and all of them are right? What if he isn't a deadbeat? What if he really is this badass they all seem to think he is?"

She shook her head. "It doesn't matter."

"What do you mean? It means he had a reason, a purpose for being gone all the time; he was keeping people safe from magical dangers. He was helping people, Mia. That's not nothing." I pulled into the driveway, and parked in the garage. "Let's go in through the front door. If Allie's still asleep we should let her stay that way. She probably doesn't get a chance to feel safe."

Mia shook her head, but she followed me. "What good is it to help people if you're ignoring the family who needs you? What good is it to help others if the people who have a legitimate claim on your time and attention need you to show up, just once, to show everyone else on the playground that your kid isn't worthless? He could win the Nobel Peace Prize, but he never once did anything for me, his own kid, when I needed him. He wasn't just a deadbeat who didn't help Mom out with the things we needed, but he was *gone.* It doesn't matter why."

And that hurt me, too. I'd spent so much time over the last couple of days helping Aiden, helping Allie, helping Bert, that I'd forgotten my oldest friend needed me to be a listening ear. She needed me to lean on, to listen, and to tell her she wasn't overreacting, whether she was or not, when she got upset about having to call her father. She needed me to make sure she wasn't in the dark. And she needed me to be there for her, whether I was talking things over with Aiden or not, to help her feel like she was important. Not just for a symbolic reason, but because we thought she was an intelligent person who could contribute more than just a symbol to protect.

"I'm sorry, Mia," I said. "You're right. Then again, maybe he's trying to apologize. He can't change the fact he was gone when you were a kid. He can't go back in time and show up to your fifth grade play or your second grade ballet recital or your tee ball games. He can't change it. Maybe he's forfeited the right to demand anything of you, but he can't fix all that's in the past. He can only try to make it better going forward."

She walked into the living room and sat down on the couch. "Janie, you were so lucky to have a dad who was there. Your dad was awesome. He would have done just about anything for you. I never had that."

"You had your mom." I followed her lead, sinking down in the overstuffed armchair facing her. "She's not a bad person, and she always tried hard."

"She did. But she had to work all the time. She worked two jobs, and sometimes she picked up other things on the side. How do you think I made it through college? I've got huge student loans to pay back when I get done, and she's done everything she could to minimize my financial burdens during school, but there's a limit when she's got her own bills to pay and no help from him. She wasn't around much either, because she had to work. I couldn't ask her to be there for the stuff I needed, because she was already stretching herself so thin to make it all work, to make sure I never wanted for anything and to keep up the appearance we were on the same financial footing as everyone else."

Oh, man. I'd known her mom was always working, but had I been that dense? I guess I had been, and I'd had no idea Mia had always felt so alone.

I swore that it was time to start making it up to her.

CHAPTER TWENTY-NINE

I started going through the refrigerator and trying to see what I could put together for lunch. The one good thing about having a social climbing stepmother who was secretly a faerie queen was that she believed in hiring domestic help. She was also appearance conscious enough to be absolutely sure in the caterers and cooks she hired. I'd stayed out of her way by hiding in the kitchen, so I'd learned a lot just by watching. One or two of them had taken me under their wing and taught me enough basic cooking that I knew what I was doing in a kitchen.

I was also blessed because Doris had been in the house and had stocked my fridge when I hadn't been paying attention. I had given her a key after I'd come back from the trial in front of my stepmother, concerned that someone from F.A.B.L.E.S. would need to deal with the portal in the basement. I wondered if Aiden had said anything to her about Tobias, but I didn't have time to worry about it at the moment. I started working on a mixed green salad, and putting together a quick cold strawberry soup that could chill for the rest of the morning. Luckily, Doris had left behind one of her famous pies, and I figured I could pop it in the oven to warm it up before we cut into it.

Mia made herself scarce. I felt bad for her, and I knew her well enough to know she was miserable. She never really talked about her father, and here he was, barging into her life at exactly the moment when some of her fears were being realized; she was going through exactly the same kind of emotional inner turmoil I'd been through the year before. I knew she was churned up. I knew she felt alone, and I hated I'd made it worse. I hoped she would remember I'd been trying to protect her. I hoped that if we had a decent lunch with her dad, not only might she get some answers for some of the questions she'd lived with since before I'd met her, but maybe she's realize how lucky she was to have a father still alive.

Bert hopped out of my purse while I was fussing about the kitchen, and it didn't take long for him to fall asleep. Soon, the noise of the whirring blender pulsing the frozen strawberries was drowned out by the loud, sonorous snores of Bert, who was sprawled across the kitchen counter. I could have Metallica play a concert on his head, and he'd never notice.

I bopped around the kitchen, glad for a few minutes to relax. I checked the patio and saw Allie had woken up and left, the books neatly in their freezer bag and the clothing I'd lent her folded on the chaise lounge. I felt bad I hadn't been able to do more for her. Sooner or later I was going to have to push the issue with her, but I didn't want to do that until she felt more comfortable with me.

Once I had lunch in the fridge to chill, I wandered into the library. It didn't take long before I found the biography of Hans Christian Andersen that Aiden had been looking at the other day. I began flipping through it looking for references to his sister.

There were almost none.

However, there was an indication he did have a half-sister, who was raised outside of the home, and the two were never close. There wasn't much explanation as to why. There was some suggestion Andersen's father bragged about royal connections, but nothing to substantiate them. There was a mention of the mother having issues with alcohol, and maybe the sister as well, but it seemed like the biographer had gone well out of his way to mention them. I took another book off the shelf and kept flipping. I found the same curious lack of information, and found an autobiography of Andersen. It seemed he mentioned them even less than the scholars who wrote about his life.

What could make someone so unhappy about their family as to almost hide them by lack of mention? Was Hans Christian Andersen so embarrassed by them that he didn't want anything to do with them, or was he attempting to protect them? How could there be so little about them? It was almost like someone had tried to systematically erase them from his life. As much as I'd love to erase my own stepmother and the stepbrother who was trying to take over her throne I somehow figured there was no way I'd ever be able to delete them from my own life story; it was too integral, too well known in the faerie world.

How had he done it?

I was saved from my own mental wanderings when the doorbell rang. It was Aiden, coming back to be present for the lunch we'd scheduled with Mr. Andersen. I shared with him what I'd found.

"I guess I never thought about that, but you're saying the nightingale Winterkiss sent might be right about the sister because you couldn't find anything about her?" he asked.

"No. Not quite. I'm saying we need to see what Mr. Andersen says. His information might match up with it, or not. I'm just saying it's an odd coincidence. And it makes good sense, which is something else we can't forget to apply here no matter what else might be going on."

He nodded, his nose deep in the books I'd pulled out.

"What do you know of Mia's dad?" I asked.

"I've never met him. I've heard of him, of course, but most of what I've heard has been reports of how he's protected people or how he's some kind of Bruce Willis in *Die Hard* kind of action hero. I don't know anything about him as a person. I don't know anything about his relationship, or lack thereof, with Mia, and I don't know anything about his personal life. He's kinda known as a hero in our circles, but that doesn't mean he isn't a complete prick."

"Aiden, just because you don't have a good relationship with your father is no reason to assume all dads are assholes. Mine was pretty awesome."

"And Mia's dad was never around. I'm not saying he was good. I'm not saying he was bad. I'm saying that no matter what great things I've heard about him, there's just no way to measure who he is or how he is as a dad from the stories we've heard. He might be the biggest badass around and still be a . . ."

The doorbell rang again. I answered it.

"A jerk, a deadbeat, an asshole, a prick, a douchebag," said the man on my front step. "I deserve all of those things and more from my daughter, but I'd ask anyone else to wait a bit before they call me names. This conversation isn't going to be an easy one."

He was tall, like Mia, and I saw he had the same sparkle in his eye that Mia had when she was amused by something. Otherwise, they didn't have a whole lot in common by appearance, but this had to be her father.

"Are you Mr. Andersen?" I asked.

"I am. And I believe I recognize the young man standing in front of me. Aren't you Aiden? I know your mother, Doris."

Aiden blushed. It almost seemed like someone getting recognized by their hero. I wondered how he really felt about having this man in my house, and I wondered what his take on all the stories and all of the heroics would be. He was right in that none of it made him a better father to my best friend, but this guy might know something about how I could keep her safe and *that* I did want to know.

"You're right. I'm Janie Grimm," I said. "I'm Mia's roommate."

He stood on the front porch without crossing the threshold. I wondered about that. "Is there some reason why you can't come into the house?" I asked.

I'd made the mistake once of asking a faerie-being into my home without realizing they were *(a)* magic, or *(b)* intended me harm. I wouldn't do that again. I guess it wasn't completely out of line to believe someone might be here impersonating Mr. Andersen in order to get closer to Mia.

"You'll excuse me if I do not extend you an invitation."

He grinned. "You're smart. And you're learning quickly, Ms. Grimm. I heard what you did to your stepmother. I wish I'd been able to help your father before his death."

My jaw was hanging open. "You knew my dad?"

"Yes, I did. I was in South America dealing with something I couldn't put off when he got sick, and I was injured. I didn't get released from the hospital in time to be able to do much to help him, and for that you have my apologies. I'm glad you were able to step up and stop Queen Eva before she could harm anyone else."

Before I could say much of anything Mia appeared at the top of the steps, probably coming out from her room at the sound of the doorbell.

"Dad," she said, in a flat voice.

"Mia," he said, stepping across the threshold without an invitation. "We have so much to talk about."

Even though he'd crossed the threshold without a problem I heard a whirring noise coming from Aiden's back pocket. It was one of Aiden's magic detectors, which had picked up on something magical the minute it had gotten close enough to be triggered.

Boy was this not getting off to a good start.

CHAPTER THIRTY

The one thing I could say for my stepmonster was that she'd definitely drilled etiquette and manners into me.

"Mr. Andersen, I must ask you to surrender any magical items as you come in the house. For our own personal protection and because of the threats we've dealt with we take security seriously," I said, stepping between where he stood and the stairs where Mia stared down at him. Aiden pulled the gizmo making all the noise out of his back pocket and the thing got even louder.

Mia's dad pulled out a necklace with a heavy medallion and held it out for testing. Aiden's device beeped and whirred louder when it was next to the medallion. Aiden waved the thing all around Mr. Andersen's body, and it kept buzzing, but it never got as loud as it did when it was near the medallion. The medallion was the magical device he was carrying, but there was no way to know for sure, and I said so.

"Miss, I'm impressed," he said. "That medallion was a gift; it wards off curses and provides some protection from most magical attacks, but it's not absolute. I never once thought to take it off, because from Mia's call I figured there was danger here. I'm glad to see you taking it seriously."

Aiden jumped in. "If you know who I am, then you know who I work for. Can I ask you to let me hold the medallion while you're here? I don't recognize this, and I don't know what danger it might be." He reached out his hand.

Mr. Andersen gave him a wry smile. "I'm sorry, but from what I know of your parentage it might not be a good idea for you to hold it. I'm not saying I don't trust you. I'm saying it might well try to harm you because of the magical blood you carry. It's not a good idea."

"I'll hold it," I found myself saying. "I'm complete 100 % Ohio born, all American, full blood human. If what you say is true, I should be able to hold it so that you and your daughter can have a discussion without any of us feeling like our safety is at risk."

He handed it over, but I could tell he was reluctant.

Bert came hopping into the room, his eyes red-rimmed, but open. He was yawning until he saw Mia's dad. "Tobias? It's good to see you. Dude, you're getting older and you look it."

He grinned back. "Well, Englebert, without a magical curse keeping me young this is the best I can do. I daresay you still enjoy a bit too much beer from time to time?"

Bert grunted. "Not as much as I used to. And don't call me Englebert. It's a truly stupid name."

How much of an alcoholic was that frog? Maybe my wallet didn't want to know. I'd just be grateful it wasn't all that bad, because I couldn't afford to keep him drunk even if he didn't have the capacity of a full sized human. It made me wonder what stories and skeletons he had hidden in his past, but we had enough emotional crap to shovel over lunch today for me to ask much about it.

"Why don't we all go in the kitchen and have some lunch. Mr. Andersen, I'm sure you'll understand why we're being so cautious, but we'd like to be sure we all know what we're facing. We need to know if Mia's a target and, if she is, then we're all in the line of fire."

He gulped, and I saw it, but he didn't say anything as he followed us to the kitchen. I served up the quick lunch I'd put together for everyone, and we all sat eating in silence as we waited for one of them to start. It rapidly became obvious he was trying to let Mia get comfortable and she was being too stubborn to say a word. This wasn't starting off well.

"Sir, I hate to step foot in what is obviously an awkward situation, but we need to know. Is Mia a target for the Seawitch?" I asked.

He stopped, his spoon halfway to his lips. "The Seawitch has escaped?"

"You didn't know?" Aiden asked, stopping to wipe up spilled soup from his shirt. I hadn't even seen him spill, but it wasn't unusual. I handed him a napkin.

"Yes, we've gotten word from two different sources within the faerie court that the Seawitch has escaped and is looking for revenge against someone. We think Mia might be the target, but we're not sure. That's why she called you. Regardless of whatever the two of you need to talk about, this is fairly pressing and we just can't wait to ask."

He cleared his throat, wiped his mouth with his napkin, and laid it back in his lap. "You want to know if we're related to Hans Christian Andersen."

"Yes, I do," I said, ignoring the death stares I was getting from Mia. Hey, she didn't have to talk to him but we needed the information, and if I waited for her to talk we'd be here until we were ready for the old folks' home. "I didn't think Andersen had kids, so we're kinda lost."

"He didn't."

"So, how?" I asked.

"Well, you might have read somewhere there was a sister, but there's not a lot on the books about her. Her name was Karen, and she did not have a great relationship with her brother."

"That explains why there's not much in the books about her," Aiden interjected.

"Well, that only partially explains it. See, Hans senior was what I am; a magical bounty hunter, a kind of special forces cop, if you will, and he was constantly trying to handle the same kind of things I face on a regular basis. He and his wife had an illegitimate daughter before they married. Her name was Karen. Hans did not put his name on her birth record, and the two let it be known around town she belonged to someone else out of concerns for her safety as his daughter. He swore he would never tie himself down again, but sooner or later word got back to him that Karen's mother was not doing well, that Karen was being cared for by relatives, that her mother was drinking heavily, and he made the decision to give up his work and settle down."

Well, this was certainly not the same kind of story I'd seen in the biographies about the son. I got up to refill drinks, trying not to distract from his story.

I must have been successful, because he continued. "Hans senior had some experience as a shoemaker, but he wasn't very successful and the family was always broke. He tried to settle down. They married and had a son, but he felt guilty for years at giving up his work; there were so many people who needed help. He tried to continue on his own, on a more local basis, but it didn't work out.

Threats started coming in to the family at about the time Karen was brought home to live with them, but it didn't last long. Hans junior was just starting to read and begin his schooling when his father died at the hands of the Seawitch. The family covered it up; the wife began taking in washing and laundry, and began to slowly drink herself to death."

I saw Mia sitting upright, now, more and more interested in her father's story. "So what happened?" she asked, her lunch forgotten in front of her.

"The son, who became Hans Christian Andersen, remembered the stories his father told him, the fables and myths his father read to him, but he didn't understand the importance of what his father was trying to teach him. His father didn't want his son to have to make the kind of choices he had, so he had begged his own family to stay silent. There are rumors of ties to the Danish royal family, and there might have been, but no one has been able to prove it. Hans was sent away to a school for poor children, and left for Copenhagen to make his fortune at 14. He was gone by the time the Seawitch figured out his father had left children behind."

"But Karen was still there, wasn't she?" Mia asked.

"Yes, she was. And the Seawitch came back, so Karen ran with her husband and her children. She tracked down her now famous younger brother, and begged him for money so they could hide."

"I assume they got away," Mia commented. It looked like she was trying for nonchalant, but she was failing miserably.

"You assume correctly," her father said, a smile on his face. "Because if they hadn't, we wouldn't be here; you and I are descended from them."

CHAPTER THIRTY-ONE

That hadn't been an earth-shattering revelation. I'd expected something of the sort, but it explained a lot of things. that had been happening. It explained how there was a connection between my roommate and the Andersen tales coming to life all around us. I still had questions.

"Sir, maybe you can tell us, though, what it means for Mia, and for all the rest of us? None of us are going anywhere, but we need to know why, all of a sudden, this is an issue."

Aiden nodded at me. I got the feeling if I hadn't asked, he would have.

"Well, suffice it to say, the family stayed away from the Andersen name for a generation or two, and then went back to it when the Seawitch learned the family's new surname. They moved across Europe, and there are many descendants, but very few of them have continued in the family business, as it were. As long as someone is doing the work it seems the family has remained relatively safe."

Mia stayed quiet for a moment, but she was thinking so loudly I could almost hear the gears turning inside of her head. It didn't take ESP to know what she was about to say. "You're saying you stayed away, kept doing all that dangerous work, left Mom and me to fend for ourselves, in order to protect us?"

He let out a long, drawn out sigh. "I could try to take the high road here, and claim to be noble and good and brave. There's some truth in saying I left in order to keep you safe, but there's more to it than that. Your mom and I loved each other, but there were a lot of things that went wrong with our relationship. Like most things that end, there's a reason, and my being gone all the time on different missions wasn't easy to take. She couldn't explain my absence to everyone, and I couldn't bring myself to give it up. We loved each other a lot. It just didn't work out."

I couldn't meet Aiden's eyes. This was my biggest fear in

commitment; that no matter how much emotion, how much caring, how much desire between two people, there would always be something that could break it up. I hadn't exactly had a good role model for a successful relationship in my life given that my mother had disappeared when I was young, and my stepmother was, well, evil. He and I had gone round and round about how to get past my concerns about his background, how magic might come between us, and all the other in-betweens, but now wasn't the time to delve into all of that. Mia's outrage distracted us all.

"So you're telling me all of this magic crap was more important to you than staying and working things out? That it was more important than the daughter who needed you? That it was more important than the wife who worked two and three jobs to keep us together? How dare you!" She slammed her fist down on the table making the silverware jump.

"That's not what I'm trying to say. I'm trying to tell you about your heritage. I screwed up. I know it. I was a lousy father. I was an even lousier husband. I'm the bad guy here. I'm not asking for your forgiveness, because I don't deserve it. I might not have been able to be there for you, but right now what you're facing is something I can help with. I can be here to help protect you from the danger you are currently in."

"And if I said to go soak your head?" she asked, a dangerous tone to her voice. "What if I said that you've never been here for me, and I don't need you now?"

I wanted to tell her she was crazy. If my dad was a bad ass and I was in danger I'd forgive him just about anything. Then again, I just wanted my dad back. He hadn't been a bad ass. He'd just been a mild mannered professor . . . who'd just happened to have three iron trunks of strange and assorted weaponry stashed aside in the attic for me. Or had he known I'd have to face all of this one day?

Before I could say anything, her father took charge. "Mia, I never was much of a father to you, but this is a danger that comes from being my daughter. You've made some great connections here, in finding a friend in a Grimm, and in finding connections with F.A.B.L.E.S., and even in having Bert here to help. You've done all this on your own, and I'm proud of you, but I can't say that you're fully prepared for the danger you might face, and I can't in good conscience leave here without knowing you're safe. This is what I do. Let me do it for you."

Long silent seconds stretched into minutes while she considered what he said. I wanted to beg her to let him help, but I'd already stretched my friend privileges by how I'd acted with Jonah. Just as I was about to explode with wanting to tell her to let her dad help her, she finally spoke up.

"Fine. Whatever. I can't tell you to stay away, because I don't know just how bad this is going to get. I'll take whatever help I can until we get through this, because you owe me for all the band concerts and recitals and ball games and everything else you missed. You owe my mom for all the child support payments you missed. And that's just the tip of the iceberg. You don't get to suddenly feel good about yourself just because you can help with this one thing. It doesn't make you even. It doesn't make you a good dad."

He sighed. "Nothing can make up for all the stuff I missed. I'm not trying to magically fix everything, but this is something I can do."

Aiden stood up. "Well, if nothing else, maybe you could walk the outside of the house and check the salt line we put down. I'm wondering if there's anything else we could be doing in order to protect the house from anything the Seawitch might send. Could you take a look with me?"

The two of them headed outside onto the patio, talking about protecting the house and putting down barriers to magical attacks. I snorted as they talked. If I ignored the fact they were talking about magic, they could be two suburban guys discussing their lawns and the pros and cons of fertilizer, or the merits of different security systems or the types of electronic fence that could be buried for the kind of dog I had enough yard to have. I shook my head. Since when was that kind of domestic detail on my mind? Was it just the fact of owning a house, or was I feeling like I was putting down roots in the house I'd hated for so many years?

Mia sat at the kitchen table, shaking her head at the two of them. "And here it starts."

"What do you mean?" I asked, as I cleared away some of the dishes.

"Well, Tobias Andersen loves to come in and take over. It always seemed like whenever he did make the time to show up that Mom and I had to drop whatever we were doing, whatever we had planned, to fit in the time he had allotted to give us. And here he goes again, showing up, elbowing his way in here, and now he's the one we're deferring to. Some things will never change."

"Mia, if this really is his field of expertise then maybe it doesn't hurt to let him into your life enough to use it to protect you. He might not have been good at anything else, but this is his thing. Do you want to turn him away and then need him?"

"Why are you rooting for him? How does he deserve it?" she asked.

"I'm not saying he deserves it. I'm saying I don't want anything to happen to my best friend. If part of that is asking your dad for help then I'll do that. If I have to go to the faerie courts I'll do that. If I have to spread salt throughout my yard it's going to happen. And, don't forget, I still have my dad's trunks upstairs. We'll go through them later, and see if there's anything we should be using or showing your father to get advice."

She narrowed her eyes at me, getting up as if she was about to storm her way out of the room.

"What? I'll put up with whatever craziness he causes in you if he keeps you alive. That's my test, and that's my decision," I said. "Where else would I get a friend who understands me as well as you do?"

She sat back down at the kitchen table, sighing as her shoulders drooped. "What can I say to that? I'd do the same to you."

I heard a pecking noise at the glass door. It was the nightingale. If I remembered right, Bert had called her Jenny. I wondered what news she might have of Winterkiss's position on our escape hatch.

Chapter Thirty-Two

I opened the sliding patio door, and saw Jenny hesitate. I couldn't figure out why, and then I saw the salt line right at her feet. No wonder she had hesitated.

"Don't worry about it," she said. "I'd do the same if I was facing the kind of danger you've got coming at you."

I wondered if she was upset or somehow offended that I wasn't letting her in, but I knew she wouldn't be able to cross the salt line and maintain her ability to help us, and there was no way I was breaking the line. I wondered what we'd do when it rained. I made a mental note to ask Aiden about it, but he was still walking the perimeter of the house with Tobias. I'd have to do it later.

"Did you get any answers?" Mia asked. I should have known. She and I were a lot alike; I'd been the same when it had been me. Ignore the emotional upheaval long enough to figure out what one was facing. I just hoped she didn't get blindsided like I had when my stepbrother kidnapped me. I planned on staying pretty glued to her side until we were through this.

"Winterkiss sends me to say she trusts your judgment not to bring through any persons or beings who might bring harm to the court or its members."

Alarm bells were ringing in my head. I didn't like the way she'd worded that, and said so. "Are you telling me I can bring in anyone I want as long as I'm responsible for their actions? Or are you telling me that if someone or something sneaks in with me I'm liable for whatever they do as well? What happens if someone I'm not aware of gets in with me and they harm someone or something without my knowledge?"

If a bird could roll their eyes, she did it. "I didn't know humans were as exacting and specific as high court faerie."

Mia and I exchanged a look. "Lawyers," we said in unison.

"We're studying to be lawyers. Our jobs are in the details. And

I've learned that paying attention to the details pays off when dealing with the faerie courts."

The bird snorted. Really, she did.

"Look, Jenny, I don't yet know what danger we're facing. It's hard for me to agree to take responsibility for someone or something I might not realize has hitched a ride, or someone or something that snuck in behind me. I don't know if Winterkiss is trying to set me up; that's not what I'm saying. I am saying, though, I don't want to be an easy scapegoat if something goes wrong."

She shook her head, and stretched her wings, ruffling her feathers. "I can't say as I blame you. You're smart. I'll be telling her that. I have the authority to tell you that you shall have the protection of the court should you need to hide with us. Winterkiss herself guarantees your safety. She will also guarantee safety to whomever has been determined to be the target of the Seawitch. Your friend Aiden has safe passage, thanks to his father. Bert is an ally of the courts. Anyone else will have to negotiate for their own safe passage."

I couldn't ask for much more than that, but I was going to, anyway. "If there are persons with us who have acted to save us, or against the Seawitch? Will they get safe passage, or are they fair game to anyone who might eat them?"

She twittered. I assumed it was her version of a laugh. "Just because they do not have safe passage does not mean they are completely at our mercy. Who has been teaching you our ways?"

I ignored the question. "I think we can live with that, at least for now. I appreciate her help. Can you tell me what measures are being taken to secure the portal in the basement?"

"You would have to ask Geoffrey the tailor about this matter. He has negotiated with the High Council regarding the portal, and I do not know what the negotiation entailed. I was not involved, and I do not believe Winterkiss was present, so there is nothing I can tell you about it from my own knowledge."

This double-speak and couched language was giving me a nasty headache. Would practicing law be this nutty? Of course, I knew the answer was probably yes, but then again, I'd probably be an expert at it by the time we graduated if I kept having to deal with the faerie courts. Was that the silver lining here?

I was hoping it was more than that.

"Look, Jenny, we appreciate your help here, really, but we've got some drama going on here of our own," I said, before I caught Mia's eye. She was shaking her head; not a lot, but enough for me to realize she didn't want her secret spilled to a member of the faerie courts. I hadn't planned on saying anything, because she was right. Who knew what they wanted to see happen? It was just as possible Winterkiss or Geoffrey wanted to hand Mia over to the Seawitch to satisfy her, and curry favor with the court. Or worse. And no, I didn't want to even think of what *worse* could be.

"Say no more," she said. "I can't stay long, anyway. I'll just tell Winterkiss you appreciate her offer, and hope not to need it."

"Thanks," I said, "and that's the truth. I'm hoping this all turns out to be more hype than anything else."

Jenny turned and flew off, but I heard an ominous squawk from the air above us and looked up.

The sky was starting to go dark, and the clouds were getting ominous. "Aiden," I called, yanking the door shut against the oncoming summer storm.

I didn't hear him as I ran through the house, looking to see if we'd left any windows open. I called again. "Aiden!"

Mia followed me, a worried look on her face. "Dad?" she asked. Neither one of them responded.

We hurried through the house to the front door just as it blew open and the two of them jumped inside. A blast of wind and rain followed them, and a tidal wave of water followed. Aiden fell against the antique coat rack beside the door, and Mia's father grabbed the door trying to close it behind them. It took both of them, as well as Mia and I jumping in, to get it closed.

"Andersen . . . Andersen . . . Andersen . . ." I heard the wind moaning outside. "I must get rid of the Andersen . . ."

Did I just hear the wind speaking in a sing-songy, whiny, moan? It couldn't be the wind. That meant . . .

The Seawitch had found her way to our door.

Son of a *bitch*.

We were running out of time.

And we still didn't know exactly why the Seawitch wanted to hurt my friend.

No time to worry about that at the moment, however. The wind whipped and twisted and howled as we slammed the door shut and threw the locks.

"What kind of weapons do you have?" Mia's father demanded.

"Sir, I don't think we have anything that can stand up to this," I said, yelling to be heard over the din of the storm outside.

"Stop calling me sir. At least call me Tobias. And you're Bob Grimm's daughter. I know he had weapons; I begged him to be prepared."

I lost the last part of his statement in the wind outside and the rushing sound of my own inner screaming. He knew my father, but somehow hadn't saved him.

"Dammit, girl, where are the weapons? Don't just stand there like an idiot. We need to arm ourselves and figure out what to do."

I let him trail off as I ran for my room. He was right. My father had left me weapons. Three iron trunks full of weapons.

What he didn't know, however, was I had something else in mind, something given to me by Aiden's father. It was still wrapped in an old t-shirt, residing quietly and unused in my backpack, where it had remained since the day all this had started.

I was going for the Tinderbox.

CHAPTER THIRTY-THREE

I heard yelling behind me, but I ignored it. Aiden was on my heels as I ran up the stairs, so close I almost tripped over him once or twice, grabbing the railing to keep from losing my balance. Bert met us at the top of the stairs.

"What's going on?" he asked.

I hadn't even known he'd gone upstairs, but I didn't have the time to ask. "Bert, move out of the way. We need weapons, and we need them now."

He hopped out of the way as Aiden slipped on the antique throw rug in the hallway, sliding feet first into the bedroom. I stepped around him and threw open the latch to the first trunk as I slid the backpack onto my back. He grabbed a crossbow and I grabbed a few weapons I didn't know names for.

Aiden, as clumsy as he was, knew exactly what he was doing. He grabbed weapons, handling them like they were weightless, gearing himself up for a fight.

We hurried back down the stairs where Mia and her father were leaning up against the front door, as if still holding it closed. I knew they'd locked it. How bad was the wind? And who in their right mind was going to believe this was a normal summer storm? Even here in Ohio we did get flash summer storms when the heat and humidity got oppressive, but it really hadn't gotten bad enough for something like that just yet. It was still early June; such storms normally didn't hit until the dog days of late July and early August.

We dumped the weapons on the floor in front of them as Mia's eyes got bigger and bigger. Her father looked over all of it nodding his approval, but he still hadn't seen the backpack and had no idea what I might be planning until I pulled it out and opened it.

Geoffrey had told me the Tinderbox would provide help if I needed it.

What I did not expect was what actually came out.

It was a pair of rubber, waterproof rainboots with smiley faces on the toes. One pair.

How in the world was this supposed to help? There were four adults and a frog in the house. We couldn't all fit in the boots. Even if I wore one, and Mia wore the other, we'd each have a wet foot. And Bert? Well, he'd fit neatly in one, and no one would be able to see him. Never mind that it would keep him from hopping into mud puddles, but wouldn't do anything to prevent the rain from filling up the boot and flooding him out. And he wouldn't be able to move anywhere if he was inside the boot itself. Exasperated, I exclaimed, "What the hell is this?"

"Oh. Wow. I don't think I've ever seen those before," Bert said, edging ever closer to where the boots had landed on the rug in the front hallway.

Mia's dad picked up one of the boots. "Seriously? They have smiley faces on them? You've got to be kidding me."

Aiden was laughing. "I did tell you that you never knew what you'd get with the Tinderbox. And that faerie magic has a very odd sense of humor. You don't quite know what could come out. And yet, these could be very useful."

As what? Footgear to run out in the storm, which I had no intention of doing? I said as much.

"No," Bert said, laughing. "Those are the Galoshes of Fortune."

"What the hell is that?" Mia asked. "Are you seriously telling me these cheap-y plastic and rubber boots are a magical faerie relic or artifact that's supposed to somehow save the day while we have some kind of weird weather magical storm outside the house? Are you nuts?"

"Quite possibly," her father said. "These boots, however, aren't going to fit me. I daresay they won't fit Aiden, and Bert's not able to wear them, like Janie said. It's going to have to be one of you girls. I'm biased, but I think Mia wears them."

"I agree," I said, without any hesitation. "It's got to be Mia."

She shook her head. "Why are we talking about going anywhere? Why can't we just wait out the storm? I mean, we've got some time before work tonight, and if we had to we could call in. I hate to do it, but it makes sense."

Tobias shook his head. "Honey, this storm could outlast all of us without even batting an eye. And I don't mean it could last until tomorrow, or next week. It's a magical storm, so it lasts until the magic user behind it either gets bored or gets tired, and if it's the Seawitch, there's enough potential power there for it to last well beyond all of our lifetimes. This means that sooner or later we run out of food, the power will go out, or a whole host of other problems meant to flush us out. I can almost guarantee we will not be able to wait her out. We're human. There are limitations."

"So what should we do?" I asked. I was so not the kind of girl who would just sit around and mope, waiting for something to come in and save the day. And if we could get this taken care of so we could get to work, so much the better.

Mia kept protesting that she didn't need protecting, but her father stepped in. "Mia, she's after me, too. I'm sure she sees you as the easier target since you didn't know about all of this. I'm sure she thinks that if she takes you out I'll be upset and not thinking clearly and she'll have her chance at me then. I'm sure she's going to try to hurt us both."

The wind and the storm howled outside as she glared at her father. "Why didn't you tell me? Why couldn't you have warned me this was even possible? Why didn't I have some kind of idea that I could be a target, and why did I have to spend the last year convinced Janie and I were seeing things when you could have told me these things were real long ago? Where have you been?"

He sighed. "Now is really not the time. I never wanted you to have to deal with all of this. I hoped you would live your entire life in complete ignorance of all of it, and you would one day get married, change your name, and that the Seawitch would remain locked up long after you and I were gone, so we would escape her wrath and our descendents would be hidden again. I can see now I was wrong to hope for all of it. I should have prepared you for this. I'm sorry, but I'm here now and we will live through this. I promise you that we will get through this and we will make it."

"Don't promise things you can't deliver, Dad. You've done that for a long time, and I've long since given up on your promises. So don't promise me anything. Prove it to me. Prove to me that you picked up some useful skills and some useful things in order to keep me alive, and keep me from getting eaten by the Seawitch, and I'll start believing the things you say again."

I saw him swallow. She was being difficult with him, but I didn't blame her. She was being hard on him, but he deserved it from years and years of not calling on her birthdays, or showing up for her prom, her graduation, or anything else that had been important to her in her life. It might not feel fair to him, but I was with her on it.

He stood a little straighter. "This is something I can do for my daughter. I might not have been able to be there for all the milestones in your life. I might not have had the opportunity to help you and your mom financially all these years. I might not have been able to do a lot of things a father should do, but I can do this if you listen to me, do exactly what I say, and let me do it. Don't argue. I know what I'm doing."

I was glad someone did.

CHAPTER THIRTY-FOUR

After much debate and arguing, we got Mia into the smiley face galoshes. I put on my pendant, Aiden had a similar one, and Tobias had his medallion. We were as protected as we were going to get.

The wind howled and the rain started. "So, um, Aiden, um, what happens to that salt line if it keeps raining?" I asked. "I'd think it would wash away, and if it's gone, then she can come in, can't she? I mean, we'd be sitting ducks for whatever she intended to do to us."

"No. This is a magically created rain. It's something the salt will repel, and even if the salt line erodes away, this is your home. Technically, the only faerie being that could cross the threshold is your stepmother, and the last I heard, she's still under lock and key. The Seawitch would have a better chance of getting through if she went through the portal in the basement, and Winterkiss has that closed off. We should be okay, but Mr. Andersen is correct in that we can't outwait this storm. We need to be willing to move. I'd say the best thing to do here is to salt our pockets and wear our items, put Bert in a protected pocket or purse, and make a break for it."

Mia cut in. "Make a break to *where?* Wouldn't this kind of storm follow us wherever we go? What's the point unless we can stop the storm? And if we did take off and it did follow us, aren't we hurting the people who might be wherever we run to? I hate to be the naysayer, but isn't it a better idea to stay put and see if anything can come to help us, especially since our threshold is here?"

I grabbed a rain slicker out of the coat closet and put it on, pulling up the hood as I waved for the others to help themselves to whatever might be inside. "Look, Mia, I don't know about you, but I can't just sit here and hope something comes to the rescue. I think we'd be headed to the F.A.B.L.E.S. headquarters, and the people there would be the right ones to figure out how to handle this. We'd be running to help, not from the witch."

Her father was picking through the weapons I'd brought down from my father's iron trunks, arming himself with several wicked looking iron weapons. I made a mental note to look up what some of them were; with nasty hooks and spiky balls and chains and blades, I had no way of distinguishing what he might be taking and what he was leaving. I knew one was a morningstar, but only because Bert had told me that last year. Aiden picked up a pointy looking spearhead. I didn't pick up much, mostly because I didn't know how to use any of it. Mental note; I needed to do something to change that.

While the others turned me down, Mia grabbed a coat. It was a pullover with a hood, a relic of an old softball team she'd once played on in high school, but with a pocket reminiscent of a hoodie sweatshirt with its pouch front pocket. Bert asked tentatively if he could hitch a ride inside, and she nodded without looking too closely at him. He noticed. So did I, but neither one of us said anything about it.

We headed out the door, with Tobias spreading salt ahead of us and Aiden spreading it behind us. "What's that for?" I asked.

"It prevents the magic from following us." Aiden called, over the rush of wind that blew past us as we hurried to the garage and the car. We all piled inside, and Aiden insisted on leaving his passenger side window down as I drove. I couldn't figure out why until he began sprinkling salt behind us as we pulled out of the garage and onto the street. It worked; the storm had all but stopped by the time we got a mile or so from the house.

No one said much of anything as we drove. I hoped we would be able to come up with a game plan, because I was really wishing I'd be able to sleep in my own bed that night. How could one sneak back into one's own house later if a magical faerie witch was stalking outside?

I didn't have time to do much wondering, because it was a short drive to the warehouse F.A.B.L.E.S. used as a headquarters. Aiden let us all in, and I noticed several members of the group were already there. I assumed he had called them before he'd even come to my house, but I could have been wrong. Maybe they already had a meeting set up or maybe they were just hanging out, but there was no way to tell at the moment.

Harold was sitting at a table with his nose in a dusty old book, his gray ponytail bobbing as he nodded to himself. Stanley was dressed all in black, a jowly ball of dark clothing that looked like a black blob instead of a stealth ninja. He wore a black beret, dark sunglasses, and head to toe black clothing. I didn't have the heart to tell him that his shadowy clothing wasn't going to work to hide him from danger; he lived for conspiracy theories and alternate explanations.

"Welcome," they said, in unison, before looking at each other and laughing.

Okay, that was creepy, but their smiles were genuine. They were an odd couple, but they'd been best friends for sixty years; Harold, the voice of reason and Stanley, the imaginative paranoid. Somehow, it worked for them. While Mia and I weren't that different, I hoped we were still friends as many years down the road. I could put up with a lot of insanity in my life if I knew I'd still have my best friend at the end of the day.

Speaking of my best friend, Mia had a hard look on her face as she watched her father shaking hands with Harold and Stanley, being greeted as a conquering hero and awed figurehead. I hadn't felt that way about him when I'd met him, but I hadn't heard all the stories of his exploits to be impressed by him. Something else I'd have to ask Aiden about later. That mental list was getting longer and longer by the minute.

The rain had completely stopped, but my coat was still wet, and my shoes were soaked from tromping through the rain to the garage. Mia's boots, on the other hand, were nearly pristine. The Galoshes of Fortune were, at the very least, pretty awesome at keeping one's feet dry. I wondered what kind of magic would be involved in getting a pair of boots that were that good at repelling water; most of the boots I wore were from the thrift store, the clearance rack, or neighborhood garage sales, and they never lasted long without soaking my feet. Then again, I was pretty sure I didn't want that kind of magic on my feet for any length of time. I wondered how long she should wear them. My pendant was something I'd been warned not to wear when I was at home because it caused bad dreams due to the magic involved.

Would she end up with some kind of weird foot problem if she wore them too long? How would she explain magical athlete's foot or faerie magic fallen arches? I snorted to myself on that one, but it didn't mean this wasn't a legitimate concern. She was too busy frowning at her father to appreciate my internal chuckle, but until we knew for sure the danger we'd faced earlier was gone I thought she should keep the darn things on her feet. It just wasn't worth the risk.

"So, we made it here. What do we do now?" I asked, hoping to get Mia focused on something other than how much she disliked her father.

Harold came back over to us when I asked the question. "Well, you made it here without the storm following you. You've got a salt line around the house and a fairly strong threshold, so the house should be pretty safe, and the hope is that by the time you're ready to head home the Seawitch will realize she needs to look elsewhere to find you guys, and you'll be able to get back to your own house to sleep tonight. If nothing else, maybe you'd be able to crash at Doris's house."

Aiden nodded his agreement.

That was a good thing, and we did have to get moving, because we had to be at work in the next hour and a half. If nothing else, everyone agreed, going to work would give more time for the Seawitch to realize we weren't at the house and go looking for us elsewhere.

I could only hope. I really didn't want to spend the night on Doris' couch.

CHAPTER THIRTY-FIVE

We made it to work early, and started in with the phone calls we were slated to make that night. Neither one of us had much in the way of powers of concentration, but we managed to get through the first hour or so of our shift without too much trouble. As we finally made it to our first break, it wasn't surprising to find Jonah was waiting for us as we came out of the office to stretch our legs.

He seemed agitated and concerned.

"Aren't you supposed to be in the audience watching to rehearse your lines?" I asked.

"Not every single night, but I do have to be here in the theater in case something happens to one of the actors during the performance. I snuck out to come see you guys. Someone told me you wouldn't make it to work tonight and I got concerned."

"Who told you that?" Mia asked. I was proud. The events of the last twenty-four hours had obviously had an effect on her; she was questioning everything. Then again, I was, too. Who could have told him we wouldn't be coming in unless he'd talked to Aiden? And Aiden hadn't come in to work yet tonight, calling in to say he'd be late in order to keep doing research and survey the house while we finished our shift, so we'd know if it was safe to go home later. No one had mentioned our afternoon, and no one else at the theater box office knew we'd even gotten the morning off at the courthouse.

"I don't know. I must have heard it somewhere. It's a theater; gossip isn't exactly a spectator sport around here. I swear, sometimes I think theater folks won varsity letters in gossip when they were in high school, and by the time they're professional they've gone pro in busybodiness."

What could I say to that? I'd heard the same thing about lawyers. Even so, it smelled all kinds of fishy to me. One look at Mia's face, and I knew she felt the same way even if she did act happy to see him. We all walked away from the office. After a while of sitting in a chair chained to the phone by a headset there was always a desire to stand up and move.

"So what's up, Jonah?" she asked.

He jerked like he'd been shot. "You don't want to spend your break hanging out with me?"

I backed off, walking close enough to hear their conversation and keep Mia in sight without being the proverbial third wheel. I owed her that much after being a jerk the other day. I might have been a concerned jerk, and I might have had a good reason, but she deserved my support in her love life. Hey, I was dating someone I liked. She deserved to figure out what she wanted as well, especially after the emotional upheaval of the afternoon. It wasn't everyday one had to host a luncheon with one's deadbeat dad.

"It's not about that. It's been a long day, and being at work is just making it longer. I'm ready to crash for the evening," Mia said, sitting down on the bench in the lobby where we'd walked to stretch our legs.

"Well, are you heading straight home after work?"

Alarm bells clanged in the back of my head, the hairs on the back of my neck stood on edge, and it took just about everything I had to keep my mouth shut. If she said we were going home, we'd be on Doris's couches for sure. I hoped she knew that, but I was also trying to give her the space and trust she deserved from her best friend. She'd been right yesterday when she'd been so upset with me.

"Well, we haven't decided yet. We thought we might go out for a drink or something, or maybe just out for a late dinner. And then, too, we talked about visiting a friend, so we haven't decided yet."

Good on her, I thought. Being carefully nonspecific was probably the safest thing she could do.

"What if I asked if I could join you?" he asked.

"I'm not sure that's a good idea tonight, Jonah," she said. "I've got some family drama I'm dealing with. As much as I'd like to spend time with you, I just am not real sure it's a good idea tonight."

"What do you mean? Anything I can help with?"

She stood up from the bench. "No. Honestly, I'm not sure anyone can help with this one. It's stupid family drama that no one deserves, and I wish it would just go away. I'd hate to have to deal with this on a regular basis. Suffice it to say I've got a relative who won't just go away and stay away no matter what I ask them to do. Janie and I may well do something tonight to avoid them or we might go deal with the matter head on, but there just isn't anything I can ask someone to help. Janie's a different matter. She and I have been best friends since high school."

"What about that dorky guy who works as an usher. I keep seeing him hanging around you guys as well."

"Aiden?" she asked. "He and Janie are kind of a thing, although I'm not sure how official that might be."

I didn't know either, so I was glad she was as confused as I was about it. That was yet another thing I should probably add to my mental list of things to talk to Aiden about; how to explain where we were in whatever relationship we might have. Regardless of what hang-ups either one of us might have it only made sense for the two of us to be on the same page as to how we explained it to other people.

"So, are you seeing anyone?" he asked her.

"No."

"That's good to hear." He sounded relieved.

So far, so good; normal early dating language from a guy that was good-looking and employed. So why was my internal oh-crap, danger-Will-Robinson, hinky-stuff meter going off like a fire alarm in the back of my head? Something was all kinds of wrong about him; I just didn't know why. I'd been willing to give him another chance, hoping I was just paranoid from all the stuff that's been going on in my life. I knew Mia; she liked him. I just didn't think she should trust him, but I didn't have any proof.

Mia leaned back on the bench where they sat and told him she wasn't seeing anyone, but that her life was complicated because of some family issues. I felt sorry for her. At least with Aiden, he knew most of my family issues without having me explain them. He was *in the know* on the magic stuff, so I hadn't had to explain or worry about his reaction. And yet, I had the feeling Jonah knew something about what was going on.

They continued to exchange small talk, with Jonah pushing her to make plans with him that night and Mia making all kinds of excuses about not being able to get together with him without telling him her plans. I could watch him getting frustrated with her, but I didn't expect him to look quite that desperate.

"Mia, why won't you let me just tag along tonight? I just want to spend some time alone with you and getting to know you better. What's so wrong with that?" he whined, which knocked him down a few pegs or so in my mind. What a weenie.

She got up from the bench, and I took a few steps closer. "Mia, we've got to get back to work. Break's almost over," I said, giving her a nudge and an excuse to step away from him and get her bearings before we went back to work.

He followed us, like a puppy dog, back to the office where we needed to grab our headphones and start making our calls again, but he didn't take the hint. "I need to see you tonight, Mia. It's important."

What could be so important when she'd blown him off so many times? She said as much at about the same time I was thinking it, but she was so much more diplomatic about it than my internal monologue.

"I wouldn't insist, but I have to. Can I take you for coffee after, or meet you at your own house? We should spend time together, and I don't want to wait."

Suddenly, I wondered if he had some connection to the faerie courts we weren't aware of. Given the attack earlier today, it seemed all kinds of suspicious that he wanted to specifically meet her tonight.

Unless her was trying to pin down her whereabouts for the Seawitch to make another run at her.

That was a terrifying thought.

CHAPTER THIRTY-SIX

S he agreed to meet him at a coffee shop across from the law school, a ten minute drive from the theater and far enough away from large crowds, but she put a caveat on meeting him: unless she got a call from a family member needing something. He agreed to meet her right after the curtain came down on that night's performance, which would end about an hour or so after our shift ended.

I was glad she was being careful. I made a point to send a quick text message to Mia's father just before our shift started back up informing him that he needed to call Mia's phone right at eight p.m. and tell her that he needed something, anything, to give her a legitimate excuse to blow off Jonah. Faerie beings had a real serious problem with going back on one's word, but they had a healthy respect for people who could negotiate their way out of something without officially breaking a promise. I'd used that to my advantage last fall with my stepmother; I'd give Mia every opportunity to use it for her own protection as well, if I could.

We finished our shift and headed out to the car. As we got to the Escalade in the parking garage, I smelled it.

It was the smell of magic. I would never again be comforted by the scent of old books and peppermint that had always reminded me of my father. I'd learned last year magic smells comforting and enticing to humans who figure out how to notice it, like an olfactory trap that speaks to the individual attractions and desire of each specific person who smelled it.

"Mia, look out!" I called, running for the car with the keys already in my head. "Get to the car!"

She didn't respond, but she took off running. I hit the door lock button on the key fob as we ran, and we got to the car fairly quickly.

It was when I stopped to open the door that I realized I no longer had a shadow. At the time I couldn't do much more than register it in my head as I slammed the driver's door shut and started the ignition, throwing the car into gear and hurrying for the ramp to get out of the garage. Mia's cell phone went off at the same time.

"Gotta go, now!" I called, flooring the gas as she tried to answer. It was her father. I only heard her side of the conversation.

"Dad, I can't talk right now."

I flew down the ramp to the exit scraping the side of the Escalade as I went, but I didn't care at the moment.

"Dad, I don't care what you need I'm a bit busy. Janie smelled something in the garage, and we're running. Is it safe to go home?"

Bert stuck his head up from my shoulder bag, which sat on the floor at Mia's feet. "What if it's not safe? What do we do?"

She shushed him. "Dad, where should we go?" She was quiet for a minute then hung up the phone without saying good bye.

Luckily the gates were up to handle the number of people who would be leaving the performance in an hour, so I didn't have to stop. The car bounced as I hit the curb, an abrupt turn into the street as I hurried away from the garage. I needed to get as far away from the place as possible.

We were three blocks away before we got stopped by a red light. I saw a police cruiser approaching, and there wasn't much traffic. I considered running the light just briefly before I realized just how dumb that might be.

I took a deep breath, willing my heart to slow down enough to breathe normally.

"What just happened?" she asked.

"Magic," I said. "Plenty of it, and strong enough to be sure no one could miss it if they knew what they were looking for."

She looked at me sideways. "Does that mean you don't suspect Jonah anymore? I mean, he's stuck at the performance, and it's not over yet."

She had a point, but I didn't think it proved his innocence. "From what I've been told, the Seawitch is female, but that doesn't mean she isn't working with others. I mean, the judge had magic in his office, and he's a guy."

"Are you saying Judge Neederhorn is out to kill me?"

"I don't know." I looked down at my watch.

"Or someone at the courthouse?"

"I don't know."

"So, then why are you so convinced it's Jonah, especially since the Seawitch is female?" Mia asked, exasperation coming through in her voice.

"Didn't you hear what I said?" I asked, as a car passed in front of us with a green light instead of the red we were facing. The headlights passed over us, and I noticed, again, there was an issue with our shadows. We didn't have one. Either one of us.

Bert stuck his head up, and noticed the same thing just about the same time I did. "What have you guys been messing with? Why don't you have shadows?"

The light turned. "I don't know, Bert, but that's a problem once we figure out where we're headed. Mia, where did your dad say to go?"

"He said the house isn't safe, but he hasn't found a secure place yet because he's not sure who is working with the Seawitch. Why don't we go to the law school? I mean, yeah it's late, but the doors will still be open and we'd have a place to go rather than just run around in the car using up gas all night."

I didn't like the idea of going into the school itself, because our greatest asset at the moment in running away was the car with the three quarters full tank of gas. If we went into the school we'd be running on foot and not a lot of people. There were some law school classes in the summer but there really weren't a lot of them, and if there were no classes tonight the building and most of the residential campus houses around the law school would be empty. That wouldn't help a whole lot if we had to make a break for it.

We parked in the empty parking lot behind the school, where there wasn't a lot of traffic, and no one following us. Once we stopped the car I rolled down the windows. It was June, after all, and there was a nice little breeze coming through. It was a chance for us to catch our breath, regroup, and wait for an idea as to what to do next.

"What about Allie?" she asked. "What if she's at the house? Isn't she in danger as well? Shouldn't we at least drive by the house to see if she's there and get her out of there if she is?"

"I'm not sure we'd see her if we did drive by. She cuts through backyards and alleys. I've never seen her in the front of the house. She knows she needs to watch her back, because I'd asked her to watch the house."

"Enough with the talk about Allie, who isn't here, and likely isn't even at the house," yelled Bert. "Why the hell don't you guys have a shadow? Who stole your shadows, and what are they asking in return?"

CHAPTER THIRTY-SEVEN

"Why is it such a big deal that you're not seeing our shadows?" Mia asked.

I'd noticed it, but I'd been a bit distracted by the amount of magic I'd been smelling and getting the heck out of Dodge before some kind of magical attack could get us. I nodded along with her question.

"There's a Hans Christian Andersen story about a man whose shadow disappeared one night, and he had to re-grow his shadow. Before he was able to complete such a thing, the shadow returned and slowly manipulated the man into becoming the shadow's own shadow, taking over his life and eventually having him killed. Losing your shadow is a serious business, ladies. You'll need to see what Aiden and the F.A.B.L.E.S. guys can do about it."

Yikes.

"How did the shadow manipulate the man into becoming his own shadow? And why would anyone or anything want to do it?" I asked. "Our lives are not quite all that exciting. I mean, does someone really want to take our place in a part-time internship for an insane judge, or are they angling for our seats in Commercial Transactions class in the fall? I mean, really, none of it makes sense."

"Janie, don't be dense. Who, in the magical world, wouldn't want to take the place of the last living direct descendant of the Grimm Brothers and the daughter of Tobias Andersen? You guys don't understand. Even if you two are getting a pretty good reputation for protecting yourself in the face of magical danger it just means those who have reason to hide from the powers that be see you guys as a safe face to hide behind. And who knows? The magic that can free your shadow is a powerful charm only shadows can perform. Another shadow, one with darker, ulterior motives, could well have convinced your own shadows to allow them to take over as a way to take over your lives. What if the Seawitch was involved? That could be a plan to attack your father, Mia."

Double yikes. I didn't like those implications. From the look on Mia's face, she didn't like it either.

"Bert, what do we do? How do we get our shadows back?" she asked.

I saw him puff up his chest a bit, his still bleary eyes wide as he realized he could impress her by helping us. I wanted to give him any help I could but, at the same time, I knew in my heart Mia didn't think of him in that way. No good would come from encouraging him, but I couldn't ignore him; he didn't deserve it. He needed to have some things he could do well with, so he could start digging himself out of the emotional black hole he'd dug for himself, at least before he finally gave up on impressing Mia.

"Well, there's a magic that can speed up the process of re-growing a shadow. You'd have to get Doris and Harold and Stanley together. Even if they don't know how to make the potion necessary, I do."

As he talked, I saw a bright ball of light over the top of the law school building. "What the hell is that?" I asked, pointing.

"Oh, my God," Mia said. "The coffee shop I said I'd meet Jonah at is just on the other side of the street, right where the light is. What's going to—"

She was cut off by a whooshing sound that got progressively louder, like a train arriving in an enclosed station, followed by a loud explosion. "Shit." I started the car again as the light in the sky dissipated.

I pulled out, again in a hurry, as we heard sirens and fire engines coming our way. As we pulled up to Brown Street in front of the law school, we saw it.

The coffee shop was engulfed in flames with fire licking its way out of the building and black smoke rising in a thick column into the night sky.

"That could have been me," Mia said in a small voice as we drove by, watching people run from the building.

We drove by slowly, looking around. The only people on the streets were the ones running from nearby businesses. There were a couple of people who were down on the sidewalk, hurt, and there were others trying to help them. I saw one or two on their cell phones, as if they were calling 911. Someone had; I could see the approaching lights getting brighter as they got closer and closer, the red and blue announcement of their arrival lighting up the sky. We pulled to one side, parked by the sidewalk and watched. Without talking, both of us knew we should not get out of the car; there were already people helping those who were hurt and help was on the way, but there was just no way to know what faerie magic was there checking to see if whatever this was had gotten its targets.

Us.

There was no way around that. It was late, but not overly so; there were people, but not as many as there could have been. It was a weekday night during the summer, and the coffee shop and those businesses and eateries around it were very much targeted towards the college students who were mostly home for the summer. During the school year, and especially on weekends, the places would have been packed.

The smoke was a noxious black cloud, and the people on the street were coughing. I rolled up the windows and turned on the air conditioning so we wouldn't breathe it in. I didn't trust the smoke not to have magical properties.

Mia called her father again. They talked, quietly, as I watched people hurrying back and forth, running down the street and calling for help. When the first ambulance and police cars appeared I pulled away from the curb. Mia hung up the phone as I did so.

"Where are we going?" I asked.

"Doris's place," she said. "There's a bunch of your old people meeting us there to try to deal with our shadow issue. We'll talk to them about what just happened. We just need to get there."

The sirens screamed and wailed behind us as we left the area, heading away from the explosion. I wanted to drive past my house and see if things were okay; see if it had stopped raining over the house, and see what was going on, as much as I could. I wouldn't be able to see the back of the house or to see if Allie had shown up, but that was as much as I could do without throwing up a big sign to whatever magical entity was after us, saying "come and get me, I'm dumb and I give up."

Something, however, bothered me as I drove away. Something was bad, wrong about the situation. I kept thinking of the fire, the explosion, and the people on the streets screaming and crying and calling for help.

No one had come from the coffee shop itself.

And something else was odd.

There was no screaming inside. The silence told me there were no survivors. And we'd planned to be inside, because there was no way I'd have let Mia go alone to meet with Jonah.

We were supposed to be dead.

We were supposed to be taken out completely. Which told me Mia wasn't the end goal. She was a means to an end, and I was just collateral damage. There was a bigger goal. The Seawitch, if she was behind this, was after bigger prey. It could be that she was after Tobias. Or Bert. Or Aiden, or the rest of the F.A.B.L.E.S. crew. She could be trying to flush us all out, or try to take over the area in the mortal world as a way to solidify power to turn around and take over in the magical world.

But if she thought we were dead she probably thought we were out of her way. I wondered if we could use that to our advantage, somehow. I wondered why we were so dangerous to her, what made us so important to get rid of.

And then I had a terrifying thought as I pulled up in front of my own house. The rain had stopped and it looked peaceful and quiet with the lights off and no movement that I could see.

What if she was trying to get us away from the house so she could work on getting to the portal in the basement? Did she know it was there? And did she know Winterkiss had moved the portal on the magical side to come in right behind the throne? Was this her secret plan to take over? Or was there something more sinister at work here?

I didn't know, but I did know the best way of figuring it out was to get to Doris's and talk to the others about the right way to handle all of this. I was out of my depth, and I was ready to take as much help as I could get.

Chapter Thirty-Eight

"I don't want to go to Doris's house, yet," Mia said. "I want to go back to the theater. Jonah will be done at the play soon. I want to confront him about what just happened. Besides which, if anyone was tapping our phones they would never expect us to go back to the theater if they heard us say we were going to Doris's. Maybe that's safer for everyone else."

It didn't sound like the world's best idea, but I could understand what she was thinking. I'd want to confront him too. And she had a point about us not going where we were expected to go. It had saved our lives by not going to the coffee shop earlier. And I was sick and tired of running around in circles while we still didn't have all the pieces put together.

From the floorboard, I heard, "I want a piece of him, too."

Oh, great. We had a frog who wanted revenge.

I wondered if Aiden had any of his magic detecting gadgets with him. We could sure use them if he did. I wanted to use them on Jonah to see if there was anything about him we had missed. I felt like I'd let my friend down by not seeing the danger in what was going on.

"Ok, we'll go back to the Schuster Center," I said, turning the car around and heading back downtown.

I had a bad feeling about this.

We pulled back into the parking garage, the same one we'd run from earlier in the night, and took stock. Mia was still wearing the Galoshes of Fortune, their smiley faced toes grinning up at us in a mocking yellow cheerfulness that contrasted with the frustration and anger we were both feeling. I had my bag with my cell phone, my wallet, and Bert, along with a couple of metal pieces we could use as weapons. I'd grabbed my screwdriver, the same one I'd used to defeat my stepmother, and slid it into my back pocket. Mia had a hammer she did the same with, and we each had a bag of salt in our front pockets. I had the magic repelling necklace Aiden had given me last year around my neck. And the tinderbox was hidden in the bag with Bert.

We were about as ready as we were going to get. We slid back inside the service entrance and went looking for Aiden as the play going on was coming to its final scenes. The usher at the front allowed us to go inside as we showed up, saying Aiden was on stage right with a flashlight at the handy for patrons who might need to get up in those final moments.

I snuck down the steps to where he stood leaning up against the wall in his usher uniform, his flashlight at his side as he watched the last part of the play. Jonah was sitting in the right section just five rows ahead of where Aiden stood. I recognized the back of his head and his identity was confirmed when he turned his head slightly, looking toward the usher who was mirroring Aiden's position at the front row.

I whispered to Aiden that we needed to talk to him. He gestured to the usher at the front, who nodded, and then he followed us outside.

When we got back to the lobby and opened the doors into the bright light, there wasn't anyone around except the female usher at the stage door. We walked toward the theater entrance to get far enough away for her not to hear what was going on.

"Aiden, an attempt was made to kill us just a few minutes ago. Mia had agreed to meet Jonah at a coffee shop down by the university after the show, and just a few minutes ago, it was blown up. It doesn't look like anyone survived."

If I'd been expecting any specific kind of reaction it wasn't the one I got. His jaw hung open, his eyes wide. "Why in the world did you guys agree to a meeting like that without calling in some kind of backup?"

"Not to state the obvious, but if we'd had backup we'd all be dead, including our backup. No one survived the fire. No one was still inside. There were people outside who were hurt, but I don't think anyone inside had any kind of warning. What would you do against a giant ball of white light that suddenly shot down and blew up the coffee shop you were sitting in? I'll tell you, you wouldn't have seen it coming," I whispered angrily, hoping the usher couldn't hear us.

"I still think you took a really stupid risk by even going!" His face was red, and he was angry. I got it, because I think he was scared I could have been hurt more than anything. I'd have felt the same way about him. And that's when I realized I needed to stop holding back from him. The faerie court stuff was never going to go away in my life, and it wasn't fair to hold his parentage against him if life was always going to hand us lemons in the form of magical faerie hinky stuff on a regular basis.

I grabbed him by the cheeks, and kissed him to shut him up. "I get it, Aiden, and I'm as shook up as you are, but there are other things to figure out yet tonight. How long do you have to stay after the show ends?"

"I can get one of the guys to cover me if we need to go now. It's not a problem."

Mia shook her head. "We're not going anywhere until I get to confront Jonah."

"Jonah?" Aiden shook his head. "You think he had something to do with what happened at the coffee shop? Wasn't he supposed to be there with you?"

She shook her head. "Not until after the show was over. It would have been timed for about when we'd have been sitting down with coffee to wait for him to show up. I think the attack was timed just perfectly for us to be there without him, rather than for him to be attacked and killed along with us. I'm suspicious. And he'd pushed awfully hard to figure out where we were going to be after the show tonight. I want to ask him about it, and I want to do it here, in a public place, with you guys present. I want to ask him about it while you use one of the magic detecting whoziwhatsits that Janie told me about. I want to know if he's human. And I want to see his reaction."

I did too.

Aiden nodded. "Fine. I think this would be a bad idea if he really was working for the Seawitch, but because I don't actually believe he is I understand it's important for you to talk to him."

"Why do you think he's so innocent?" she asked. Clearly she was mad, worked up and ready to spit nails at Jonah the moment she saw him.

If nothing else this could be interesting, I thought. I trusted

Aiden's judgment, but at the same time, Mia had a pretty good argument for suspecting him.

"Look, guys, the only way we get an answer to what's going on is for us to get him out here and ask him some questions," I said. "We can argue all day about who is right and who is wrong, but none of that actually answers for us what is really going on. So, Mia, you and Aiden go get him. I'll wait here with Bert. Let's get him out here and ask."

"No," Aiden said.

"What?"

"No, Mia doesn't come with me, inside. I'll go get Jonah and bring him out. Just because I don't think he's actually guilty doesn't mean everyone else in the theater is innocent. I hate to say it this way, but if someone else is the guilty party I don't want Mia in a place where getting her attacked might also mean a lot of innocent people in the line of fire, and I don't want her out here alone. Janie, you stay here with her." With that, he was gone, disappearing inside without giving us a chance to argue with him.

He was right to be concerned, but Mia wasn't happy. She paced and prowled back and forth in the empty lobby waiting for him to come back, her face flushed and her fists curled into a ball by her sides. She wasn't paying attention to anything around her, which I thought was careless, but I was definitely paying attention. I reached into my bag, bumping Bert who protested, but got my hands on the tinderbox just in case I needed it.

Who know what might come out of it if there was danger, but it was probably the most powerful weapon I had at my disposal to protect my friends. I wasn't going to ignore it if we were up against something potentially even more dangerous than my stepmother.

CHAPTER THIRTY-NINE

Aiden came out with Jonah who had an obviously befuddled look on his face.

"What did you tell him?" demanded Mia, her hands on her hips as she confronted Aiden.

"Nothing other than someone tried to hurt you tonight at the coffee shop while you were waiting on him," he explained.

"Well, I think someone was trying to make sure we were dead rather than hurt. I don't think it's someone that likes me very much, and they wanted to make sure there was no coming back from it. They want me dead, or at least out of the way."

Jonah's reaction didn't look like he had any clue. Either he was a better actor than I thought, or he was truly surprised. Of course I'd never actually seen him on the stage, so I had no way of knowing what he had going on. I was willing to give him the benefit of the doubt and keep talking, but there was no way I was taking my hand off the tinderbox in my bag until I was sure that he was no longer a threat to my friend.

"Look, Jonah, there's been a lot going on today. Someone set us up. The coffee shop no longer exists. It pretty much exploded and everything blew up. No one got out. It was timed to go off while we would have been inside waiting for you to show up."

For him to fake the look of surprise on his face he'd have to have been a much better actor than an understudy in regional theater. No one I'd ever met had the skill to fake that reaction.

"*What?!*" he exclaimed. "That's not possible! Why would anyone do that?"

Mia stalked forward like a lion going after its dinner, stealthy and yet predatory at the same time. I was glad I wasn't on the receiving end of that even though I was sure it would be a pretty awesome cross-examination technique. It was intimidating without being overtly threatening, but I knew she was bottling up one hell of a lot of rage over what was going on around us. "Why were you so insistent we get together tonight?"

"Because I thought you were losing interest in me and if I didn't move fast I'd lose my chance. You acted really interested the first couple of nights and then suddenly tonight it seemed like you were suddenly interested in someone else," he said, throwing his hands up in the air as she got closer to him. "I was afraid that if I didn't insist you would think I wasn't interested, and I can't think of anything except figuring out how to get to know you."

A plausible answer, and one that completely fit his behavior. She'd been all over the place lately, what with the lack of sleep, the emotional upheaval, the threat, and her father suddenly in her life. Never mind trying to keep up with the craziness of working a split work shift. Mia's behavior was on a roller coaster, calm and rational one minute, then angry and hostile the next. I didn't doubt he was having a hard time figuring out what to do about when to make his move, and he was feeling a bit desperate. I had thought she'd been coming on strong, and then all of a sudden she was very cool to him after she and I had argued about not telling her the entire picture. Maybe that was a bit of self-survival for her, but it would definitely be confusing for him.

"Okay, I've been off lately. Who did you tell we were meeting at the coffee shop? Who got that information from you?"

"I don't know," he said. "There were a couple of ushers who walked by later and said congratulations because they'd heard I had a date. Andrea Scolari overheard them and asked me if I'd lost interest in her, even though I never had any interest in her in the first place, she's just that stuck on herself. And one or two of the other understudies asked me if I'd asked you out yet, because I'd been trying to get up the courage to do it. Was I supposed to keep that a secret? Everyone's been here; we've got a show going on. It couldn't be related to that, no one has left."

"Believe me, it's about Mia," I said. "There's too much else going on for this to be a coincidence."

She nodded. Aiden nodded. And then Bert stuck his head up out of my bag, and nodded.

"What the hell is that?" Jonah asked. "Why would you have a frog in your bag? And one that nods its head?"

"Talks, too, if you can believe your ears," said Bert. "Pleased to meet you."

"Are you *kidding* me?" Jonah hollered, backing away from us.

"Not in the least," Aiden said, as he motioned Bert back into the bag. "There are things going on you can't understand without taking a big leap of faith. And it's because a lot of those things are happening that I can tell you it's more likely than not the attack on the coffee shop was meant to kill Janie and Mia. They are targets. They know it. Something or someone is out to kill them."

"This isn't possible. You guys are going nuts."

"No, we're not. But we have all been where you are, and you're not going crazy. It's true, there are things out to kill us, and the sooner you embrace that fact the sooner we can get to the bottom of this. Now, was there anyone who seemed especially interested in the fact you had gotten Mia to agree to meet you?" I asked.

His eyes were wide, but he didn't get much chance to respond.

The usher's face had changed, morphed into something otherworldly and dangerous. It reminded me of a sea monster with tentacles and gills instead of skin and a nose. He came at us, a whooshing, sucking noise coming from his mouth, and I felt a vacuum coming from him.

My hair began to lift, pointing in the direction of the usher, where the suction was pulling it up in the air. The fountain in the center of the lobby started to lose water, as it rose up in the air and was sucked in by the powerful breath. I saw Bert hanging onto my bag for dear life as it rose up in the air. I grabbed the handles just as it slid from the bench, keeping one hand inside on the tinderbox. I couldn't risk letting go, but I also couldn't risk Bert.

"Mia! Grab Bert before he loses his grip. We've got to get out of here!"

Aiden pulled his necklace out of the collar of his shirt, but, like mine, it wasn't a complete protection from the sucking wind. Mia and Jonah and Bert were having to fight even harder than we were to stay on their feet, but it wasn't like we were having an easy time ourselves.

I sat there wracking my brain for anything and everything I could do and everything I thought of came down to one thing.

I'd have to use the tinderbox.

Mia grabbed Bert as I whipped it out of my bag. I tossed the bag at Aiden, who grabbed it and nodded at me as I yanked the tinderbox open and pointed it at whatever it was the usher had become.

I heard a clanging sound, like a lot of metal clanking together all at once. I cringed, but held the tinderbox open as the sound got closer and closer. Jonah and Aiden pushed Mia behind me, and them, as the tinderbox shook in my hands. I held on as a full sized tin soldier came out the end of the bone tinderbox.

I couldn't figure out how that had happened, and I started to turn it around like an idiot to look at the opening, but I was able to stop myself as another tin soldier came out, then another and another. An army came out of the tinderbox, one by one, faster and faster. It was like the tinderbox was actually vomiting the soldiers out.

The soldiers marched toward the usher, blocking the wind as we were able to get ourselves together. Jonah's jaw hung open, but there was no time to explain. We had to get the tinderbox closed and get out of there before anything else showed up to attack us.

No sooner did I have the thought than other ushers appeared and began morphing into the same slack jawed sea monster with tentacles that the first one had turned into. There were five of them charging towards us and trying to suck us in, and failing because of the wall of tin soldiers effectively keeping the wind and suction from doing much more than ruffling our hair. I slammed the lid back on the tinderbox and we took off running out the door and heading for the parking garage. We needed to get out of there and regroup.

I guess Jonah had realized we weren't crazy, after all.

CHAPTER FORTY

It was a short, quiet, but determined drive to Doris's house. All the lights were on, and there were several cars in the driveway. She lived in South Park, a neighborhood near the university with plenty of student housing, but there were several old Victorian era houses with beautiful architecture in the neighborhood. Much like many neighborhoods in Dayton, the area had buildings that had seen better days, and others were clearly long term residents who had made the place a home. Some parts of the neighborhood were being seriously rehabbed, but I preferred the older houses with their dark woodwork and crown molding and delicate scrollwork on the large wooden porches rather than the modernized fakes. I'd been there several times with Aiden for Sunday dinners or for F.A.B.L.E.S. meetings, and the house just had a well-lived aura of *home*. Doris had a way of making anyone feel welcome no matter what had been going on before we got there.

We got out of the car. I recognized Aiden's little car, a beat up Volkswagon Bug that had seen better days, presumably just dropped off from the repair shop; Doris's Buick—which had been mine, I'd sold it to her to replace her dying station wagon after I'd gotten the keys to my stepmother's Escalade—and several other cars. As we walked up to the back door, I smelled pie.

Bert called from my bag. "We're in time for pie? Maybe some good will come out of this day after all!"

I had to smile. He was right.

Mia looked like she was devastated. Of course, an attack on your life was definitely something that could throw anyone off kilter in a serious hurry.

Jonah, on the other hand, was quieter than I expected. He was certainly quieter than I had been when I'd learned about magic, and quieter than Mia had been when she'd been let in on the secret. I didn't know what else to do besides bring him with us; it wasn't like we could leave him there to face the whatever-those-things-were that had attacked us. On the other hand, I now fully believed he didn't have anything to do with it, at least on purpose. Someone must have overheard him talking about Mia and either told the Seawitch, or the Seawitch herself was in the theater. That was a doubly scary thought.

Doris welcomed us with open arms. "Oh, my. Is everything okay? And who is this?" She gave me a big hug and kissed Aiden's cheek as we came in the door.

"This is Jonah. He's Mia's friend from the theater. He was with us when we were just attacked," Aiden said to his mother.

"What?" Tobias came into the kitchen. "You're talking about the coffee shop, right?"

"No," Mia said. "We went back to the theater afterwards to talk to Jonah since I was supposed to meet him there for coffee not too long after the place exploded. It looked like whoever did it wanted me to think Jonah did it if I survived, but didn't want him to get hurt. And there's the added bonus of people knowing he was supposed to meet me there, which would have made him the prime suspect."

I could tell he hadn't even thought of the possibility. His eyes widened, but then his shoulders slumped and he nodded. "Enough people heard me talking about meeting Mia that the cops would have eventually knocked on my door. I was at the theater all night, so I think I'd have had a good alibi and absolutely no motive, but I'd still be tied up dealing with all of that while the person responsible got a free pass to finish out whatever nefarious plan they might have had." Jonah's face hardened. "I can't let them get away with that no matter how crazy all this might sound and feel."

"Bravo," Stanley said as he shuffled into the kitchen. "Don't let the bastards get you down!"

Doris shook her head. "Let's all go into the living room. We have a few things to sort out, plans to be made, and some things to catch up on. Don't get him started or we'll never get through it all and it is getting late. Mia, Janie, both of you have work in the morning. I assume you'd like to get some sleep?"

Sleep. I hadn't even thought about it, but suddenly I felt ridiculously tired. "Before we go too far, Doris, you need to know Mia and I have lost our shadows."

Tobias jumped in. "There's a potion that can be made to re-grow a shadow overnight, and I suggest we start brewing it immediately. The girls can't be vulnerable to a lack of shadow if they go up against the Seawitch. That could be disastrous. We can talk about everything else while the potion is brewing."

We shuffled everyone into the living room, and Tobias and Doris put their heads together with Harold about what needed to go in the potion, while the four of us sat down on the couch. Bert hopped out of my bag as soon as I put it down. Jonah had questions about him, and I answered as best as I could but I wasn't so distracted as to miss Bert butting into the discussion in the corner about potions. It looked like an argument, but I didn't have the expertise to figure it out so I stayed out of it. Bert went with the others back into the kitchen to get things started.

"Maybe it's a good thing Bert went in the other room. I'm sure explaining why he's a frog gets old after several hundred years. At least we can help him with this round," Aiden said, as he leaned back in his mother's overstuffed chintz couch. "I feel for the guy."

Now was so not the time to bring up that there was another reason to feel bad for him, namely his unrequited love for Mia. So I didn't. "He doesn't want anyone feeling sorry for him. He's actually quite helpful in a lot of situations, and if there's a potion we have to take I'm glad he's having some input in what goes into it. I just hope it tastes better than the last potion I had to drink."

Aiden chuckled, and helped me explain the rapidly growing hair I'd had to cure by a potion last year when I'd been suffering from Rapunzel Syndrome. "Is that why your hair was suddenly normal again?" Mia asked.

I nodded. "It was completely disgusting and I thought repeatedly I was going to gag, but it was worth it in the end; I was able to go back to school the next day as if nothing had happened. Except for drinking a disgusting potion and sleeping on the dirt floor of a hut in a faerie realm."

She chuckled. I was glad to see it. She really was wound tight, and I just didn't know exactly what to do to help her at the moment, not just with the Seawitch, but to help her as a friend would. If making her laugh and relax a bit would help, I'd start juggling Bert.

Stanley came in asking particulars about our height and weight. I was used to his blunt directness, but Mia blushed a bit when she answered. Of course, what woman wants to answer questions about her weight in front of a guy she'd been flirting with? It remained to be seen if anything came out of all this, especially given the situation, but even if there was no possibility to be had it would still be difficult to bring oneself to answer that kind of question. I squeezed her hand.

"Mia, I'm sure they wouldn't ask if they didn't need the information for the potions. And I don't know for sure just how bad walking around without a shadow is, but there's no way I want to find out the hard way. If they can fix it, I'll be straight with them about what the scale showed me this morning."

She gave me a weak grin. Jonah smiled at her, an embarrassed look on his face. She reached over and took his hand. "So, now that you're in the know, do you have any questions?"

"Yeah, I've got a few. For starters, why the two of you? How did you figure all of this out? How can you protect yourselves against something so crazy? How do you have a normal life when all of this is going on around you?"

Good questions, all of them. I opened my mouth to answer but he kept right on talking.

"And you do know that the frog has a thing for one of you, right? I haven't been able to figure out which one, but he's definitely working on a major crush," Jonah continued.

Oh, crap.

CHAPTER FORTY-ONE

W hat could I say? "I know," I nodded. "But don't embarrass him. He's been through enough. No one is leading him on, believe me, but no one should crush him on purpose, either. And he's been a huge help to us. He knows it's almost impossible for a frog and human relationship to work, so he's realistic, and he's a good friend. Don't make it harder for him than it already is."

Jonah nodded. "I didn't mean anything by it. As an actor, you learn how to read an audience pretty well. Ask someone who's onstage; they've probably noticed things about people in the front rows of the audience just from watching them, and they're adjusting their performance bit by bit by how the audience reacts to them. I just didn't know if you guys knew."

"I didn't," Mia said.

"Why do you think he got drunk the other night? He was upset and he knew there wasn't a good answer to his feelings, so he drank more beer than is good for him and threw up all over the sink. He knows there's no good outcome. There is no white picket fence for him as a frog. Wouldn't that make you reach for a bottle? It might do that to me." This was saying something because I didn't like to drink, and Mia knew that.

She nodded at me, and didn't say anything else. I was sitting there hoping no one would ask if I knew who Bert was in love with; I didn't have the heart to say it out loud, knowing he could come in at any minute. It would be like betraying his confidence, and I knew I'd never feel right about it.

Doris came bustling back into the room with three steaming mugs of liquid. "This one is for Mia," she said, handing over *Grandmas Rule* mug to her. "This one is for Janie," as she handed me one with smiley faces. "And this is for Bert. I still don't think he needs this, but he's insisting."

I hadn't thought about Bert being with us when we'd lost our shadows, but he had been. It made sense he'd want to be cautious, too, but then again, I wasn't so sure he should be adding more magic or potions when he was already affected by a witch's curse that had made him into a frog. I said so.

"Janie, this is my decision, and I need to be able to help you guys. What if I'm the weak link, here? I can't live with that," he said, as he leaned over the mug and started gulping in big, thirsty, loud swallows.

I couldn't argue with him. "Do we stay here, tonight, Doris?"

"Yes. I have guest rooms. You can sleep in Aiden's old room, and Mia can sleep in my daughter's old room. The guys will just have to sleep on the couch here in the living room and in the recliner. In the morning, we'll go with you back to your house for clothes for work, and then we'll see what happens next."

It sounded like a plan.

The potion wasn't even close to as bad as the one from last year, but it was another one that required us to drink all of it at once. I felt my stomach filling up before I was even halfway done. Damn. I'd really hoped I'd have had room for pie before bed.

Once finished, I felt like I sloshed my way down the hallway to Aiden's childhood bedroom, complete with G.I. Joe posters, baseball posters, and model airplanes hanging from the ceiling. In one corner I saw Star Wars space craft arranged on a shelf in front of a model Death Star. No question he'd been a typical boy as a kid. Nothing in the room screamed that his father was high court faerie. I'd have loved more time to look around, but I was suddenly exhausted, and Aiden was encouraging me under the Millenium Falcon sheets as I fell asleep almost before I lay down.

I awoke with a start the next morning, and it took me a bit to figure out where I was; I wasn't used to waking up in a twin bed in an unfamiliar house. I sat up, still fully dressed, and noticed someone had taken off my shoes after I'd fallen asleep. I figured it had been Aiden since he was the one who had pointed me to his room and his bed before I'd passed out. I slipped them back on and headed for the kitchen. I was hoping there was coffee.

There was.

Mia was already up and sipping a mug. Aiden was rubbing his eyes and looking for a refill while Jonah stood in front of the pot as if willing it to brew faster. Doris was wearing a ratty bathrobe and fuzzy slippers as she sat at the kitchen table with Harold and Stanley, all of them with steaming mugs in front of them. No question, then; I'd missed the first pot and would be stuck waiting with the guys for the next pot to finish brewing.

As I stood, waiting, I turned in the morning sun streaming through the window. I could see my shadow, faint as it was, on the floor. "Looks like it worked," I said.

The others at the table nodded, as if was an afterthought, as opposed to the reason why we were there in the first place. Mia looked around and moved to the sunlight, looking and finding that hers was back as well.

"Thanks, guys. I don't know how bad it would be if our shadows were gone when we faced the Seawitch, but I'm glad I don't have to find out the hard way," she said to the others, and going over to give Doris a big hug. "I don't know what we would have done without all of your help."

"I agree," I said. "Did it work for Bert as well?"

A lot of throat clearing followed that question. "We don't know," Harold said, shushing the others. "He hasn't come out yet."

The brain wasn't quite kicking over yet and I hadn't had my customary morning cup of wake up juice, but I still knew there was more going on that they weren't telling me. I must be developing a keen deductive mind. That, or they were just really, really bad at hiding something.

Or what they were hiding was just that bad.

"What did you guys do?" I asked, as I realized Tobias wasn't in the kitchen. "What have I missed?"

Mia looked around. "Where's Dad?"

The coffeepot finished brewing and we all started pouring as I heard a commotion in the other room. Tobias came storming in. "Where did that frog go? Is he hiding?"

Mia and I exchanged a glance. "What do you mean? Where's Bert?" she asked.

Something told me I wasn't going to be very happy at whatever was going on.

Tobias sighed. "He crawled into the bathroom last night after he took that potion, and now he's not there. Anyone have any idea where he went?"

Before anyone could say much of anything, Jonah looked up. "Anyone have an idea why there's a naked man on the back porch?"

We all hurried outside.

He stood on the back patio, with his hands on his hips, facing the backyard with a giant grin on his face. His dark hair was rather scraggly, as if he normally wore a ponytail that was mussed from sleeping and hadn't yet been tied back. There was a giant scar across his back, like a burn scar, over his shoulder blades. There was another scar, as if he'd been slashed with a sword, over his ribs. He turned, wobbly, to face us in all his naked splendor.

Eye contact. It was important to keep eye contact. I told myself that more than once, but it was hard to do so with a very naked, very good looking man in front of me. He had very clear pale green eyes that looked right at me, as if he knew me. Out of the corner of my eye I saw Doris blushing, and I saw Mia trying to do the same thing I was doing.

Aiden stepped forward. "Who are you and what are you doing in my mother's backyard with no clothes on?"

"Don't you recognize me, Aiden?" he said, in a voice I recognized.

It was Bert. In human form.

Oh, damn. This was a wrinkle I hadn't thought about. And I knew exactly why he'd done it.

He'd done it to impress Mia, and now he was standing buck naked in front of her.

CHAPTER FORTY-TWO

A iden ran inside, coming back with his own ratty bathrobe and talking Bert into it.

Mia just kind of stood there, a look of shock on her face as Bert stared at her right back. I had to turn her around and get her back inside, while Jonah followed us asking all kinds of questions I just didn't feel quite up to answering yet.

Aiden stayed outside with Bert, as Doris and Harold and Stanley came tromping back inside. I assumed Tobias was also outside, as I didn't see him coming back into the kitchen. That would be an interesting chat between the now-man with a crush on his daughter and the dad who is trying to be more of a dad. I was glad I wouldn't be a part of that conversation.

"Doris, what do you know about this?" I asked.

She was wringing her hands and looking down at her feet. "I told him I didn't think it was a good idea, but he insisted."

"And why keep it a secret from everyone else?" Mia asked. "Don't we get to know what potions the people around us are taking? I'd hate for someone to get hurt, or to take something that renders them incapacitated, or makes them more vulnerable. This isn't the time to experiment!"

Doris nodded her head. "I've been working on it for quite a while. It wasn't like we just cooked this up last night. When I mentioned to him that he needed to take something regarding the possible loss of his shadow, he wanted to do both, at the same time. It seemed like he was in a hurry to get it done."

I'll bet he was. He had watched yesterday as Mia learned that Jonah wasn't as guilty as we'd first thought in the magical shenanigans in our lives. He'd seen her, if not completely fall for the competition, but warm up more than she had, by giving Jonah a chance by agreeing to meet with him, and then believing his shock and surprise when confronted with allegations that he was out to get us. I shook my head.

Bert wasn't thinking straight. Just last fall he'd talked about being hesitant to become human again if it was at all possible; for him to change his mind like this had only one explanation. It was because of Mia.

"Regardless of whatever else is going on, we need to start thinking about going to work," I said. "We only have an hour and a half, and we need clothes for the courthouse."

Doris nodded. "I'm sorry, Janie, Mia. I don't mean to invade your privacy, but last night Tobias, Harold, Aiden, and I left Stanley and Jonah to watch over you guys while we headed over to your house to get you a change of clothes for work today. If someone was watching the house we didn't want you getting trapped inside. You both have a suit hanging in my bedroom. I even ironed them for you."

I didn't know whether to feel weird about her being in my bedroom where Aiden had spent the night before and her going into my closet, or be grateful that she'd thought ahead. I decided the best course was to say nothing and go jump in the shower. Apparently Mia thought the same thing, because she followed me back to Doris's room, silent as I hopped in the shower first, then heading straight in without a word when I was done. I didn't know what she was thinking, but I'd known her a long time. It was sometimes good to let Mia come to her own decision without picking at her.

As long as I'd given her all the information, that is. I wondered if now was the right time to tell her Bert had a big ol' crush on her, and decided that was information she'd figure out on her own in time. I so did not want to get into the middle of all of that.

I came out of the bathroom, pulling my hair back into a ponytail to get it to look a bit more professional than the wild tangle it would come from taking a shower and not having my own hairspray or hair dryer. Doris had an old lady hair dryer, which looked like something straight out of a fifties hair salon, and I was worried I'd electrocute myself if I tried to use it. Of course, I made sure to put Aiden's necklace back around my neck. I wasn't going anywhere these days without it, even if I did take it off to sleep at night.

When I came out into the living room it seemed the guys had talked the now-human Bert into jeans, an old grey University of

Dayton t-shirt, and a pair of flip flop shoes. His wild hair had been tamed into a ponytail, and he looked more like a campus hippie than a former prince. Then again, he had better posture than I'd had, well, ever. *Probably from hours of parades and etiquette lessons,* I thought, before I realized the Bert I knew probably wouldn't have put up with much of that. I wondered if he'd been the same cynical wiseacre when he'd been human before.

He stood up when I entered the room, making me rethink the whole etiquette thing again, and said the first thing that came to his mind . . . or at least it seemed so. "Janie, you're shorter than I thought you were."

I guess it could have been worse.

"I'm sure I look a lot taller when you're less than six inches off the ground. Well, as soon as Mia is ready we need to get to work. Aiden, can you drop Jonah back at the theater?"

He nodded his head.

"What are we going to do with Sir Hops-A-Lot, here?" I asked. "It's not like I can take him with me in my purse anymore unless he's developed the ability to shift back and forth at will."

"Hey, I've got a name," Bert protested. "It's not like I'm invisible here, I'm just human now."

"Yes, you are, but that brings its own set of complications. You don't have any identification; you have no driver's license. You might know magic and the faerie courts, but you don't know the ins and outs of human life yet. You can't drive a car. Do you know how to use a computer? We have to go to work, so no one can just hang out with you and teach you how to do all of those things all day," I said. "I'm sorry if that sounds harsh, but I just don't know if you thought all of this through. It's bad timing, Bert."

He made a face at me, an inscrutable look of exasperation and frustration that I recognized even though his face wasn't green and amphibian any longer. Yeah, I knew he thought it was better timing than I did. I'm sure he felt like he would lose all chance for happiness if he didn't act right away, but the problem was that I wasn't real sure it was going to work. In fact, I was pretty sure it wouldn't.

Aiden spoke up. "He can hang with me, today. I don't have

anywhere to be except at the warehouse before I go to the theater tonight. We'll deal with it when we reach that point. Right now I think we all just need to get going."

Oh, great. All three guys in Aiden's tiny car driven by the biggest klutz in the city with rising levels of testosterone, at least in the one that used to be a frog. Not my idea of a good time but, then again, I didn't have time to worry about it. Aiden was going to have to keep them from killing each other, at least until he could get Jonah dropped off. I had all kinds of respect for him. He was going to need as much patience as he could muster if Bert was newly human and ready to strut his stuff, so to speak.

Mia and I headed for my car hoping we'd be able to have a fairly easy and productive morning, one way or another. The drive to the court house was silent, and even the morning rush hour traffic wasn't as stressful as the whirling thoughts in my head that didn't seem to have a good solution.

I was just hoping the rest of the day wouldn't be as off the wall as the morning had been. An early morning sight of a naked former frog was about as much as I could take.

Chapter Forty-Three

We were in the courthouse with just minutes to spare to start our shifts, but there was no judge in the office to meet us. We sat in the waiting area for a bit staring at the statue of the judge, the painting of the judge, and all the different photographs of the judge. Yet again, I thought this guy was nuts. I wondered if I'd have that thought every day for the rest of the summer.

An hour after our morning was supposed to start the judge came through the door wearing a pair of earth-friendly sandals, khaki cargo shorts, and a madras shirt. He went to the closet and pulled out a set of somber black robes before inviting us into the courtroom to take notes on the motion hearing he had set that day.

When we went into the courtroom it wasn't hard to see the lawyers there were frustrated with waiting; heck, we were, too, but the judge didn't waste any time getting down to business. Mia and I sat in the back, legal pads at the ready. He had told us to take notes of what was going on, so we could discuss the case with him later and so we would have notes to use in case there was a research project we would be assigned from the hearing.

The hearing lasted most of the morning. The gist of the hearing? Well, there was a man who had been charged with drunk driving and was claiming the results from the breath test should not be held against him, along with all of his statements to law enforcement, the field sobriety tests, and pretty much every piece of evidence the prosecutor had laid out against him. If his lawyer had forgotten any singular piece of evidence against him I'd have been shocked.

As boring as all the minutiae of the hearing could have seemed to others, Mia and I were both engrossed in what was going on in front of us. This was what we wanted to do. This was what we were spending so much time, money, and effort in school to learn. And this summer's internship was supposed to be exposing us to exactly this. We were in heaven.

I had to give the judge credit; he at least acted like he knew what he was doing. He ruled on objections and kept the hearing moving at a swift enough pace that we were done within a few minutes of the lunch hour. He dismissed the attorneys and the parties and recessed for the lunch hour before calling us back to his office.

When we walked into his office I smelled magic, but I couldn't tell where it was coming from. There were still material samples all over the place—as there had been earlier in the week—but I noticed nothing that looked remotely magical about the judge. There was nothing in the room that stood out to me, as I sat down in his office chair and pulled out the legal pad ready to take further notes. Mia did the same.

"Ladies, I had you sit in that hearing, because I wanted you to see a hearing and because I also am expecting briefs from the lawyers in the morning. I want you pick up those briefs, read through them, and then discuss them with me when I come in. We don't have a morning docket, so you'll have time to get through them, outline whatever questions you might have, and we'll have time to discuss it all before the tailors get here with my new robes. I can't wait to see what you guys think of them!" He sounded very excited. "They are supposed to be the best robes money can buy!"

Oh criminy. I hoped like mad they were exciting enough robes for us to have something positive to say about them. He'd been obsessed with them all week.

"Once we've all seen the robes I'll take you two out to lunch if you have the time. You've earned it this week, given that you've done work at home and had to deal with my crazy schedule. It's on me. And you can ask whatever questions you might have about the bar exam, law school, internships, the courthouse, or anything else you might want."

We exchanged glances. Under normal circumstances the two of us would have jumped at the opportunity to pick the judge's brain about exactly those kinds of topics. We would have, at the very least, been excited about the idea of a free lunch along with personal attention from a practicing lawyer, much less a judge. At the moment, however, all I could think of was that being out and about in public could be dangerous for Mia, for me, and even for the judge, until we got all of this stuff figured out. As it was, though, I couldn't think of a good excuse that I could use to say no.

"It's settled then. We'll have lunch tomorrow and then you guys will be able to enjoy your weekend after that."

Had this week been so out of whack I'd completely forgotten that tomorrow was Friday? I had to stop myself from shaking my head at him. "We'll be there, sir. And maybe have some research ideas for you for answering the briefs that the attorneys will file. Is there anything else we can do for you today?" I hoped he'd say no.

He must have read my mind. "You guys have put in plenty of extra hours this week. Go home. Enjoy your day. Be here bright eyed and bushy tailed for a morning of research, checking out my new robes, and then a free lunch. You've earned it."

We slunk out of his office, almost waiting for him to call us back in and tell us he'd forgotten to assign us some kind of research to do for the evening. He didn't.

In the whirlwind of the past week I'd forgotten exactly why I'd been so looking forward to working with a judge, and today's events reminded me why I'd been so happy to take the job. I loved being in court. I liked the mental challenge of it. And I was more impressed today with the judge than I'd been just a few short days ago.

We headed for the parking garage and left. Mia still hadn't said much all day. I wasn't prepared for what she did say when she finally opened her mouth and said it.

"So who's the one Bert's got the crush on? I wonder why he felt like he needed to turn into a human so urgently. Is there something going on that I don't know about?" she asked, as I entered the highway through all the summer construction.

The orange barrels and cones were everywhere so I ignored her question. Ohio has four seasons, rain, snow, wind, and road construction. It seemed like every surface road in Ohio was under construction at this time of the year. I slid in between the barrels at the entrance ramp, and headed away from the courthouse. Then I couldn't put it off any longer.

"It's you, Mia. He is in love, frog legs over heels in love, with you. I believe he turned himself human, despite whatever risks he might have faced, because he couldn't compete with any other human male out there for your attention and your affections."

"Wow," she said. "I figured it was you. He's always checking on you, offering to bring you things, and just in general that you were so close to him."

"It's not me."

"How do you know that?"

"He told me."

She sat in silence as I drove. I was sure it was a lot to process, especially since she'd expected the truth to be the other way around. I didn't know quite how else to tell her and I felt a bit guilty about spilling Bert's secret, but it wasn't like it wasn't going to come out anyway. I had a feeling he had a plan for trying to win her affections.

I just wasn't sure it was a good one. So far I was less than impressed with whatever plan he might have.

Absent whatever Bert was planning there were also a few other things left on our plates, like knowing whatever Jonah's role might be in all of this, like knowing what Tobias wanted from my friend, like making sure Allie was okay since we hadn't been at home last night, and like figuring out what in the world we were going to do with a human sized Bert in a house with two women.

I figured we had our work cut out for us.

CHAPTER FORTY-FOUR

I was going to drive by my house no matter what else was going on. I hated the idea that we'd run the other day. I wanted to fight what we were facing. I just didn't know how. Even so, no matter what was going on, no matter how smart it was to stay away. I couldn't help it.

I turned down our street looking for signs of anything being out of order. It was a tree-lined street in an upper class neighborhood. It wasn't the neighborhood I would have chosen, but it was feeling like home now that my stepmother was out of it and I was feeling protective, combative, and just downright stubborn. I tried to explain to Mia.

"I completely understand," she said. "I kinda feel the same myself."

"Yeah, but that doesn't mean it's a good idea for you to go with me. I can take you back to Doris's house and come back with Aiden, or your dad, or Jonah, or Harold, or Stanley, if you'd feel safer," I said, as I circled the block checking to see if anyone or anything was following me or watching the car. I saw nothing.

"I'm not afraid," she said.

I could hear a bit of fear in her voice as she spoke, but I guessed she was entitled to it. Heaven knows I remembered feeling the same way when I went to confront my stepmother about what I'd learned about her plan. I'd been terrified and determined at the same time, but I'd at least had backup.

As I rounded the block and came back to the driveway I still didn't see anything suspicious. I saw the normal mid-day traffic, people coming home for lunch, a mom outside with two very young children on the front porch of her house, and the postman walking his rounds. I saw nothing out of place, nothing suspicious, and nothing to worry about. But what had I *missed* that should have been right in front of my face all this time? Who was actually magical that I just hadn't figured out? I shook my head. I was going to talk myself out of this before I'd actually stopped, and I couldn't let myself do that. I pulled into the driveway and hit the button for the garage door opener.

I pulled inside without incident, and closed the door behind us before getting out of the Escalade. So far, so good. We gathered our things, and locked up the car, stopping inside the door to the back yard in order to peer out the window for anything that might be amiss. I saw nothing, but I couldn't see the entire yard. No matter what angle we tried we couldn't see everything.

"It's no use," Mia said. "There's no way to be sure. Either we're going in, or we're getting right back inside the car and leaving. We either need to go and check on things, or we need to get out of here. We should be safe once we get inside."

She was right. Even if the salt line Aiden had laid had been washed away there was a threshold on the house to would keep out any faerie being who tried to sneak their way inside, unless they came in through the portal in the basement, and I thought we had the portal under control due to our deal with Winterkiss.

Speaking of Winterkiss, we hadn't heard from her lately. She probably had no idea we'd had to leave the house the night before, or that the Seawitch had found us. I wondered if there was a way to track her down and ask more questions. But there was no time for it now. I opened the door to the back yard and began hurrying toward the back door.

The back patio was a mess. Whatever storm the Seawitch had wrought, it had blown the patio furniture all over the place. I didn't see it until I was almost to the door.

There was a lump on the back patio behind an overturned chaise lounge. The cushions had landed on top of whatever it was we couldn't see. I started over to investigate when Mia grabbed my arm.

"Don't," she said. "It could be a trap."

"Mia, you might be right. I need you to go in the house and grab the phone. If you're behind the threshold and it is a trap, then you'll be safe and can call for help if something happens to me. If the threshold doesn't hold against this magic, run to the basement and through the portal. Tell Winterkiss you are there asking for assistance on my behalf."

She started to argue.

"Just do it." I cut her off. "Mia, you're the target. I need to see what this is. Get inside."

She shut up and unlocked the door, stepping inside and closing the screen door. "This is as far as I'm going. I've got my cell phone if I need to call."

I nodded, and headed over to whatever it was on the other side of the overturned lounge chair. After pulling off the cushions, I uncovered Allie, unconscious, with a huge goose egg on her forehead. That was new; the bruises I'd noticed before were starting to yellow around the edges, but this was fresh and looked painful. "Allie?" I asked, shaking her shoulders.

"Oh my," Mia said. "It's the street girl who has been visiting, the one you've been sharing food and clothes with?"

I realized at that point she'd never actually met Allie. It had only been me, Aiden, and Doris who had seen her, talked to her, fed her, and interacted with her. "Yes, it's her. Stay where you're at. She's pretty small. I'm going to drag her into the house, but don't you dare come out to help. It might be what the Seawitch is waiting for, to draw you out where you're not paying attention and give her an opportunity to attack."

I looked up to make sure she was paying attention. She didn't look happy, but she gave me a barely perceptible nod. I shoved the overturned furniture out of the way, and grabbed Allie under the armpits to drag her backwards into the house. She flinched as I moved her, but didn't wake up and didn't fight me. Mia opened the door so I could drag Allie in. I got her as far as the kitchen, and didn't have the strength to go much further. Mia ran for a pillow from the living room as I grabbed a freezer bag to fill with ice.

I filled the bag, added a bit of water, and wrapped a dishcloth around it, not forgetting to shut the door behind us. Before I stopped to apply the ice bag to Allie's forehead I grabbed the saltshaker off the table to pour a line of salt at the base of the door and line the windowsill above the sink. I didn't know if it would do any good, but it couldn't hurt. When Mia came back in I considered leaving her in the kitchen to take care of Allie while I went through the rest of the house doing the same to all the doors and windows, but I knew if Allie woke up and saw an unfamiliar face she'd freak. I had to stay with her, no question. I explained my idea about the salt to Mia and she nodded, taking the salt shaker as well as a couple of the canisters of salt Aiden had left behind the other night to get it all done. There were a lot of windows and doors in the house.

I knew she'd feel better with something constructive to do. I didn't know how much good it would do, but I'd take whatever I could get at the moment. I applied the ice bag to Allie's head while I waited for Mia to come back.

Allie opened her mouth a bit as I touched the ice to her head, but nothing came out. She tossed and turned back and forth a bit as I tried to ice down her forehead without too much pressure on the swelling on her head. I was pretty sure she had a concussion. If nothing else, she'd have one hell of a headache once she gained her wits.

It took a while, but soon her eyelids fluttered open. She started to panic as she woke up, pulling away from me as I tried to help her until her eyes focused enough to recognize me. I saw her wince in pain, and was glad I hadn't turned on the kitchen lights yet. The sunlight coming through the window, I couldn't do much about.

"Allie, are you okay? I asked. "What happened to you?"

She shook her head.

"It's okay. You're safe now, with friends. It's just me and my roommate. You're in my house, and we'll keep you safe. Who hurt you?"

She shook her head again.

I sighed. I'd known somehow that pushing her for information could be a bad thing, but in this case we needed to know if it was related to her own problems or to our drama. "Allie, I need to know. I wouldn't push you if I didn't have to, but there's stuff going on with us that could make any information you have very valuable to us. There's a reason I asked you to watch the house. Do you know why?"

She didn't respond, just stared at me through half-open eyes.

"Well, the reason I asked you to watch the house is because someone has been threatening us. My roommate's had some drama the last couple of days. I need to figure out if you got hurt because of our situation or if there's someone who has come to our house to hurt you."

She opened her mouth to start talking, but nothing came out.

"I can't hear you," I said. "Can you speak up?"

She tried again. Nothing came out. Her mouth was moving, yet there was no sound coming from her throat. I wondered if she'd been choked, but there wasn't even a hoarse rasp coming from her.

"If I got you a pen and piece of paper do you think you could write it down?" I asked, thinking quickly.

Allie nodded. I left her lying on the kitchen floor as I snatched the notepad we used for a grocery list from where it stuck to the front of the refrigerator with a magnet, and grabbed a pen from my bag and handed them to her.

I wasn't prepared for what she wrote.

Seawitch.

CHAPTER FORTY-FIVE

Oh. My. God.

Seriously? Was she magical? How had I not noticed? I hadn't smelled magic on her once. She had never once flinched about coming in the house. Her only flinching had been to Aiden when she'd been surprised by his presence. Had she recognized him? Was she faerie? Was she dangerous to Mia? Was I making myself crazy?

Yeah, my brain on a hamster wheel, if the wheel was powered by a hamster who'd taken a big whopping dose of crystal meth.

"What do you mean?" I asked.

Seawitch was here last night. Asked for Andersen girl, she wrote.

What could I say? How did I even start asking for questions? "Allie, I have to ask. Are you working for the Seawitch? And how do you know who the Seawitch is?"

Not really working for her. And she showed me what her power is.

"What's that mean?"

She killed someone who was hurting me to prove that she was magical and I believed her. She wants me to work for her. She wants to use me to get to you and your friend.

"When did this start?" I asked. Had I invited her into my house without knowing she was a danger to me and to Mia? How could I have been so stupid?

Two days ago. Took me off Brown Street, near the university. Promised me safety if I could deliver you and your friend to her.

"What do you mean 'promise you safety'?"

Not important.

"Yeah, actually, it kinda is," I said, handing her the ice bag and leaning back on my heels. "I know you're reluctant to tell me all the details, but right now I need to know what the threat is that we're facing. Allie, you know me. I've helped you. I've suspected for a while you might be a runaway . . ."

Her eyes widened. I assumed that I guessed right.

"Look, Allie, I haven't told anyone. I haven't even told Mia. I think you're in trouble. And I've been hoping you'll get comfortable enough with me to tell me what's going on, so I can help you or at least point you in a direction where we can find you help. I'm not talking about calling the police, although that might be the right thing to do eventually. I'm talking about finding you a place to stay, a safe place, getting you someone to talk to, and getting you off the street."

Her eyes got even wider. She ripped the page off the pad and balled it up, writing on the next page. *How did you know?*

"The way you reacted to Aiden, the bruises I saw, the jumpiness," I said. "I put it together with a few other things, and I came to the conclusion that someone's been hurting you. I think, maybe even sexually, you've been hurt. And I want you well. I want to do what I can to help you get out of this situation."

What do you want in return?

"Nothing."

I don't believe you. He said no one can help me.

"He, whoever he is, is wrong. He's trying to keep you dependent on him by trying to convince you that you don't have any other choice," I said, putting the ice bag back on her head. "I've never asked you for anything, and I never will. Let me tell you something, though. My stepmother treated me terribly growing up. She even broke my arm once just for refusing to do her twisted version of chores around the house. She's make me scrub the bathrooms with a toothbrush, pluck feathers for pillows, and all kinds of weird stuff. When I finally complained it was too much, she hurt me. I was thirteen.

"I'm not kidding myself in thinking it's anything close to what you're going through, but I can remember feeling stuck in a bad situation and not knowing where to find help. I was just a kid. Eventually, I grew up, and I ended up getting her put away for a long time." I just didn't explain what I meant by *put away*. I wasn't sure how much of the magic stuff she'd been exposed to just yet. "The point is, I'm trying to help you in a way that no one tried to help me."

She didn't say anything, and she didn't write anything for a minute. Then, she slowly picked up the pen. You're not wrong on any of it. It's true, all of it. But right now, not important. Must not give in to the Seawitch.

"I agree with you. You're inside. There's a lot we're doing to protect ourselves. You're as safe here as we can make you. What did the Seawitch ask you to do?"

Mia came into the kitchen, but was out of Allie's sight since she was still on the floor. She was completely clueless when she wrote, *Wanted me to get close enough to lure you into a meeting with her. Refused. Stole my voice for refusing.*

I didn't know someone could do that, but we were talking about magic, so I guess anything was possible. "I tell you what, Allie. My roommate just came in the kitchen, so I'd like to introduce you to her. And I'd like to introduce you to some people who can help you with figuring out maybe how to reverse this magic. You met Doris the other day, right? She's good at helping people figure out how to solve problems caused by magic."

She nodded.

I gestured to Mia, who came around the kitchen island and said hello to Allie. "I'm Mia. I hear Janie's been helping you. She's been my best friend for years. She's pretty good at helping people even when they're not sure they need the help."

Together we helped Allie to sit up, steadying her as she swayed. I was grateful for Mia's statement. I hoped it meant she had forgiven me for keeping things from her earlier this week. I had been trying to protect her, but I'd been wrong to keep her out of the loop.

"Allie, there's a place I heard about at the law school that might be able to help you with some of the things you might be facing. It's called Safe Haven. It's got all kinds of resources and people who specialize in helping girls who have been through things like you have."

Can I stay here?

Oh, boy. I glanced at Mia, who shrugged.

"Well, I'll tell you what. We'll try it for a bit, but none of us know each other very well so it might not work out. I've got a couple of conditions. I want to take you to a clinic and get checked out. You can't go back out on the street. And if the guy you were talking about figures out you're here, you will call the police and see about getting a restraining order against him. I won't force you to call the police until you're ready, unless that happens. You get why, right? It's about all of our safety."

She nodded.

Mia nodded. "I'm good with that. I'll add one more thing. I think you met Doris?"

Allie nodded.

"Well," Mia said, "We stayed with her last night because we were trying to throw off the Seawitch. If things become too dangerous here promise me that you'll stay with Doris if she'll have you. If we ask you to go there it's for your safety, not to kick you out. We won't ask unless it's necessary and, if it is, it's likely we'll be headed there ourselves."

She nodded, and gave me a small smile.

"Why don't we get you to the living room where you can lay down on the couch and be a bit more comfortable? This floor can't be all that great." I smiled at her, and when she agreed I handed Allie the ice bag. Mia and I each took an arm and helped her to her feet. She swayed a bit, but between all of us we finally got her to the couch.

She still had the notepad in her hand. Can I get something to eat? I'm starving.

Even if she did have a concussion a good appetite had to be a good sign. I agreed to make her a sandwich, and Mia sat with her in the living room to keep her awake while I went into the kitchen. I made a sandwich and called the free clinic downtown to try to set up an appointment for her.

As I put the mustard back in the refrigerator I also called Aiden and filled him in. Things were hitting a little too close to home for me to keep moving forward without asking for back up. And if I was going to ask for it, Aiden was the only person I'd call. I'd have to remember to tell him that as soon as life slowed down long enough to have that relationship discussion with him.

Yeah, he meant that much to me.

CHAPTER FORTY-SIX

A iden agreed to come over, and Doris came with him. I didn't want Allie to be overwhelmed, but I did want her to see familiar faces and I wanted her to know we were working on a solution, not just to the Seawitch being free but also about her own voice issues. It just made sense that we could start working on all of it at once.

I got Allie an appointment for Monday, with strict instructions to wake her once an hour due to the head injury and take her to the emergency room immediately if she seemed confused, disoriented, or had balance issues. It was the fastest I could get her in, and I hoped she could wait that long because I didn't think she had medical insurance and I knew I didn't have the money to cover a big emergency room visit for her. I'd hate for her to have her clean start marred by big debts before she even got started.

Once she was resting comfortably, I pulled Mia aside. "It seems to me the house is fairly secure. I don't see any damage anywhere, and I don't see any place the Seawitch might have gotten in. You see anything?"

"Yeah, there's a pretty deep ditch on the north side of the house, but it doesn't even come close to the foundation. I don't know what caused it, but I could guess. No matter what, it looks like the Seawitch couldn't touch the house even if she tried." She smiled. "Something about that just makes me happy."

I grinned back at her. "Me, too. Aiden and Doris are on their way to see what they can do to help."

"Good."

I checked back on Allie, who had fallen into a light doze, and woke her up long enough to have her touch her nose and silently recite the alphabet to make sure she was okay. Doris and Aiden arrived within a few minutes, and Doris was immediately clucking over Allie.

I shrugged. I guess once a mom, always a mom. I couldn't help but wish I'd known whether my own mother would have been so caring and kind. If she hadn't passed away maybe I'd have had a normal childhood with a regular mom instead of a childhood with a mean, emotionally distant, abusive stepmother who hated kids. I shook my head. Allie deserved as much kindness as we could give her. I doubted she was even eighteen yet, and had probably still seen all kinds of things she'd rather not repeat; likely things I couldn't even imagine.

Aiden touched my hand as he walked through the living room, doing double duty both to get my attention and still give Allie as much space as he possibly could. I think it hurt his feelings when she'd cringed and flipped out at his presence before. I followed him into the kitchen.

"What in the world were you two thinking of to come back here when the house was just attacked last night? Are you insane? For all you know, the Seawitch is watching the house just waiting for you to return with Mia and stepping right back into a trap," he whispered at me, his voice low so his mother and Allie wouldn't overhear our conversation. Mia had stayed with Allie in the living room.

"I was thinking that I no longer want to live my life in fear. This is now my home. I cannot bring myself to hide and to run, because then she's already won. And you know Mia feels the same way. I let her decide. And if she'd begged me to go into hiding I'd have gone, because it's her fight this time."

"You knew it was a better idea to stay away, and you let her come back here? Why would you do that?" he asked. It was almost like he hadn't even heard me.

"And whose idea was it to let Bert turn himself human? I mean, seriously, as if Mia's not got enough on her plate right now who thought it was a good idea for Bert to pile all of his own issues on her at the same time? I mean, am I the only one here thinking someone should have stopped him? Someone should have told him that now was not the time to put his own wants or desires ahead of everything else. Someone, namely you and your mother, should have told him he should not make her deal with this on top of everything else," I said, getting angry at him.

"Did you tell her?"

"Of course I did. She thought he was in love with me, and she couldn't figure out why he'd done it." We were nose to nose, spitting angry whispers at each other. I think this might be our first fight, and I had no intention of giving in.

"Don't you think it was his to tell? Have you ruined any chance he might have for happiness?"

"No. She's not in love with him."

"She's in love with Jonah, the dude from the theater? I mean, I like him and all, but that doesn't mean he's the right guy for her!"

"Doesn't she get to make that choice?" I snapped back. We were getting louder as we went, but at that point I didn't care.

"Doesn't he get a chance to give her a choice?" he yelled.

"What are you saying?" I asked.

"I'm saying you need to decide yourself what you want. I've tried being patient, and I've tried being just the friend. I've tried being just your magical go-to guy and your backup, and that's not enough for me. I know you've been through a lot. I know you're in school, I know it takes a lot of your time and energy, but, Janie, I'm in this for the long haul. I just need to know what you think. I can't be the only one trying in this relationship." He swung his hand out emphasizing his point.

I rescued the bowl of apples he nearly knocked off the kitchen island. "You think this is about us?"

"No. It's about Bert. It's about Mia. But we still have issues that need to be resolved as well. I know you don't want me to say it, but I love you. I love everything about you. I love your stubborn prickliness when you don't want to hurt someone's feelings, your sense of right and wrong. I love how you seem to collect people who love you no matter what you're doing. I love how you wrinkle up the skin just above your nose when you're not quite sure of what I'm saying. Like you're doing right now."

I reached up. Crap. He was right. "Aiden, we've been through this. My reluctance isn't about you or anything you've said and done. It's that we're charting new territory here. Your parents couldn't make it work. My dad was victimized by my stepmother. What relationship have you seen work with people with our backgrounds without falling apart spectacularly and massively in an implosion that takes down the people around them? There are too many people depending on the two of us these days. Are we making ourselves more vulnerable by even trying? Is it right for us to be together when there's so much magic out there that could hurt other people?"

"And you think staying alone is going to fix that? Are we nuts?" he asked. "All the fighting we're doing to protect people doesn't mean a whole hell of a lot if we forget the kinds of things we're fighting for. One of the things I'm fighting for is to keep you safe and with me."

I knew he felt this way. He'd never made it much of a secret. And I felt the same way about him. No matter what my own personal hang-ups. No matter what roadblocks might stand between us. "Is that why you didn't talk Bert out of it? You'd have done the same if it was me and you?"

He nodded.

"Lucky for you, I'm not Mia. And you're not Bert. Because . . ." I only stumbled a bit, but it wasn't as hard to say as I thought once I got started. "I love you, too. The only problem with their situation?"

"She doesn't love him, does she?" he asked.

"No, she doesn't," I answered, as I stepped into his arms. He wrapped them around me. "You're lucky. He's going to get his heart broken, and he's not going to know what to do with himself." Bert as a frog, drunk and throwing up in the kitchen sink, I could handle. I wasn't quite sure how to handle a human-shaped heartbroken Bert.

I can't quite figure out how Aiden and I always ended up having romantic moments that always ended up with us talking about other people's problems. Maybe that was part of why I always felt like nothing could ever come together for us. We'd have to try to do something about it the next time. Then again, maybe it was just us, the way things would always happen for us. While I didn't like the thought I disliked the idea of us not having those moments even more. I was through hiding from my feelings. I wanted Aiden, and I knew magic was part of it. As long as we had magic together I could handle the rest. Bert's shenanigans were the least of it.

Aiden kissed the top of my head. "I couldn't talk him out of it when I'd have done it myself. Say what you might about me, but I'm not a hypocrite."

He wasn't. And neither was I.

CHAPTER FORTY-SEVEN

A s good as it felt to hear Aiden actually say that he loves me, and as good as his arms felt around me, I couldn't stay here forever. I had to check on Allie. I had to check on Mia. We had to make sure the house was secure. And I was starting to formulate a metric ton of questions in the back of my head. Something wasn't adding up right.

"Aiden, is there a way we can talk to Winterkiss? Is there something we can do to help the faerie courts gain control of the Seawitch again? I mean, I assume she's immortal, that we can't kill her. What can we do to imprison her other than to salt the entire neighborhood? I think all the amateur gardeners might have a problem with that." And I wasn't kidding, either. There were several older ladies who were serious rose gardeners that lived down the street. Visions of what they might say or do if I started spreading salt everywhere . . . well, let's just say it wasn't a pretty thought.

"I think we can do something about it, but it'll take some thought," he said. "And I'll probably end up having to contact my father, something that's never a good idea."

"You do know they moved the portal in the basement, right? You can't use it to just go looking for him. It comes out in the back room behind the throne room in my stepmother's court."

He gave me a horrified look. "Why in the world did you agree to that?"

"I wasn't asked."

He stepped away from me and started pacing, back and forth, in what space was available in the kitchen. "Normally both sides have to agree to the moving of a portal."

"But they only moved one side," I said. "Why would they need my permission if my side of it wasn't being moved?"

"Doesn't matter. They always get permission from both sides before they move anything. Then again, they don't necessarily need permission from the actual owner. Anyone left in charge of the house could have given permission."

We both looked at each other at the exact same time both of us knowing exactly who had given the okay. "Bert."

"Where is that little shit?" I asked. "I'm going to kill him." I wondered what bottle he'd crawl into next if he figured out all of his master plans were falling apart. It was one thing to clean up after a drunk frog throwing up in the sink. It was another to have a full grown man drowning his sorrows and vomiting all over the place. And there was also the cost of what it would take to get him drunk now that he was full-sized. It would be two or three times what it had been as a frog, and I didn't have the extra money to keep him in beer. It wasn't like he had money of his own, and I was absolutely not going to pay for it.

"The last time I saw him, he was still with Mom, but I think Stanley and Harold were taking him out to get him some other clothing. I think they were heading to the Goodwill store down on Fifth Street. That's not that far away. Let me call Harold's cell phone and tell them we're all here. I can insist they all get here immediately. We need to know why he's working with Winterkiss, and what Winterkiss promised him to get him to agree."

That was a scary thought. As much as I didn't like the idea of Bert going behind my back, I liked even less the idea that he owed something to the high court, or that he'd made some kind of deal with them. What hold might they have over him? What had he promised? Was there some kind of angle Winterkiss was playing? Or were Mia and I somehow being set up to be pawns in some strange back room drama Winterkiss was manipulating Bert into playing? Or was Bert the chess master moving us around? Were either one of them working for the Seawitch?

Either way, I couldn't believe Bert would sell us out, no matter what anyone said. There had to be something he had gotten out of the deal, there had to be something he couldn't turn down, there had to be . . .

My brain wouldn't stop running in circles even as Aiden whipped out his cell phone to call Harold and get them to the house.

I went back into the living room to check on Allie while Aiden was on the phone. Doris sat next to her in one of the overstuffed chairs

I'd replaced my stepmother's fussy elegant furniture with, her fingers tangled in yarn that she was winding into a ball.

"Sorry, dear. I'm not trying to make a mess, but I always have some kind of project all over the place. I figured you needed someone to sit with Allie, so I'm going to sit here and straighten out the mess in my yarn bag while I stay here. That way you girls and Aiden can still go to work tonight without worrying about anything. I'll be right here, watching over her, and watching over your house."

I smiled at her. "No problem, Doris. Thank you. Where did Mia run off to?"

"She went up to her room. She said she wanted to be alone for a bit."

I was running for the stairs. I didn't have a good feeling about Mia being alone considering Bert's deal regarding the portal, the magical attack on the house the day before, Bert's professed love for her, and the drama surrounding her father. Wait a minute. I had no idea where her father was. I burst into her room Mia lay on her side on her bed curled up in a ball. She jumped as I entered the room.

"What is it?" she asked, on full alert.

"Something's going on. We're missing something important here. I just can't quite figure out what it is." I plopped down on her bed near her feet.

"What is it?" she said again, sitting up. I could tell she'd been deep in a funk, probably turning the last few days around in her mind, but I didn't have any answers for her situation, either. Or maybe it was all the same.

"Mia, there's just so much going on, and it all seems related but it isn't. But it is." I filled her in on the movement of the portal, and my suspicions that Bert had something to do with it. "I just can't believe Bert would sell us out. He's always been so helpful, and he's been a friend."

"But he's magical. I agree with you, Janie. I have a hard time believing it as well, but let's face it, he's been affected by magic for longer than he was human. It's bound to do something wonky with his thought processes. Is he bound by something we don't know about? Is he working with something else? Someone else? There's just too much we don't know." Mia sat in front of me, picking at the seams on the quilt that covered her bed. "There's too much about *him* we don't know."

"But it's *Bert*. How do we doubt him? He's given great advice all the way through all of this, for you and for me. How can we suddenly think he could do anything to hurt us? That could endanger us? How can we think he's the problem here?" I asked. "I just can't believe it."

She shook her head. "I feel like I've misjudged him anyway. How did I not know how he felt?"

"Would it have changed how you felt about him?" I asked. It seemed such a simple question, but it wasn't. It was an honest one.

She considered it, the seconds ticking away as she sat quietly. "No," she said. "I'm not in love with him. He's a friend, and I care about him, but I don't know that I will ever love him like he loves me, regardless of the magic, the curses, the portals, or the fairy tales. I'm sorry for him, but I don't love him, not like that."

I reached over and patted her hand. "Mia, you can't ever plan who you love. And you can't fall in love just because someone else wants you to. You have to meet the right person and be open to it at the same time in order to fall in love, a solid love that you can build something with."

"Are you saying something? Are you in love with Aiden?"

For once, I could answer the question honestly, with no hesitation and no doubts. I knew in my heart that I loved him and we'd work together to get through any kind of barrier life, or magic, might put in our paths. "Yes, I am."

"Have you told him?" she asked me.

"Yes, I did. Just a few minutes ago, in fact."

"You're lucky. You've found the right guy and you've finally found a way to be open to love; Aiden's pretty great. I can't bring myself to be open to anyone. The right guy could be standing right in front of me, but I'm too afraid of ending up like my mother, working her fingers to the bone to support me because the man she loved couldn't stick around long enough to take care of his responsibilities. I can't ever allow myself to end up like that."

I didn't know quite what to say. I understood her feelings more than I could even say out loud. I hadn't wanted to end up in a loveless marriage, like my father with my stepmother, but then again, I couldn't say it was loveless. I still didn't know if he'd actually fallen for her, or if he'd been magically compelled into loving her, or if he just settled for someone who would make him comfortable after my mother was gone.

I shook my head. I could play amateur psychologist sleuth hour with my family's past later. Right now I had my answer about her feelings. Now I just needed to go confront a love-sick former frog turned human.

And he wasn't going to like what I had to say to him about it.

CHAPTER FORTY-EIGHT

"Hello?" I heard a familiar voice calling from the front hallway. The traitor frog had returned.

"Mia, stay here."

"No problem. There's a part of me that would love to watch you go after him, but I'm afraid you won't get the information out of him if I'm standing there. You go ahead. I'll be listening around the corner. He won't see me."

I started to protest, but she had a right to know what was going on; she was the one being targeted in all this. I nodded, and walked out of her room to head down the stairs.

He was standing in the front hallway with three large brown paper shopping bags. Harold and Stanley were right behind him, and Tobias was walking in at the same time. I walked up to Bert as he was thanking them for the shopping trip, and reached up to slap him as hard as I could across the face.

He dropped his bags on the floor. "Ow," he said, raising one hand to his cheek. "What the hell was that for?"

"What in the world possessed you to agree to moving the portal in the basement? How could you have agreed to have it moved closer to the throne? How in the world did that seem to be a good idea?" I asked. "Oh, and that's just the first set of questions. I have more."

"Well," he said, retrieving his bags. "Someone from the court approached me about it. I thought it was smart, so I said yes."

"Did you know Winterkiss has limited the number of people who could come through the portal into the court? Did you know her moving the portal into the court would be a trap for anyone she didn't agree to allow in? If something attacks this house and we have to escape using the portal, do you understand it's not a real escape? Anyone not covered by safe passage could be held for the rest of their natural lives, or until they are so insane they don't have a clue what they are running from in the first place? How can you do that with people's lives?"

He stared at me in utter shock. "What are you talking about?"

"Winterkiss's emissary told us the only people with safe passage were me, and whoever the Seawitch's target was. That's me, and that's Mia. No one else."

"I didn't make the deal with Winterkiss. I made it with Geoffrey. And there were no deals or restrictions on the number of people who could come through the portal. There was nothing else about the portal in our deal. I don't know what you're talking about. Geoffrey would never have made such a deal with me if it meant his son wouldn't be safe. He wanted to move the portal so his son would have a protected hiding place."

He was right about that. Geoffrey would never purposely endanger Aiden, regardless of any other flaw he may have, or not; he wanted Aiden safe above all else. I wanted to believe him.

"What else was part of the deal, Bert? What else did you tell Geoffrey? What did you promise him? And what did you get in return?"

He blushed. It didn't look so good on him. "Don't ask me."

"I have to, Bert."

Aiden slipped into the room behind me. "We need to know. It's a safety concern, now, Bert. It's not just about you anymore. It's about all of us. Who is changing the rules on us? Who is really in charge over there? And what's the deal between Winterkiss and Geoffrey?"

Bert sighed. "Neither of them are in charge. Both of them want to be. I made the deal with Geoffrey, but if Winterkiss is limiting his deals, then Geoffrey is losing the struggle for whoever he is working for to take over the court, and we don't know who that is. It's not safe there, no matter what. The portal is not a good escape hatch. You can't rely on safety, even if Winterkiss has made a promise to you about safe passage, because the whole court is in disarray. There's no telling who might be in charge, or what you might be walking into. The tide might have turned again, and someone else might be in charge that won't honor Winterkiss's promise. No one sits on the throne, so the court is not bound by each other's promises. Only a monarch can bind the entire court."

My brain spun with all the possibilities. While we'd all been sitting here trying to figure it all out, there had been a veritable civil war brewing in the court. I'd known there was conflict. I'd known about a power struggle, but I'd also been distracted enough not to think about how it might affect all of us here in the mortal realm. It wasn't something that had been at the front of my mind. Now, it definitely was.

But there was still one thing that was bothering me. "Bert, what did you get from Geoffrey in exchange for moving the portal? That was a big deal. There had to be a good price he'd been willing to pay. What did you get in return? What was worth risking our safety to get? Moving the portal puts us right into the lion's den, so to speak. If the portal had stayed where it was we could have still avoided the court, because we wouldn't have been inside of it. We could have gone looking for another portal. You had to know that, because you're not dumb enough to think otherwise. You know the courts and magic well enough to think things through in more than one way. So what did you get for it?"

His shoulders slumped. "Adder root and tinderbane. Those were potion ingredients that one can't get in the mortal realm. I needed a connection to get them."

Those had to have been in the potion he took to make himself human. Geoffrey must have appeared and struck a bargain with Bert at his lowest point, while he was mooning over Mia. "Bert, when exactly did he show up?"

He looked at me sadly. I knew he must have been desperate. He would never have done such a thing to anyone, made any such deal, if he could have thought of any other way to compete with Jonah for Mia's affections other than to become human, but he had never had a chance to win her heart. He had just been desperate. I felt my own heart crack a bit, and swallowed hard. It didn't matter if I understood his desperation. He had put all of us in danger.

"I didn't mean anything by it, Janie. I just had to break the curse I was under. I had to become human, so I could at least try to find a way to see if Mia could just once feel something other than friendship for me. I needed to know if there's anything I could have done to step in, to have a chance before it was too late. I saw how she looked at just about every male out there other than me, and then I saw how she looked at Jonah. And I knew if I didn't do something then I wouldn't have any way of approaching this topic with her. I had to do it. No matter what it might cost me," he said, sadly.

"No matter what it might cost you?" I asked. "What about what it might cost everyone else? What if your deal cost other people their lives or their free will? Did you even stop to think about that? Or about trying to ask around to find out if your deal was worth it or not? Did you ever even think about talking to a friend to see if it was worth the gamble?" I yelled.

"Like who? Most of the close friends I used to have, that I used to talk about girls, what I wanted, and such, they're all dead. They've been dead for centuries. There's nothing that I could do other than take the risk."

"You have no other friends, do you? What am I, chopped liver? What about Aiden? Or even Doris, or Harold, or Stanley? Even though they might not have known how Mia felt about you they might have at least given you advice on whether or not to make such a deal, and I can say I don't know that any of the others would ever have advised you it was a good idea to make this deal," I said, hands on my hips.

Stanley cleared his throat, his jowls quivering as he timidly took a step forward. It was almost as if he was afraid I'd hit him, too. "He did come to me."

"And you advised him to do this?" I asked.

"Not necessarily. That's not what we talked about. It's not how the conversation went. I poured him beers on your back porch one night, about a month or so ago, where he poured out his heart as I poured him more beer. He's been heartbroken, haven't you noticed? Or have you been too wrapped up in your own petty problems that you haven't given him or his issues a second glance? This isn't something recent; he made the deal with Geoffrey a while ago. He just decided to finally use the potion ingredients and become human."

As I looked at Bert, I realized Stanley was right. I'd been pretty wrapped up in finishing up the school year and in figuring out my own internal struggles with deciding how to handle my own feelings with Aiden, moving into my stepmother's house, and getting started on the internship and summer job. I'd sent Bert over to my stepmother's house alone in the last week or two before the move so I would have had quiet to study during final exams and he would have time to make sure the house was safe for us to live in before we actually moved. I hadn't thought about someone getting to Bert, because I hadn't thought it was possible for him to be someone who could have been gotten to, be bought so cheaply.

Apparently everyone had their price, and Geoffrey had found Bert's pretty easily.

CHAPTER FORTY-NINE

B ert was almost in tears as he told me he'd been in love with Mia almost from the moment he'd met her, and that he'd tried to hide it from the moment he'd realized his feelings. He'd done an incredible job; I'd had no idea. He hadn't believed it would ever be possible, but he also never thought he'd get all the ingredients to make the potion to become human again unless he found a way to the faerie realm. He couldn't figure out how to do it, then Geoffrey had shown up, offering to solve the problem for him. It had seemed too good to be true and it turned out it was.

Mia finally came out from behind the corner.

"Oh, God, you heard it all?" he wailed.

"I did," she whispered, as she crossed the room, and came to him. "No one in my life has ever done anything so outrageous to show me that I was loved. And I will always have a tender spot in my heart for someone who is willing to risk so much for me, but, Bert, you don't understand. Your transformation doesn't change anything about my feelings. I don't love you, not like you want me to. I can't. I'm not sure I can love anyone the way you want me to love you, but I know for sure I can't love you that way." She hugged him.

"Oh, I am such a fool!" he said.

"Well, you are entitled to your own happy ending and I'm glad you're doing something to get it, it's just not me. I can't help you with that." Mia patted his back. "I will do everything I can to help you find what you're looking for, but I'm not the girl for you. I wish you'd tried to say something before you took this risk."

"And if I had? Would that have changed anything?" he asked. "Would you have been able to love me if I hadn't made this deal?"

She pulled back from her hug. "No. It has nothing to do with you, Bert. It has to do with my own issues. I'm not sure I can love like you want. And you deserve better. You deserve the real thing. I'm not it. I don't love you like that, and that did not change because you were human or frog or whatever. It just is. But if you'd asked, if you'd have looked around and asked before you made that deal, then the portal might still have been the safe passage we'd been relying on as a backup.

Do you understand you might have made us vulnerable? Our deal with Winterkiss and with Geoffrey to secure the portal to keep people from surprising us from the basement might not hold. And now, because of your deal to move it, it's vulnerable to anyone who gets enough power in the faerie court to take it over. And whoever that is can come right into the house, right under our own threshold, and can defeat any of the defenses we might have already set up against it."

He looked horrified. "I'm sorry, I didn't mean for such a thing to happen. I only meant to try to take my life back. It hasn't been my own for so long, and I finally thought I'd found something to make it worth becoming mortal and human again."

Aiden finally stepped forward. "Actually, I have an idea. We might be able to mitigate the danger if we secured a salt line with iron around the portal."

Harold didn't like the idea. "Isn't that going to piss off whatever comes through?"

"I don't care anymore. Winterkiss and my father have been playing games with our lives. We are not their playthings. We are not their toys. If they want safe passage into our world they will have to also bargain with us. And right now I don't really care what they think about it."

He started toward the kitchen, gathering the last of the salt supplies and a bag of nails, and heading for the basement steps.

"What are you doing?" Stanley called. "Aren't you making matters worse?"

"I don't care at the moment, Stanley," he said. "If it's Winterkiss who comes through then she'll have leverage to negotiate further entry into this world. If it's my father, well, let's just say I've got plenty of questions I'd like answers to. Either way, I call that a win-win situation."

I didn't disagree with him; in fact, I was completely on board. The others followed us to the basement like a herd of elephants down the wooden stairs, clattering and clacking with the sound of shoes as all of us hurried down the steps. "What are you doing, Aiden?" Doris asked. "You're going to set off all kinds of problems with the faerie courts if you lock down the portal completely."

"I'm not going to lock it down completely. I'm going to set a salt circle around it. Anything magical can come through the portal, but it can't go anywhere once it's here. It will be bound by the salt circle until and unless it bargains with us to get out or decides to go back. We'll reinforce it with iron, and we'll have someone stand guard down here at all times to make sure there's always someone here to reinforce the *no*. And I'll say right here, right now, in front of all of us, the only persons with the power to negotiate this line are myself, Mia, or Janie."

"Are you saying you don't trust the rest of us?" Harold asked.

"No, I'm not. I am, however, saying you guys have been sympathetic to other issues we're not facing at the moment. The only thing I'm thinking of is Mia and Janie, and their safety. So I'm setting this up so the only people who can break it or negotiate around it are the people who are most affected by it. It seems to me that's the most expedient way of protecting everyone and yet accomplishing what we need at the same time." He started to spread the salt, and I wordlessly picked up the nails and followed him.

Everyone started arguing all at once, but the deed was done. No one broke the salt circle. I felt the magic close with a snap and we were done. We should have thought to do this long before, but rather late than never I supposed.

"It's done. The house is secure," I said.

"No, it's not." Tobias leapt into the conversation despite having been so quiet before. "We need to re-salt the perimeter. The girls did a good job of temporary safety, but with the storm we had the other night it just worked to weaken the defenses you guys had set up before. We need to regroup, and we need to secure everything we can think of. Janie, those trunks you had in the attic?"

"Yeah?"

"Where did they come from? Your father?"

"Yeah. I don't know what half of it is."

He chuckled. "I do. It's a special treasure trove of weapons your family has stockpiled for centuries. Once this crisis is over the two of you need to spend some real quality time doing weapons training, because you'll need it if more magic shows up in your life, and I think you're learning that magic is going to keep showing up for a while."

I thought that was an understatement.

We headed back up the stairs; Doris, Harold, and Stanley contritely offering to make another grocery store run in order to stock up on more salt and nails, Aiden and Tobias walking the perimeter to check the weak points of our defenses, and Bert disappeared to my father's library where he'd been sleeping when he'd been in frog form. It didn't take long before I heard the stereo.

Mumford and Sons "White Blank Page" came blasting out of the room. I wondered if he'd found my father's hidden bottle of scotch. It wouldn't be hard to find now that he had opposable thumbs; it was in the bottom drawer of the desk. The drawer had a latch with an iron catch on it, so it made it a perfect place to hide things from my stepmother, who hadn't approved of him having a few drinks in the evening when my father had been so sick. I shrugged. I hoped it gave Bert some comfort.

Allie was sitting upright on the couch as I came back into the living room. "How are you doing?" I asked.

She nodded, still unable to speak, but grabbed the notepad. *Still headache, but better. Is everyone okay? Heard yelling.*

"Everyone's fine. No one is hurt," I said, not quite sure exactly what to say to explain it all, but I figured she was doing a decent job of taking things in stride. I'm not sure I'd have been as laid back if I'd been attacked by a magical bad guy. Then again, my life had seen some weirder moments lately.

I just hoped it didn't get any weirder any time soon.

CHAPTER FIFTY

Four o'clock rolled around pretty quick and it was time for us to go to work at the Schuster Center for the Performing Arts. Selling theater subscriptions just didn't seem all that important at the moment, but I was going to have to take out a mortgage on the house just to pay for all the salt we kept buying from the grocery store. We needed to come up with a better way of dealing with real life and magic messes at the same time, but I didn't know how I was going to do it tonight. I needed the paycheck. And the distraction from everything else wouldn't go amiss, either.

I was exhausted. It seemed like we'd been running from one crisis to another all week. Doris stayed at the house with Allie, who was still resting from her injuries. Tobias stationed himself in the basement, and Bert still hadn't come out of the library. That bottle of scotch wasn't going to last too much longer, and I was sure I was going to have to shoo him out at some point at least to shower some of the stink off. I wasn't looking forward to it.

Jonah was waiting for us when we came out of the office for our first break. Mia's face lit up when she saw him. He hugged her. As much as I still felt like he was an outsider, I couldn't treat him badly just because I felt bad about Bert being heartbroken. What could I do? It was a good thing he wasn't with us. Maybe that was the silver lining about him being human: he could no longer fit into my shoulder bag to go with us and have to watch Jonah trying to impress her, or her being impressed by him.

"Is everyone okay?" he asked. "I hadn't heard from you guys and I got worried. No more problems at the house? Did you guys go home? What's going on with the naked guy?"

Bert. He wanted to know about Bert. Of course he did; he probably wasn't completely clear yet that Bert thought of him as competition, whether it was a true competition or not. Thank goodness Mia had already addressed that issue earlier in the day.

We spent our break filling in Jonah quietly, hoping that no one was listening in, and hoping that no one was actually paying attention to the three of us. Aiden stuck his head into the conversation at one point to check on us, but he had to go deal with a sick ticket holder who had stumbled out of the theater on the way to the bathroom right past us in the lobby as we talked. Jonah made us promise that we'd wait for him or Aiden to walk us to our car after our shift was over.

Given the last couple of days, we agreed.

The rest of the evening passed uneventfully. I think both of us were actually ready for something to leap out from behind a door or curtain and start a fight. We kept jumping at shadows, just waiting to be attacked or killed or threatened, but nothing happened.

Aiden appeared with Jonah the minute the show was over, and they insisted on riding with us to the house. We got back to find Allie still on the couch, intermittently dozing and eating, nursing her banged up head. Doris was in the kitchen furiously cooking up a storm as she fed everyone at the house. Bert was still in the study, having yet to come out and be sociable. I couldn't believe it; he was now listening to Joni Mitchell. I didn't even think I owned any of her CDs.

Tobias was outside in the yard with Harold and Stanley. A new salt line had been laid around the flowerbeds, and they were outside with some kind of thick metal fencing wire. I hoped it wouldn't be visible from the street. I had a funny feeling the neighbors would complain if we made it look like some kind of fortress with inexpertly laid wire fencing.

"How much did that stuff cost?" I asked, as we walked up to the house.

Tobias shrugged his shoulders. "I took care of it. It's the least I can do for my daughter since I wasn't around very much when she was a kid. Take a look at what I've done."

It was impressive. I hadn't seen what he was actually doing until I got closer. He was using the fencing wire to put up a pattern in the yard that would be right on top of the soil. Eventually, the wire would become part of the grass and allow us to prevent any magical beings from the faerie court from coming up to the house unexpectedly, and would be less likely to wash away with a rainstorm like a salt line would. The fencing wire was just outside of the salt line, so there were actually two different lines of defense to prevent an attack from the outside.

"Wow," I said. "I never would have thought of most of this. This is incredible. Is this stuff going to rust? Are we going to have to replace it?"

"It should be good for at least a few years, and it should be low enough that the grass around it will grow up through it. I'd be careful this summer mowing the yard, but it should eventually rest at the base of the grass and be completely out of the way for you."

Mia didn't say anything but I saw the smile at the corner of her mouth. He'd impressed her by doing something to help her without being asked. I got it; she just wanted him to be the kind of dad who would show up and fix the leaky plumbing and check the oil in her car. She wanted a reliable dad, one who would be around to help her out, to listen to her, and to just flat out protect her. It was the kind of thing she'd always wanted. She wanted him to be there.

I gave him a thumbs-up behind her back as we went in the house and smiled at him. He needed all the encouragement I could give him in order to keep on making my friend happy.

We went back inside, the echoes of Bert's music getting louder as we went. Mia shook her head. "I'm going to the kitchen to get some of whatever Doris is cooking. It smells incredible."

I headed for the study. Someone was going to have to kick that frog in the rear end. Whether he was still a frog or not, I did not have time to deal with him acting like some lovesick teenager. I rapped softly on the door, opening it as I stuck my head inside.

"Bert, you've got to stop this. You need to come to your senses and start living your life again," I said, as I eased myself into the darkened room. "I know you're hurting but there's got to be something that would make you feel better."

"More scotch," I heard, in a scratchy hoarse whisper.

I looked a bit closer into the darkness. He was sprawled across my father's leather sofa, one leg up on the arm rest and the other one splayed across the floor. It looked uncomfortable, but then again, I wasn't drunk and forlorn and hiding in the dark. "Bert, grow up. I'm not getting you any more scotch. In fact, I'm not getting you any more alcohol until you shape up."

He groaned.

"Bert, look, I know being human didn't turn out to be the magic fix you thought it would be. I can't help you with that. What I can help you with, though, is realizing you can do good for yourself, for Mia, for all of us, if you get off the couch and start helping us." I crossed the room, sitting down in Dad's leather recliner, facing him.

He looked up at me. "You just want me to help you. You don't care about my feelings. You told Mia about how I felt about her, and made a fool of me."

"I beg your pardon, Mister. I'm here because I'm your friend, but you're acting like you're a junior high girl with her first crush. I did not tell Mia about your feelings to make a fool of you. I told her because I knew she didn't have those feelings for you, and I wanted her to let you down easily. I wanted it to be easier for you, not harder. I wanted you to be able to move on with your life without pining over her forever."

He sniffed, and I realized he'd been crying.

"Bert, I could have told you, if you'd asked, that becoming human again to get her attention just wasn't going to work. I can tell you this because Mia is one of my oldest, dearest friends. I know her. And I've also come to know you. And the two of you just don't fit together. She knows it. I know it. And I think, deep down inside, you know it, too," I said. "But see, here's the thing. Regardless of whether or not there's any room in her life for romance or whether she's going to turn around and instantly fall for you or not, there's something bigger you can do for her than anything else."

"What's that?" he asked, sitting upright and ready to march out to do battle, if need be. I just hoped it was an army of drunken frogs. That might be just about as much battle as he could handle at the moment.

"You can be there for her. Right now, she's building a real truce with the father who abandoned her as a child. She's in danger. And she's having to work and find time for what passes for a normal life around here. Never mind the fact she's got a roommate who has professed his undying love by using magic to court her. Talk about a full plate . . . and also a whole lot of craziness running around. We still don't know where the Seawitch is, or how to find her, or what to do if we did find her. You can help with all of that. And regardless of whether or not you and Mia do ever end up falling for each other, you're the kind of guy who would much rather be the one who helped save her than the one who made her life harder."

He stared at me for a moment. I could hear the wall clock above his head clip-clopping a steady beat as my words swirled around in his brain. "You're right," he said.

That might be the first time in a long time.

He stood up. "I can help her. I can do research with Aiden. I can help lay down the fence the others were putting in."

"And," I said in a conspiratorial whisper, "you can also help protect Mia from any danger that might be out there. You can also help me to keep her safe. You can promise right now to help, to be there for her, and to prevent her from killing her father. You can be a listening ear when she's tired or upset, or whatever else might be going on her head."

He was nodding.

"In short, you can be her friend," I said. "Right now she needs as many honest and true friends she can get. Sure, you hoped she would return your feelings, but she didn't. That doesn't mean she doesn't care for you. And it doesn't mean she wants you completely gone. You have an opportunity here to show her that you are bigger than this, that you care for her no matter what, and that you can be her friend regardless of any hurt feelings or disappointment you might have. She needs it right now. What happens when her father leaves again? Because he's going to. No matter how much she is warming up to him, his job is going to take him away."

He nodded at me. "I can do that. And you're right. No matter how much Tobias wants her to forgive him, he's going to end up leaving again because he'll have to. She's going to have to understand it doesn't have anything to do with her, and everything to do with the fact that the rest of the human world needs him."

Well, it was true. And if it got Bert up off the couch and helping then I didn't feel bad about it. But it was the truth. I knew Tobias would be leaving. And as little as Mia had interacted with him I could see her heart melting, even if just a little bit, toward her father. I didn't know how she'd take it when he inevitably left.

CHAPTER FIFTY-ONE

Doris had been busy. The whole house smelled like heaven as she had spent most of her time in between checking on Allie on putting together enough food to feed a small army. Which was, of course, a good thing, because we had a small army of people at the house working on safeguards and protective measures on the house, and all of them were surely getting hungry. She'd made piles of sandwiches, a vat of soup, and if I wasn't mistaken, there were pies still in the oven.

She'd even gotten Allie up from the couch to help. I went over to where Allie sat at the kitchen table, putting together the small mountain of sandwiches. "How are you feeling?" I asked.

She grabbed for the notepad and pen still sitting beside her. *Better. Still can't talk. Not dizzy anymore, just headache.*

"Good," I said. "Thank you for helping." I didn't know what else to say to her, but she smiled at me, and that smile was enough. I patted her on the shoulder and went to check on Mia.

She was standing by the window watching her father, Harold, Stanley, and Aiden fussing with the lines they were creating around the house and arguing about the best way to do whatever it was they were trying to do. She heard me coming up behind her, and turned to look over her shoulder.

"It's you," she said.

"Yes, it's me. How are you doing with all of this?"

"Which part?" She gave me a slight grin.

Okay, she had a point. "Well, let's start with Bert."

She shrugged. "He can't help how he feels. I can't feel the same about him, and I hope he knows that, but I didn't ever want to hurt him. I'm glad for him that he's human again, and I hope he does find someone he can be happy with. He deserves happiness."

"You're right."

"And I'm glad all the music has died down. Who'd have thought he would drown his sorrows in music?" She laughed.

"Well, it could be worse. It could be polka. Or rap. Or even funeral dirges," I said, continuing the joke.

She laughed. "I hope he's okay. I want him happy. It's just not with me."

"What about your dad?" I asked. "Are you happy he's here, with you?"

She turned, watching her father argue with Aiden. "I am. I'm surprised by it, but I am happy he's here. I'm glad to know the truth about him. And I'm glad to finally know for sure I didn't do anything as a kid to convince him to leave us."

I started to protest, but she shushed me.

"I know," she said. "I know in my head he didn't leave because I was bad, or because there was anything I did or said or forgot that made him leave. But I was a kid who never understood why he was never there. I lived with the insane blaming for a lot of years. I knew I could never say it out loud, but it didn't mean I didn't think it to myself. It's nice to have it affirmed now that I'm old enough to know the truth and experienced enough to actually believe it. I mean, who would have believed the truth if I hadn't already seen what had happened to you, to your father, to Bert, to Aiden, and now to me? If I hadn't already learned what magic was or that it really did exist, would I really have finally come to believe the truth about my father?"

The argument seemed to have subsided outside as all of the guys started picking up the remnants of the tools and leftover wire to come inside.

"That's true, but Mia, you do know what his job means, right? He's going to have to leave again. You know that, right?"

There was a few moments of silence. "I know."

"And you know him leaving has nothing to do with you?"

"It does and it doesn't," she insisted, turning away from the window and sitting down on the couch. "See, he's here right now, and that's good because I need him and I need his help to keep me safe. But if we get through this and defeat the Seawitch, he's going to leave. It doesn't matter if I need him or not, he's still going to leave."

"But, Mia, he's needed all over the place. He keeps lots of people all over the world safe from magic. It's what he does. Could you live with yourself if he stayed behind and someone got hurt?"

"No. And that's not what I mean. It means I never had a dad like you did. I saw what you and your father had. You told him just about everything. You talked to him when you had a bad day. You relied on him even when life with your stepmother was unbearable. He prepared you, even if you didn't know it at the time, to be able to deal with much of the things you would have to deal with."

"Huh?" I asked. "What do you mean?"

"Your trunks? That's what I mean. He put them together for you in ways that your stepmother would want as far away from as possible, and yet put them right where they would be safe for you, right where you would be the person she called to get rid of them. He hid those things right under her nose, and she could only compel people to do her bidding through the very magic that would keep them from being able to handle the trunks themselves. Your father must have suspected something, because he was able to protect them while still preserving them for you. He cared. It's something I've never seen my father do for me."

"And you think I love you less because I didn't have some elaborate plan?" Tobias said, entering the room. "You think I didn't love you with every part of my being? Mia, the biggest reason I stayed away was to protect you and your mother from the ugly truths I face every day. The magical world knows me and knows our family's past. I was hoping that no one would ever link us together. I stayed away because I love you, and I couldn't believe there was anything else I could do to protect you except keep far enough away that no one would ever realize the connection."

She was silent.

I tried to slink slowly out of the room. This was between the two of them and I felt like an intruder, even though I was in my own house.

As I left, I saw the two of them hug. I hoped that meant they were coming to some kind of resolution, at least for now. They both deserved a chance to come to some peace with each other.

I know I'd give just about anything to hug my father one more time.

My eyes weren't even close to dry as I saw Aiden in the hallway and ran into his arms. He hugged me tight, and I told him about the conversation I'd just had with Mia and her father.

"That's all well and fine, Janie, but remember not every father out there has a noble purpose. Not every one of them can live up to the standard your father set. Even Tobias had his heart in the right place. He might have been wrong, but he stayed away out of trying to protect her. He made mistakes, too. And some fathers just make mistakes without any redeeming higher purpose to their decisions."

Oh boy. I'd gone straight from one friend with daddy issues to another. In this case, though, I thought they were both wrong. The question, however, was whether or not I'd read the whole situation wrong, or if I'd missed the whole situation completely.

Either way, it was getting late. I was hungry. And sooner or later we'd need to get some rest. Even though tomorrow was Friday I had a bad feeling it was going to be an incredibly long day.

CHAPTER FIFTY-TWO

It was decided over dinner, and multiple slices of pie, that everyone would stay at the house this night with us. We'd put in enough work that no one wanted to go elsewhere, the house was about as safe as we could get it, and it was probably safer than all of us scattering to the four winds in order to get things accomplished.

Figuring out the sleeping arrangements wasn't as easy as one might have thought. Aiden insisted he was sleeping in my room with me while Doris and I both blushed, but she didn't say anything and I didn't argue. If he thought he was getting some kind of advantage by that he was sorely mistaken, but I was grateful for having him next to me. Bert, trying to be the better man, offered to share the study with Jonah, who accepted. The two of them agreed to take first watch. I hoped nobody actually needed to watch them, but Bert promised to behave when I got him alone before we all called it a night.

Despite the fact Bert had been sleeping in the study, there were two other bedrooms in the house. They hadn't been aired out in a while, but there were clean sheets in the linen closet. Doris and Allie took one room, which I remembered one housekeeper staying in for about a week before being fired by my stepmother when I was fifteen. Harold and Stanley took the last bedroom despite it being devoid of furniture. They made a nest of quilts and blankets and spare pillows in the middle of the room, and insisted Bert and Jonah wake them for the second watch.

Tobias claimed the couch in the living room where Allie had convalesced for most of the afternoon. He declined any offers of blankets or pillows, claiming the sofa was more comfortable than most of the places where he'd slept in the field over the years. He proved it by falling asleep almost immediately. I was jealous.

Once we had everyone settled for the night Aiden and I trudged upstairs. "Is this becoming a pattern?" I asked. "Am I becoming the safe haven for anyone and anything that is affected by magic?"

"If that's the case, then why is Allie here? I mean, other than being attacked by the Seawitch, there's no indication she's related to anything magical. She's a normal human girl. There's no evidence of anything else. And yet, you took her in, even when you could have just turned her over to the police. You do know she's probably been walking the streets. She's probably had to do some very unpleasant things in order to get where she is. She's probably committed crimes. And yet, she's here, in your house, eating your food and sleeping here. You're protecting her."

"She's a victim," I said, as I took a pair of pajamas out of the closet to get ready for bed. Yet again, we were doing the same awkward evening routine of being in love with each other but not yet lovers, comforting each other but not yet completely comfortable together. Sooner or later it was probably going to change. That much, at least, could make me smile. I might not be ready to change the status quo yet, but I knew I would be eventually.

"She is," he said. "But at the same time she's also got her own set of issues, her own set of problems. Taking her in does not solve those problems. It just delays them. Sooner or later she's going to have to face them."

"I know. But right now I'm more worried about getting her voice back, and she's acting stronger than she did when she was first showing up on our back porch. I think actually being able to help someone else is giving her some purpose, something to focus on other than her own problems. Sometimes that's a good thing."

"And sometimes it's just avoidance," he said. "I'm just worried. I'm afraid you aren't seeing all the problems she's going to have. I'm afraid she's staying here to hide from them. And I'm afraid you'll be in danger from more human elements after all this is over. Our web of wire fencing and salt won't keep out a pimp who's trying to get his prostitute back. It won't keep out a gang member coming to retrieve a girl he sees as his property. You live in a very safe neighborhood, but it's not all that far from neighborhoods that are way less safe and way less civilized, and those neighborhoods are within walking distance. You know she walked here every time. How can you believe the danger that follows her is any further away?"

"Aiden, you're right. I know that you are. But we've got to deal with her voice first. I know there's a place not far from here that helps girls in her situation. It's a shelter, and there are counselors and therapists and help. I've brought it up with her. I don't think she's ready to go, and if she goes now there are all kinds of questions she can't answer, that I can't answer." I stepped into the bathroom to brush my teeth and change. I came out to find him already on the bed wearing a Masters of the Universe t-shirt and a pair of baggy basketball shorts, his hands behind his head as he lay back against the pillows.

"I'm just worried about you," he said. "I don't want you to be in any more danger than you need to be. And the truth is, I don't want you to be in danger at all."

I smiled, and crawled into bed. He immediately closed his arms around me and snuggled up close. I reached up and turned off the light. "I feel safe with you beside me." And it was true.

"I love you," he said. "I want you safe."

"I love you," I said. "And I can't bring myself to turn away someone who needs help, someone I can help. I wish someone had helped me with my wicked evil stepmother. I wish someone had called Child Protective Services when she broke my arm. I wish I'd found a way out of the house. I wish my father had been able to resist her and I wish I knew how he'd fallen under her spell, but there's a pretty darn good possibility that I'll never know the answers to most of those questions."

He didn't say anything.

I didn't either.

We lay there together, curled up on my bed, holding each other tightly and waiting for morning. I didn't feel like I'd get much sleep, but I closed my eyes at one point, and when I opened them again sun was filtering into the room from the curtains. The alarm clock showed it was only six in the morning, so I had plenty of time to check on everyone and get to the courthouse by eight.

Shower first, then downstairs for coffee as the rest of the house woke up. It seemed it had been a quiet night, which let the knots I hadn't even realized I had in my stomach loosen a bit. I still felt keyed up, like something was going to happen today. Even if I was right, coffee was still necessary.

The others began trickling down the stairs. Harold and Stanley were moving slowly, as I'm sure sleeping on the floor didn't do their arthritis any favors. Tobias was acting fresh and alert, but he didn't turn down a cup of coffee. Allie was still without voice, but she staggered into the kitchen yawning and smiling at the same time. *Slept better than I've slept for a long time,* she wrote. *Thank you.*

I went looking for Jonah and Bert. The two of them had taken first watch, and I hadn't heard anyone else moving around, so I hoped they had actually kept watch instead of, well, killing each other.

As I walked through the house, I heard them. They were in the dining room talking and laughing and acting like they were best friends.

And they weren't paying attention to anything outside of the house.

"Did you guys watch anything?" I asked. "Or did you hang out here together and bond? Did you arm wrestle or something? Or measure each other's biceps? How are you two suddenly best friends?"

Jonah cleared his throat. "We're not. We are, however, burying the hatchet by getting to know each other. We aren't all that different. Both of us want to protect everyone. Both of us want to protect Mia. I wanted to know more about magic. Bert wanted to know more about the modern world. I've been showing him my smart phone and he's been telling me how to smell magic."

"Wait a minute," Mia called, as she joined us. "I don't even know how to do that. Why does Jonah get training on it before I get a chance to learn?"

I crossed my arms over my chest. Bert better have a good answer to that one. She looked pretty pissed off.

CHAPTER FIFTY-THREE

"Well, he was here. And he was awake. And he asked," Bert said.

So much for having a good explanation, I thought.

Mia didn't like it either. "I thought I was your friend, Bert. I thought you were supposed to be helping to protect me."

His shoulders shrugged. "I'm sorry. There's been a lot going on, and I have to apologize again because I was too much in my own head rather than worrying about the best way to do what I should have been doing. You're right. I should have been helping you instead of trying to help myself."

"Look, Mia, the smell of magic is individual to each person. I smell something different than Aiden does, and he smells something different than Doris does. It's about what appeals most to each one of us, generally a comforting, inviting kind of thing. Truthfully, it's a warning. It's meant to draw someone in, to make them relaxed and to welcome magic that might end up hurting us lowly humans," I said, trying to explain to get her to focus on the issue at hand and not at Bert's allegiances shifting to Jonah.

She began pacing back and forth. "Why haven't I heard about this in more detail before?"

"Mia, there was always someone with you who knew how to smell it or sense it. We should have tried to help you learn what the smell would be to you, but you were never far enough out of range of anyone else who might be able to know what was going on." Bert tried to explain, and he was right, but she'd been in turns pissed off, annoyed, and frightened all week. It was simmering in a quiet bubbling stew, ready to boil over at any minute, but still a pot to watch.

"What do you . . .?" she started.

"Real vanilla, like the kind I bake with," Doris said.

"Fresh mown grass and black licorice, like when I played Little League baseball," said Aiden.

"Old peppermints and dusty books," I said. "The way Dad used to smell." It still gave me a start when I smelled it, but it definitely got my attention. It had been over a year now since my father died, but just mentioning it gave me an odd twitch in the pit of my stomach. I liked to think of it as one last way he had to protect me.

"So if I told you I smelled the burnt sugar scent Mom's phlox used to have in odd places, would you say that would be magic?" she asked.

We all looked at each other exchanging meaningful glances. "How long have you noticed it?" Doris asked.

"I smelled it in the parking garage when we lost our shadows that night. I smelled it again when Janie got out the tinderbox and I got these highly stupid boots." She pointed at her feet where she was still wearing the rubber soled smiley faced Galoshes of Fortune. "I smelled it when those tin soldiers popped out at the theater, and when those ushers turned into whatever the hell it was they turned into. Come to think of it, I've smelled it just about every day we have been in the judge's office."

Bert perked up. So did I. "I never smelled anything," I said. "But Bert did say he noticed magic around the judge. We never did look into why."

"What if it's the judge? I mean, he wants to have lunch with us today after work. He's trying to meet us outside of the courthouse. Maybe it's an attempt to get us somewhere he can attack us," Mia suggested.

"I hadn't thought about that," I said.

"Well, between the magic you noticed in the bathroom at the courthouse at the beginning of the week, the magic in the judge's chambers, and how weird he's been acting, I can't figure out why we didn't think of it before. It has to be the judge," she said.

"But why would stuff be coming up at the theater? I mean, the judge's office is blocks away from the theater. There's no reason to connect the two," Harold suggested. "It just doesn't make sense, no matter what Stanley might think."

His shorter friend frowned at him. "Of course there's a connection. He's probably in the back pocket of one of the powerful rich people who donated to build that new big performing arts center, and he's probably actually working for them. He's probably finding a way into the city council, and is probably aiming to take over the mayor's office, and then the county commissioners, and then the state legislators and then the governor's mansion, and then, from there, who knows? He might even be aiming for the White House down the road."

I loved Stanley dearly, but even when his theories had some thread of possibility at the beginning they tended to devolve into paranoid fantasies of right wing power trip magical conspiracies that were guaranteed to take over the world. The truth was generally something less than what he had proposed, although it was always entertaining to see what slippery slope he'd fall down next.

"Stanley, I can't agree with you about the White House, but there is a connection."

He was pouting, his jowls quivering as his lower lip jutted out. Could a seventy plus year old man look like a contrary two year old? He was pulling it off.

"Stanley, it's simpler than that. The judge has a subscription of tickets to most of the fall performances. He's got the biggest package we sell," I said.

"How do you know that?" Mia asked.

I grinned, sheepishly. "Because I sold it to him the first night we were working at the theater. His home number came up on the autodialer, and he pulled out his credit card and bought the tickets without batting an eye. The computer brought him up as a long time supporter of the theater. He's had ticket subscriptions for ten years or more to the Schuster Center, to the Victoria Theater, and he's even bought separate tickets to events that weren't a part of the subscription package."

"How do you know he didn't buy just because it was you on the phone? How do you know he didn't manipulate the computer system just to put your mind at ease?" Stanley insisted.

"It's not a bad question, Stanley," I said. "But I never smelled any kind of magic. The servers for our computer network are just one room over, and the room's not that big. If someone was using magic to mess with the servers I'd have smelled it. And if they'd been in the room messing with one of our computers, our phones, our headsets, or any of our equipment, I'd have seen them. I didn't see anything, and I didn't smell anything."

"Oh," he said. "That doesn't mean it isn't true."

"Look, it could happen. It's possible. Don't want to say it isn't. But Janie's right. I didn't smell anything either when I showed up to meet the girls," Aiden said.

"And even though I didn't know it was magic, I didn't smell anything either," said Mia.

"That settles it," Harold said. "The judge is innocent."

"That's not what I said," I insisted. "I said the records of him buying tickets weren't faked magically. I don't think he knew it was me on the phone. But that doesn't mean he's innocent. The Seawitch hasn't been out of captivity long, and he has records we're pretty sure weren't faked that go back a number of years. So either he has nothing to do with this or he's working for her. Either way, there's no reason to let our guard down."

Aiden sat down at the dining room table. "She's right. The two of you should be prepared. You should salt your pockets, and take whatever you think you can to protect yourselves with you. Just in case."

"There are metal detectors at the courthouse. There's a limit on what we can take in. But that doesn't stop us from having something a bit more weaponish in the car for when we go to lunch. I assume there's no metal detectors in the restaurant where we're meeting him," I concluded. "I don't want to be paranoid. I just want to be prepared."

Everyone nodded. I think they all agreed.

Tobias was two steps ahead of us, having packed a bag of weapons and sundries to leave in the car. "This should be everything you need for now."

We finished getting ready to go. I made sure the tinderbox was in my shoulder bag. It was made of bone, so security had never stopped me with it on the way in or out of the courthouse.

Mia and I headed out to the car, leaving everyone else behind to guard the house. Somehow I felt better knowing they were all there.

CHAPTER FIFTY-FOUR

Twenty minutes later we were sitting in the judge's chambers, and the smell of cheap peppermints and dusty books was so strong it was nearly choking me. Mia's eyes were watering as well. And yet, we didn't see anything amiss.

I was wearing my necklace, the one with immunity to magic. Mia was still wearing those silly boots. We'd lined our pockets with salt.

"Ladies, I just can't wait. I'm dying to show off my new robes. I've cancelled the morning hearings," Judge Neederhorn exclaimed, just as we were about to tell him our impressions of the hearing we'd sat in on the day before. "I just can't wait another second."

Oh my. He was definitely a flake.

He shooed us into his courtroom, which was empty other than his office administrator, his court reporter, his bailiff, and the two of us, all women. "I'll be right back," he hooted, dancing his way out of the courtroom.

One of the ladies pulled out a digital camera. "I know he'll want this on film," she said, shrugging her shoulders and, it seemed, bracing herself for the inevitable silliness the judge seemed to always engender.

"I'm sorry, but has he always been so eccentric?" Mia asked. "Don't get me wrong, I like him, but he's definitely different. Or is this a recent thing?"

I could tell where she was going with this, but even if he'd gotten oddball lately it could be a sign of dementia, of Alzheimers, or any other mental faculty failure that didn't have anything to do with magic. It could be as simple as his brain no longer functioning the way it should. Or it could be the same kind of fog I was under when I was a teenager living with my stepmother. She'd altered my memories and my ability to recall certain details about my childhood on top of everything else she did. I was still getting pieces back from all of that.

"No, he's always been different. I've been with him fifteen years, and he's brilliant but he's definitely an odd duck. I've heard stories about him even before I started working for him," said his bailiff, a really nice middle-aged woman named Margaret. "It's like all of us look at a problem and we see a straight line ahead of us, taking us from Point A to Point B, directly ahead. Judge Neederhorn has a tendency to think sideways, or maybe even diagonally. Don't ask me how he does it, but he'll start talking about something that makes absolutely no sense, then suddenly he's figured out why people are really arguing about a case, and use that knowledge to talk people into a settlement. His written decisions don't always make sense until you get to the end, and then it all falls into place."

"And he's always been like that?" I asked.

"Ever since I've known him," the office administrator added. "But then again, he's a pretty easy boss to work for. He's understanding about real life problems, because he's had a few of his own. He cared for his elderly mother for years before she passed, and so he's had to be available for her needs."

We exchanged a glance. An elderly mother? Or was this code somehow for some kind of communications with the Seawitch? Were her accommodations less secure than we'd believed? Or was he simply a devoted son with a sick mom who passed away? That wasn't exactly a question I thought we could just ask straight out. Or, at least, not without looking completely mental. I kept my mouth shut.

Mia didn't.

"What do other attorneys think of him?" she asked.

It sure was taking him a while to get into his new robes. I saw one of the gray suits from earlier in the week stick their head in. "Just wait, it's so wonderful. You'll be shocked and amazed when you see how wonderful they look. They are just so magnificent." He giggled, and slipped back out of the room.

We all looked at each other in astonishment. Margaret continued. "Well, the attorneys complain about having to wait for him all the time, but he has a tendency to make their lives easier by helping them to resolve cases. He almost never gets overturned on appeal, so they know if he tells them an argument isn't going to work they know he's right. They trust his instincts so they put up with him even when it seems a little wacky, because he moves cases, and he makes them laugh."

It made sense, especially since law can be such a good old boys network, and if he made them all look good, made them all laugh and gave them entertainment, then they'd put up with a lot.

We all sat down in the first few rows of seats in the gallery where the public would sit when they came to watch a hearing, and waited. Seconds turned into minutes, turned into three quarters of an hour, before one of the gray suits stuck their head back in and informed us that the judge was "almost ready."

"You've got to be kidding me," Mia whispered. "I mean, I know we're getting paid, but this is nuts. What are we supposed to be learning while we sit here and wait for the judge to whip out his new robes?"

I smiled at her and nodded. "I agree. But like you said, we're getting paid. And we're sitting here with plenty of security around us, with metal detectors and sheriff's deputies and such. I can think of a whole lot worse things."

We sat there and waited for a total of two hours before the judge finally appeared. I was no where near prepared enough for what I saw.

The rest of the judge's staff oohed and aahed over his robes. "They're fabulous," they exclaimed. "They're so impressive. They make other robes look positively threadbare."

I was trying not to look. In fact, I was making pretty serious eye contact with the floor, and with the smiley faces on Mia's toes. I didn't have to look up much in order to see Mia was very studiously doing the same.

"Mia, Janie, come here and tell me what you think of my new robes!" Judge Neederhorn called from the front of the courtroom where he danced around in front of the bench. "They're fabulous, and they feel so incredible against my skin!"

Oh please, oh please, don't make me look up, I thought. "I can see just fine from here," is what I said out loud.

"Oh, no, you have to come here and see this material up close!" he called, as excited as a giddy schoolgirl. "You need to see the detailing and the rest, and you can't see all the incredible details if you stay all the way over there."

I kept trying to say it was okay until he insisted, almost to the point of getting angry with us. I didn't want to jeopardize my job or my not-yet-established professional reputation. Mia and I slowly inched towards the front of the courtroom, still staring at our toes as we went, hoping we didn't have to look up.

"You must come here, you must look and see!" he called, coming over to where we were dragging our feet.

"Judge, are you wearing anything underneath those robes?" Mia asked.

The rest of the staff stopped and stared at us.

"Of course not! I wanted to know what the material would feel like against bare skin!" he danced and pranced and spun about like a May queen at a spring festival.

Salt. I thought. I've got a handful of salt in my pocket. The rest of the staff acted like they saw actual material and robes. I was wearing my magical immunity necklace. Mia still wore the Galoshes. We didn't see the robes, because they were magical.

Instead, the judge was dancing and singing and prancing around the courtroom in front of his staff buck-naked.

Mia and I locked gazes, staring at each other instead of the robes, and we nodded at each other as we reached into our pockets at the same time, grabbed a handful of salt, and threw it at the judge.

I reached into my pocket and grabbed whatever was left, and threw it at the judge's staff.

They blinked hard, before staring at the floor much like we had done just a few short minutes before. "Um, Judge . . . you're naked. You know that, right? How did you get naked? We never even saw you take off your robes. What happened?" the bailiff asked.

He looked down and saw his, um, endowments hanging free for all the world to see. For all that I thought he was a bit odd, a bit different, he acted like the stereotypical person when suddenly discovering he was naked in front of all of his own employees.

He shrieked and screamed and covered himself with his hands, backing toward his office with a flaming red embarrassed blush sneaking up his chest, neck, and face, all the way to his hairline.

Well, now we knew where the magic was coming from in his office. The material the gray suits had brought in was all enchanted.

And it seemed as if normal humans would have seen the material as it was intended while those of the magical persuasion or those with some kind of immunity would see absolutely nothing. It was clear the judge had no idea, or he'd have at least worn a pair of tighty-whiteys underneath the robe itself.

On the other hand, I had a pretty good idea he'd be very covered up for the rest of his life underneath any robes he ever wore.

And for that, I guess, our work here was done.

CHAPTER FIFTY-FIVE

M ia and I headed back to the judge's chambers, knocking softly to be sure he had warning before we entered. Thankfully, he was dressed and sitting morosely behind his desk when we went in.

"I'm so sorry," he said. "I never once imagined that this would happen. I presume the two of you will be reporting me to the bar association, to the state supreme court, and to the law school for my behavior. I can only promise it will never happen again."

I felt bad for him. I doubted he'd have exposed himself to any of us on his own. I took a deep sniff, and I smelled nothing that even slightly resembled the scent of magic.

"Where are the men in the gray suits who were here working on your robes?" I asked.

He slumped, holding his head in his hands as his elbows were propped up on the desk. "I told them to take everything they owned and get out or I'd have them thrown in jail for contempt of court."

I doubted he would have actually done it; if they'd fought a contempt charge, everything would come out and be very public. The threat of it, however, seemed to have worked. They were gone and there were no longer any piles of fabric or anything else littered around the judge's chambers.

"What happened to the robes?" Mia asked.

"I could still feel them around my neck even though I couldn't see them. I reached up and could feel the hook at the neck, so I unfastened it and threw it out the window. It's gone. And I'll never try anything like that again. I will only wear robes that are already in my closet," he promised.

"And you'll never go without clothes underneath them again?" I asked. That was a sight I could do without.

"Oh, *never,*" he said. "You have my word."

I looked at Mia, and she nodded at me. "Look, we don't think you would have, well, shared anything so private with us on purpose. We won't report you anywhere."

"And you'll stay for the summer?" he asked. "Your briefs have been well-written, well-reasoned, and well thought out. I always have need of solid researchers."

"Of course. I hope you understand, however, that we will not be going to lunch with you today. Give us some time; it's just uncomfortable for us at the moment," Mia said.

He reached for his wallet. "Look, I really was going to buy your lunch today. Let me at least do so even if I'm not there with you." He started to pull out some cash.

"No," I stopped him. "If anyone ever misunderstood what happened today there could be some kind of allegation we are somehow agreeing to keep this confidential in exchange for money, and I don't want any of us to have to face that. Order in lunch for your staff with the money. Talk to them and apologize to them about what happened. Don't worry about us. We'll be okay. And we'll have the summer to get past this."

Mia nodded. I was glad. I hated the idea of ruining his career, and I hated the idea of the rest of the local legal community learning of our names somehow as related to this issue as opposed to learning of us as competent attorneys with professional reputations. It would not help our careers, and would probably hurt even if we had done nothing wrong. Better for all of us to be grown-ups, especially when neither of us believed there had been any ulterior motive in flashing us.

He let us leave early, which I felt was a good thing. My brain kept rolling with the ramifications of what had just happened. There was absolutely no magic in the judge's chambers when we left. Any thoughts I'd had that the judge was our bad guy had been put to rest despite any of Stanley's goofy theories.

I felt sorry for Judge Neederhorn. I didn't know why he'd been targeted by magic, but I was as sure as I could get that he wasn't in league with anyone who was gunning for us. If I was wrong, I'd, well, I'd buy Bert a dozen cases of beer.

We headed home, a bit shocked at the morning, but relieved to be on our way and one more avenue of attack at least crossed off the list. But why would anyone in the faerie courts have targeted a county court judge?

I drove quickly but quietly, Mia and I both contemplating what was happening in silence. Our street was silent, but when I pulled in the driveway I suddenly had a very bad feeling about what was going on.

Nothing was out of place. Nothing was in the yard. But every hair on the back of my neck was standing at full attention and throwing the most formal salute imaginable. I smelled peppermints and dusty pages so strongly I almost gagged. I noticed Mia's eyes watering as we left the garage at a dead sprint to get to the house.

I felt a wall of wind hit my chest, as if trying to prevent me from getting to the back door. I fought to keep going, to hang onto my things rather than leave my bags in the yard. I hated to leave weapons where we would not be able to use them, and I hated even more the idea of leaving the tinderbox where it could be used against us.

I saw Aiden at the patio door screaming my name. Mia was just steps behind me, and I turned, reaching back for her, but she was caught.

She screamed, long and loud, for me to get safe, when I saw Tobias, Jonah, and Bert come up behind Aiden storming out of the house and armed to the teeth with weapons from my trunks.

I grabbed Mia's wrist and began pulling for all I was worth, looking to see what had a hold of her. And when I saw what it was I nearly dropped her hand in shock.

It was Andrea Scolari, the lead actress from the current production of The Little Mermaid, the one we were selling tickets to in our night jobs. Her hair was now blue as the ocean waves with crests of whitecaps at the tips. Her eyes were dark and wild with blue as she opened her mouth to create more wind. I had the sudden feeling that ocean water was in the air around us, and I wondered about it briefly. If she was the Seawitch, then she commanded salt water . . . which meant at least half of our defenses were probably less than effective against her.

But she hadn't counted on the fencing wire laid into the yard.

I felt it under my feet and knew I was close to safety, but Mia wasn't. With one hand on my bags and another attempting to hold onto Mia, I had exactly no chance to pull out a weapon, the tinderbox, or anything else. All I could do was hold on and hope the guys could do something before my strength gave out.

Tobias yelled, drawing back the drawstring on a heavy bow and unleashing an arrow at the Seawitch. It imbedded in her upper arm, but the Seawitch pulled it out with her free hand and dropped it. I saw a burn mark on her hand just before she threw a column of water with magic right over the metal wire net on the ground and knocked over Tobias. "I will deal with you later, good sir, after I get rid of your daughter. And once both of you are gone there will be no one left of those who helped imprison me, and I'll take my rightful place on the throne!" Her voice echoed as she got louder.

Why, oh why, did everyone want that damn throne? I couldn't understand it, but then again, I wasn't someone motivated solely by the pursuit of power. I wanted a good life with a solid career, a comfortable income, someone to love me, and a family, eventually, but I was okay with life not going much beyond that. There was just no need, in my mind, for more than what was in front of me at the moment.

But whatever I wanted out of life, Mia didn't have much time left. I felt my grip slipping and my hand was cramping from having hold of her so tightly. I knew that sooner or later I wouldn't be able to hold onto her.

And I didn't know what would happen then but I didn't see a lot of options in front of me, and I started crying as I didn't know how to protect my best friend.

No one ever contemplates watching their best friend getting killed in front of them.

CHAPTER FIFTY-SIX

Tears blurred my vision as I began losing my grip on Mia's arm. "No!" I yelled. "You can't have her!"

"All evidence to the contrary, my dear," the Seawitch cackled, as she ripped Mia away from me and tossed her several yards away from the house.

The Seawitch was between me and my best friend. Our greatest chance was for me to get to where I could pull out the tinderbox. I ran for the patio to get it out, but I wasn't the only one with a plan. I just wasn't the fastest one.

As I dug in my bag I saw the Seawitch gathering power, drawing it in and aiming towards Mia. I give my best friend credit; she stood up, bravely, closing her eyes and waiting for the end. It looked like she was trying to give the rest of us time to get to safety, but I'd be darned if I was going to leave her out here alone to die.

I got the tinderbox out as Bert took off running toward Mia, jumping in front of her as the Seawitch threw a curse at her. Bert knocked Mia to the ground as the curse hit him in the back. He groaned and didn't move, but the magic was knocked back at the Seawitch, forcing her to duck. I ran toward where they were at in the yard, and together Mia and I dragged Bert back to the patio. Jonah helped pull him the rest of the way inside.

The Seawitch was angry. No doubt about it. "Your puny defenses will never stand against my magic. I shall have my revenge on those with Andersen ancestors! I will wipe them from the face of this realm forever and I will rule everywhere. You cannot stop me!" She began throwing magic at the wire barrier that kept her from crossing to kill the rest of us, howling and screaming and blasting away.

I could only wonder what the neighbors would think, but didn't have time for more than a passing thought regarding their impressions as we gathered everything up and barricaded the doors inside. Even Doris was holding a weapon. I hated that it had come to this, that everyone found themselves at my house, where we would all, almost certainly, die. It had been made very clear to me we would never outlast the Seawitch the last time she'd sent magic against us at the house, and this time she was here in person.

"There's only one option. You and Mia need to go through the portal in the basement and ask whoever is currently in power in the courts for assistance with the Seawitch. You two have safe passage. If nothing else, you should be safe there until someone from F.A.B.L.E.S. can find a way to get to you. And you might even find help, but you have to go," Tobias said, readying another arrow in his bow, and standing guard at the window.

"Dad," Mia said, "I can't leave you here."

He smiled. "I've waited a long time for you to say something like that. I never wanted to leave you, either, but I didn't have much choice. I've been fighting battles like this as long as I can remember. I hoped you would never have to. But I'm proud of you, I love you, and I need you to get safe. I'll do what I can here."

"Dad," she said, her eyes full of pleading.

He leaned over and kissed her on the forehead. "I love you. Now go."

I grabbed her hand. "He's right. We don't have much time, especially if we have to negotiate with the courts. We have to go, and we have to go now." I pulled when she stood still for a moment.

Bert was curled up in a ball in the kitchen floor as we walked away from Tobias. His skin was taking on a greenish cast and he was shrinking. As we moved, I saw his tongue snake out and trap a fly that had gotten inside.

He was turning back into a frog. Jonah stepped up, holding his hand. "I'll sit with him." Bert's hands were shrinking in Jonah's as I looked up at Doris and Aiden.

Aiden shook his head. "I don't know how to stop it. He's reverting into frog form again. We won't let him be alone, but we can't keep him human."

"I'm fine," Bert muttered. "Get her safe." He curled up beside Jonah, who tried to comfort him.

I looked to Aiden. "No time."

He nodded at me. "I love you. Go. Be safe. And see what you can do."

I whispered the words back to him, tears still spilling from my eyes. I was crying, but I still yanked Mia toward the basement to the portal, down the stairs, as she pulled and protested. "I can't leave them," she cried.

I grabbed her shoulders. "You have to. They need us to do this. None of us live if we stay. If we go we have a chance, we have a chance to save them. Do as I say and we'll be okay."

I was careful not to promise that the rest of them would. I might have just said my last good bye to Aiden, but I couldn't bring myself to think about it. I couldn't watch someone attack my best friend again, and I hadn't been making it up. Going into faerie was the only solution I could see where any of us stood a chance at living.

She broke down, weeping and wailing, but I didn't let her drop to the floor.

I dragged her through the portal, and let her collapse on the other side.

It was the only thing I could think of, and at least we were safe. For the moment.

She whimpered on the ground where I'd dropped her.

I, on the other hand, was looking around. No one seemed to be in the room with us. It was dark; the only light coming from the door leading into the next room. There was noise in that room, the throne room where I'd stood trial and pled for my life.

"Mia, get a hold of yourself. We don't have time for this. We've got to be ready, because there's no telling how long we have before they know we're here. Come on, stand up. Dry your eyes. Don't show weakness or fear. We can do this," I said, trying to get her at least somewhat ready for probably the most important court appearance of our lives.

She swallowed hard, and I dimly saw her swipe her sleeve across her face, mopping up the tears and the runny nose. I heard her take a deep breath, letting it out slowly.

"Do you think we'll ever see them again?"

I couldn't dwell on it. I couldn't think it was even a possibility to be any other way. "I'm counting on it," I said, as I edged closer and closer to the door.

Someone was talking on the other side. I put my eye up to the crack in the door, trying to see who was talking, who was in charge, and what was going on. I saw the throne, but I couldn't see who was in it. I saw a room full of nobles, some of whom I recognized from the last time I'd been here. They were all sumptuously dressed with long flowing robes and hemlines, glittering threads of gold and silver, but not all of them were completely human looking. Some had skin in different colors, from blue to green to pink, some had wings, and some were part animal. I didn't know them all.

Before I could truly take stock, however, the door flung open, and one big meaty hand grabbed the front of my shirt. I was kicking and flailing before I realized who it was.

It was Grechuk.

He was an eight-foot tall, green-skinned ogre, wearing a blousy pirate style shirt and clown-polka dotted pantaloons. He'd stopped my escape the last time I'd been here with Aiden. He'd bullied Aiden as a child. And, it looked like he was still in charge of court security.

"Janie Grimm. I hoped you would try to sneak your way back. I've been preparing for your return. Did you bring the half-breed with you?"

Oh, shit. He still wanted revenge on Aiden for making him look bad. And he wanted to look good to whoever was in charge. This could be bad.

CHAPTER FIFTY-SEVEN

Grechuk grabbed me and somehow had gotten a hold of Mia as well, dragging us both to the throne. He dumped us both on the floor in front of whoever the leader was, but I refused to stay down. He smacked me hard enough to drive me back to the floor, and I started to get up again even as Mia tried to tug on my leg to stay down.

"No," I said. "I'm not a member of the court. I will negotiate with them as equals." I turned to the throne.

A glittery woman with all-white hair sat on the throne. "I do not believe I have made your acquaintance yet, but I presume you are Ms. Grimm? And this is Ms. Andersen?"

Mia stood beside me and nodded, squinting her eyes against the bright, brilliant whiteness of the woman's eyes and hair. "I don't believe we've had the pleasure," my friend said.

"You haven't, although I believe you've met friends of mine," the woman on the throne said.

Who was this woman? Would she honor Winterkiss's promise?

"What friends?" I asked. I figured that was the more polite way to go.

"You have heard me referred to as Winterkiss. I have been working through intermediaries to offer you safety and assistance where I could."

What was I missing? I wondered. Something was afoot. "Who were your intermediaries?" I asked.

"Jenny, come forward." A nightingale flew up from the back of the room and landed in front of Mia, dipping her head in a bow. Mia nodded to her.

"And, though I did not know it at the time, Geoffrey Tailor was working in the same direction as I was. We were working separately, but we eventually became allies." Aiden's father came forward. He had a wicked looking red mark on the side of his face that looked like a burn, but he smiled when he saw me and I saw the smile reach his eyes.

"Who are you?" Mia asked. "You said we knew you as

Winterkiss. Who are you really? I mean, I get not wanting your identity known to someone who you didn't yet trust, but you offered us safe passage and we're standing in front of you, seeing your face."

She smiled. "I am the Snow Queen. I am here to stabilize the court that was left vacant by Evangeline's absence. I am to reign here, although I also have my own court. I go by Winterkiss in other realms, so I can pass without threat of harm."

A random thought jerked my head forward. "It was you, in the restroom at the courthouse. You're the one who left the layer of snow and ice I slipped on."

She laughed. "Yes, it was me. I did not mean to do so, but I was surprised that I had happened upon you so easily. I needed to test you. I needed to know what I could count on you for, in discretion, in intelligence, and in everything else important. Believe me, when I say that you passed. You sensed magic, sensed no attack, and knew not to engage, even though I was still in the restroom when you left. You showed poise and grace, and a sensible head, and I knew I could trust you to protect the Andersens from my sister, the Seawitch."

Sister? I bet those holiday dinners *sucked.* "Why did you want to protect the Andersens? And what makes you not like your sister?"

"My sister is dangerous. I love her dearly, but I do not trust her and she cannot be allowed to run free in human lands. I cannot in good conscience let her sate her vengeance," the Snow Queen said, as she stood from her throne and approached us.

"I thought the Andersen family had a tradition of protecting humans against magic. Why are you so keen to protect them? Isn't that kinda like a vampire protecting a vampire hunter? Doesn't make sense," I said.

"If the Andersen family just hunted down magical beings wherever they were found and dispatched them on sight you'd have a point, but they don't. They protect humans from faerie beings who have gone too far, from those who try to bend the rules to get their way that we cannot police, for whatever reason, ourselves. I have no beef with the Andersen family, and they have allowed those of us who respect the rights of mortals to self-determine their fates to exist without a problem."

"Then you have no reason to stand aside while my friends and her father are in danger," I said.

"I'm sorry?" she asked.

"Tobias Andersen, Mia's father, and my friends, Geoffrey Tailor's son and others, are all in my home holding off your sister as long as they can. They need help."

Geoffrey's face fell. The master manipulator was speechless. I don't think he anticipated me coming and asking the court for assistance. I'm sure he thought he had secured everything he thought he needed, but I don't think he foresaw his son in the line of fire. He should have known better, though, if he'd known that Mia was the Seawitch's target. Then again, I don't think he knew.

"You're asking me to risk the court, and all of our members," the Snow Queen said.

"Yes, I am. I am asking all of you to risk yourselves to help me," I said, turning to make my case to the court members as well. "I ask you to do this not for myself, although my friends and my family are in harms' way. I ask you to do this because it's the right thing to do. I ask you to do this to secure the Seawitch, who has designs on taking over this throne. I ask you to do this for the Andersen family, who you yourselves have said you have no complaint with. And I ask you to do this, because we are in this boat due to the original request made of me to help locate and warn the target of the Seawitch. I have done so, and she stands before you now." I pointed to Mia.

They began nodding slowly along. I turned back to the Snow Queen awaiting her decision.

She must be a much different ruler than my stepmother had been, because she nodded. "I must ask you, however, in return, for one favor."

"What favor is that?" I asked.

"No, not a specific favor, but a future favor. You have done as you were asked, and I have no problem with following the lead of my court and assisting you, but I ask for a favor in return, one that I shall cash in at some point in the future."

I didn't like it. I didn't want an open ended claim on my time, on my commitment, on my abilities, or my life, but I didn't know what else to do.

"Will you promise your favor will not intrude on my schooling or exams, and that I shall have at least twelve hours to respond to any such requests in case of prior commitments? Also, I can't do anything illegal. If your favor is for me to commit a crime I need the right to refuse. If you make this promise and do not interfere with my priorities in the mortal realm, I have no problem making that promise."

I saw Geoffrey shaking his head at me even though he was smirking. Yeah, I'd seen that look before on Aiden's face. I knew what it meant, too. He approved of my negotiations, although he didn't approve of me making the deal in the first place. What he didn't know was that I was willing to agree without it in order to save the others if the Snow Queen said no.

"Done," she said. I felt a weight settle on my shoulders. I wondered if it was a binding to my promise, and was happy to carry it.

The nobles followed us into the room with the portal and followed us through, one by one.

CHAPTER FIFTY-EIGHT

I saw the salt line around the portal as I came through and immediately began to scuff the line with my shoe. Mia saw me doing it and joined me as she followed, and the Snow Queen was the first through after her. Several others came through as I headed up the stairs, hoping I would not open the door to bad news.

The lights were out as we came into the front hallway. I led them all through the house to the kitchen where they others had been holding off the Seawitch. I smelled burning metal and peppermint as I got closer.

It looked like the Seawitch was nearly through the barriers we had erected. She had been throwing brute force magic against the line of wire fencing until it melted away, and had created a storm of water to form a lake over the remains of it. Most of the people in the house had been soaked by water that had started to leech into the house through the broken windows from the rain and the storm outside. Some of them were hurt, and I didn't yet know how bad it was.

I ran to Aiden, who seemed to be okay, as he kept picking up iron tipped arrows and shooting them with the bow I'd seen Tobias holding earlier. His arrows were keeping the Seawitch from getting close enough to come into the house itself. Tobias was sitting on the floor with a giant knot on his head, but other than being a bit dizzy and disoriented he otherwise seemed okay.

Doris was armed with a meat tenderizer waiting by the door as if she intended to whack the Seawitch in the head if she came through. Harold and Stanley each had cast iron pans at the ready, as if they planned to do the same thing. And Jonah was sitting on the floor, consoling a very upset frog. Bert was completely back to his frog form, same size, same color, same despair. Somehow, though, I got the impression he wouldn't give up looking for happiness, as despondent as he might be at the moment, and I was glad.

We didn't have to do much. The nobles sauntered outside, and the Snow Queen froze the water her sister was throwing around. The other nobles cast a net of magic around her, holding her and preventing her from doing anything else while the storm subsided outside. They brought her into the house slowly using their magic to move her across the threshold and toward the basement as she yelled and cursed at us for depriving her of her rightful vengeance.

Mia stepped forward. "I have done nothing to you, and yet your all-consuming goal was to kill me and my father. I hope you see we did not do the same. All I have ever wanted is to know my father, to have my friends safe, and to know what was going on around me. I hope you can see the irony in that your appearance in my life has made all of those things come true. I wish you many years to dwell on the complete failure of your plan to accomplish anything you have tried to accomplish."

The Seawitch wailed, and her sister froze her face, with her mouth wide open. The Snow Queen turned to me.

"I thank you," she said.

Huh? I gave her a puzzled look.

"Your actions and those of your friends did allow me to re-secure my sister. I hope one day she will see that her actions are ill-advised and will start being my sister again. I am glad to have her alive."

I nodded at her. I'd feel better if she wasn't but, hey, I think I'd made if not a friend then at least an ally. "There's just one more thing," I said, as I led them all back to the basement.

"The portal," she said, as if she'd read my mind.

"Yes. It seems a security risk for both of us."

"It is. We will close it. None of our people shall be coming into your house by the portal, and I presume then none of you will be coming into our court by that means, either. I think it's a mutual decision that benefits both of us."

"I agree. Please don't take offense if I tell you that I'm going to be building up defenses after you leave, and trying to reestablish whatever threshold I can have at this house. After today, you are not welcome here," I said.

"As long as there's a caveat for me to contact you regarding the favor," she answered.

"Jenny will be welcome and invited in only when she is here to request my assistance on your favor. At any other time, no other faerie or magical being is welcome in my house after all of you leave, save Bert." I'd learned the hard way to negotiate with caveats and exemptions, and to tie the reins on agreements as tightly as I could. I wanted my house to be my home, and I wanted Mia to feel safe as well. She wasn't far away, just down the hallway, but she was busy checking on her father, on Jonah, and on Bert.

The Snow Queen nodded. "I accept your terms."

I walked her and the others back down the stairs, and waited for all of them to go back through the portal. The swirling purple mass of air grew dimmer and dimmer and finally disappeared altogether, but just to be on the safe side I redrew the salt circle around it. I knew I felt safer for having done it.

I came back upstairs to find Mia waiting for me in the hallway.

"Thank you, Janie, for helping me to do this. I think it's over." She had a slightly flushed look on her face.

"Of course I would help you." I gave her a sideways look. "But did I miss something?"

"Yes. Jonah asked me to go out on a date with him tomorrow night after the show. And I said yes." She beamed a smile that lit up her face. "At least some good came out of the whole thing."

I didn't know what else to do but to smile back as she headed off to get towels to mop up the water. I felt sick to my stomach for Bert, who had probably had to listen to the whole thing, but I was also happy she'd found some silver lining to the whole situation. And she'd reconnected with her father. I wasn't sure if she ever thought that would happen.

Aiden joined me in the hallway as I was mulling over the outcome of the whole situation.

"You okay?" he asked.

"Sure," I said. I told him about Mia, her father, her date, and my worries about Bert. "I think they'll all be okay, but I'm worried."

"Bert will recover. And someday, he'll find a way, not only to be happy, but maybe even to be human enough to enjoy it. I have faith he'll get there," he said, as he wrapped his arms around me.

I leaned into his hug. "And I'm happy we're together."

"You mean that?" he asked.

"Of course I do. I'm still worried the issues that kept your parents apart could still sink our relationship. I'm still worried we'll mess it up. I'm still worried we'll fail, and that we'll hurt everyone around us, but I'm also worried about what I'd have to give up if I didn't try," I said, leaning my head back and smiling up at him.

"You said 'our relationship,' didn't you?" he asked. "Does that mean we're actually in one? I've been asking, and you hadn't given me an answer."

I kissed him soundly on the lips. "There's your answer," I said, moving decisively toward the future I wanted with him. "Everything else will work out."

I could think of worse ways to begin a new chapter in our lives.

ACKNOWLEDGEMENTS

Many thanks go to . . .

My parents, Alvin and Karen King, my biggest cheerleaders.

Ray and Daniel Westcott for making me smile, and reminding me every day of fun things I can put in Bert's mouth to say.

My writer's group for their enthusiasm and their encouragement.

Ashley and Jake Ballard, and Alex King and Michelle Birchak, for constantly reminding me what having siblings are all about.

Blake and Kenley Ballard for reminding me of the great fun of being a kid, and the little memories that we forget as we get old and deal with grown up stuff.

Eugene and Sandra Westcott, for welcoming me with open arms . . .

Jenna Bennett, Steven Saus, Sarah Hans, and all the other writers I've met on this journey, for friendship, networking, and all the other writer stuff we've shared along the way.

My grandparents, Loren and Dorothy King, and Merlin and Mary Jane Woodruff, for instilling the importance of family and its enduring legacy.

Celina Summers, publisher extraordinaire, and Jaime-Kristal Lott, my awesome editor, for seeing the potential in the first book and being so excited at turning it into a series. Also a big thanks to James Barnes and everyone at Loconeal Publishing for believing in these books after Musa Publishing ceased to be. This book would never have been written or published without the excitement and support of everyone there. Thank you.

AUTHOR INFORMATION

Addie J. King

Addie J. King is an attorney by day and author by nights, evenings, weekends, and whenever else she can find a spare moment. Her short story "Poltergeist on Aisle Fourteen" was published in MYSTERY TIMES TEN by Buddhapuss Ink, and an essay entitled, "Building Believable Legal Systems in Science Fiction and Fantasy" was published in EIGHTH DAY GENESIS; A WORLDBUILDING CODEX FOR WRITERS AND CREATIVES by Alliteration Ink. Her novels, THE GRIMM LEGACY, THE ANDERSEN ANCESTRY and THE WONDERLAND WOES are available now from Loconeal Publishing. The fourth book, THE BUNYAN BARTER, will be available in 2015. Her website is www.addiejking.com

61098420R00143

Made in the USA
Columbia, SC
21 June 2019